Dedication

To the memory of my beloved cousin
Jacqueline Mary Clements
31st March 1941 – 15th May 2017

Acknowledgements

Once again, thanks to Miles Cookman for the setting and the whole family for information about beer festivals and bands. Apologies as ever to the police forces of the UK for use and abuse, and thanks to the wonderful independent and idiosyncratic food and drink producers of my home town of Whitstable. Both the smokery and the cafe mentioned here are real, and can be found by trawling my social media links!

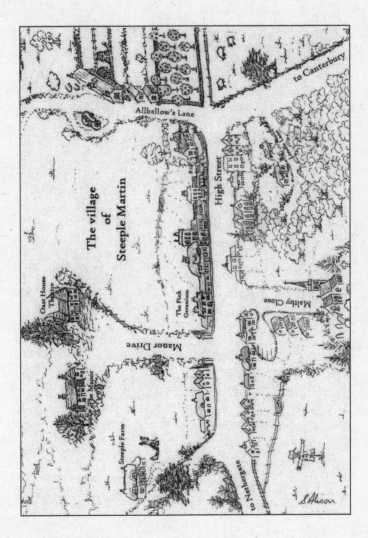

The village
of
Steeple Martin

Allhallow's Lane

to Canterbury

High Street

Oast House
Theatre

The Peak
Geranium

Maltby Close

Manor Drive

The Manor

Steeple Farm

to Nethergate

S Alison

Cast list of regular characters

Libby Sarjeant — Former actor, sometime artist, resident of 17, Allhallow's Lane, Steeple Martin. Owner of Sidney the cat.

Fran Wolfe — Formerly Fran Castle. Also former actor, occasional psychic, resident of Coastguard Cottage, Nethergate. Owner of Balzac the cat.

Ben Wilde — Libby's significant other. Owner of The Manor Farm and the Oast House Theatre.

Guy Wolfe — Fran's husband, artist and owner of a shop and gallery in Harbour Street, Nethergate.

Peter Parker — Ben's cousin. Freelance journalist, part-owner of The Pink Geranium restaurant and life partner of Harry Price.

Harry Price — Chef and co-owner of The Pink Geranium and Peter Parker's life partner.

Hetty Wilde — Ben's mother. Lives at The Manor.

DCI Ian Connell — Local policeman and friend. Former suitor of Fran's.

DI Maiden — DCI Connell's former sergeant.

Adam Sarjeant — Libby's younger son. Works

	with garden designer Mog, mainly at Creekmarsh.
Belinda Sarjeant	Libby's daughter. Lives and works in London.
Dominic Sarjeant	Libby's elder son. Lives and works in London.
Sophie Wolfe	Guy's daughter.
Flo Carpenter	Hetty's oldest friend.
Lenny Fisher	Hetty's brother. Lives with Flo Carpenter.
Jane Baker	Chief Reporter for the *Nethergate Mercury*. Mother to Imogen.
Reverend Patti Pearson	Vicar of St Aldeberge's Church.
Anne Douglas	Librarian, friend of Reverend Patti.
Tim Stevens	Landlord of the village pub.
Dr Nigel Peasegood	Village doctor.

Chapter One

Detective Chief Inspector Ian Connell stood at the tall window of his sitting room and looked out at the moonlit lake. The silver slice across the black surface was almost theatrical, a spotlight on the flagged terrace below.

It was rare that he had the time to appreciate the good fortune that had brought him here. Others might say it was the result of hard work rather than good fortune, but Ian knew that luck had played a large part in his rise through the ranks of the police service.

Tonight was the first night of his weekend off, a weekend to enjoy with friends in Steeple Martin. His bag was packed and he could look forward to being plain Ian Connell for a whole two days.

Libby Sarjeant watched as the band on stage played an encore to an ecstatic crowd. Ben Wilde, standing beside her in front of the small bar at the back of the field, was mouthing something, but Jonah Fludde had never been a quiet band, and this was their most famous – and loudest – hit from the 1970s. She shook her head at Ben, grinning.

Further away, Ian Connell sat with Fran and Guy Wolfe. Libby was still marvelling at the transformation of Ian from detective chief inspector to ordinary citizen. She wasn't quite sure she approved of the Jonah Fludde tour T-shirt he sported, but under the circumstances, as the first founder of this "Roll Out The Barrel" Beer Festival, she supposed it was allowable.

'I'm closing up,' shouted a voice in her ear. 'We're already past time. Only hope your mate isn't keeping a beady eye on the clock.'

Libby turned her head and nodded. The new landlord of the village pub and sponsor of the festival, Tim Stevens, nodded and smiled back. Next to the bar, the street food stall, run by Harry Price's restaurant, The Pink Geranium, was already closed. Libby's son Adam, who had been manning it, was in the thick of the crowd with a party of friends.

At last, after a prolonged final flourish and extended cheering and applause from the audience, it was over.

'My ears are ringing,' said Libby.

'I remember being unable to hear for at least twenty-four hours after a Who concert back then,' said Ben. 'I just hope we don't get too many complaints from residents.'

'You were properly licensed,' said Ian, coming up behind them, looking at his watch. 'And they finished almost on time.'

'Difficult to shut them up,' said Tim, pulling shutters down over his stock. 'I'm glad you were one of the organisers.'

'It was his idea,' said Ben. 'Standing in this very field.' He stretched. 'I'd better go and start stewarding.'

'I'll come,' said Guy, arriving at Ben's side. 'Are they all going out to the car park?'

'Most of them,' said Ben. 'Ian's going to look after the gate to the Manor drive.'

Gradually, the field emptied. Libby, Fran and a few other Steeple Martin villagers went round with long-handled litter pickers and bin bags, occasionally waking up an over-enthusiastic participant who had to be encouraged to go and find a more appropriate place to sleep it off.

'God, I couldn't stand this sort of thing,' said Libby, wiping a weary hand across her forehead.

'Just think of them,' said Fran, nodding towards the stage, where members of Jonah Fludde and their roadie team were packing up. 'Every time they do a gig.'

'I don't suppose they did when they were in their heyday,' said Libby. 'They had minions.'

'They've got minions now,' said Fran. 'The band members are only packing their own instruments.'

'Except the drummer.' Libby paused to watch as the drummer snapped out orders to the hapless roadie coping with the kit. Ron Stewart, frontman of Jonah Fludde, gently guided the drummer to the back of the stage and received a grateful look from the roadie. 'Ron Stewart's definitely honed his people skills. That was very nicely done.'

'Was it? I'm at a bit of a loss in this world,' said Fran, resuming her litter picking. 'I mean, that band who played last night – what were they called?'

'Ellis.'

'Yes. Which is a mad name for a band, in my

opinion. They're supposed to be famous, aren't they? And they did all their own packing up.'

'They're up and coming,' said Libby. 'And they did this as a favour, really, because they know Bel and Dom. So I expect they couldn't afford to pay roadies.'

Belinda and Dominic, Libby's two older children, had graced the weekend with their presence, despite disapproving, along with their younger brother Adam, of the name of the event. Naming the Roll Out The Barrel Beer Festival had been the idea of landlord Tim, after he had agreed to sponsor it, and met with the approval of most of the older generation.

'What does up and coming mean, these days?' asked Fran.

'Slightly more prestigious gigs in better venues, invited to appear at festivals, a record deal and apparently, being on a BBC radio playlist. Very important.'

'So we're quite favoured, then?'

'Oh, yes. Luckily, two of them had known Bel and Dom for years. Well, since college, anyway.'

'I thought they were quite good,' said Fran.

'Well, don't sound so surprised,' said Libby, amused.

By the time the site was cleared and Ron Stewart had packed his fellow Jonah Fludde members into the minibus he had hired to take them back to his house - and Fran and Guy had retired to the Manor, where they and Ian were staying overnight - it was very late when Ben and Libby walked slowly home to Allhallow's Lane.

4

'Remind me never to organise a festival again,' said Libby. 'If anyone else wants to use the field, I suggest you charge them a fee and stay out of it.'

'I think you may be right.' Ben yawned and extracted his key from the pocket of his jeans. 'And just think, we'll have the camping and car park field to clear up tomorrow, as well.'

'Oh, don't,' moaned Libby. 'It doesn't bear thinking about.'

'We could hire that cleaning company Ian suggested,' said Ben, ushering Libby into number seventeen. Sidney the cat shot out between their legs. 'Are you too tired for a nightcap?'

'Unlike me though it is,' said Libby, 'yes. Straight to bed, I think. And yes, despite the money, I think we will hire that company.'

The following morning, slightly bleary-eyed, Libby and Ben arrived at the festival field and surveyed it gloomily.

'It doesn't look much better than it did last night,' said Libby. 'What time are we letting the lunchtime visitors in?'

'Eleven thirty,' said Ben, stretching. 'Tim will be over to set up the bar in a minute and Harry will be coming to do the food stall.'

'Come on, then, we'd better get the backstage area set up for the first band,' said Libby. 'They'll be here any minute, too.'

She walked over to the stage and hauled herself up to the side.

'They haven't left it very tidy,' she called out to

Ben. 'I hope the next band don't -'

'Don't what?' called Ben, after a pause. He straightened up and frowned. 'Lib?'

Libby appeared hanging on to the scaffolding at the side of the stage.

'Don't mind a body,' she whispered.

Chapter Two

Sitting down abruptly on the edge of the stage, Libby put her head in her hands.

'A body?' Ben gaped. 'Oh, Libby! Not again.'

Libby raised a tear-stained face. 'It's not my fault!'

Ben rushed over. 'No, of course not.' He put his arms round her. 'I'll call Ian.'

Libby nodded.

Ian answered immediately.

'I'll call 999,' he said. 'Ring off, Ben.'

'Why? Can't you...?'

'No. I'm off duty. Ring off, and I'll be over straight away. No one's touched anything, have they?'

'I don't think so...' said Ben doubtfully, but Ian had rung off.

He sat down beside Libby. Tim appeared from the back of the pub and began lifting the shutters on the bar, and Harry had already raised his own shutters.

'We'll have to tell them to stop,' said Libby. 'We won't be able to carry on.'

'Oh, Lord.' Ben shook his head. 'We'll have to turn all the campers away.'

'I doubt it,' said Libby. 'If they were here overnight the police will have to question them. And I recognised him.' Her voice wobbled.

Ben looked at her sharply. 'Who is it?'

'One of the members of Ellis.'

'Oh, bloody hell,' said Ben.

Ian appeared through the gate from the Manor drive, a grim expression on his face.

'Did you recognise the body?'

Libby nodded. 'One of the members of Ellis – Bel and Dom's friends.'

Ian's expression became even grimmer. 'I'll go and have a look.'

As he disappeared to the back of the stage they heard the sound of the police siren, and suddenly the field was full of uniforms. Within seconds, Ian was back and shepherding onlookers away as patrol cars drew up in the drive. Libby and Ben watched as uniformed officers surrounded their friend and others went over to the car park and camping area.

'Mrs Sarjeant?' A red-haired, blue-eyed plain clothes officer smiled at Libby. 'Remember me?'

'Sergeant Maiden.' Libby gave a tremulous smile back.

'Inspector, now.' He beamed. 'You found the – er – fatality.' He turned to Ben. 'And Mr Wilde, wasn't it?'

'I wasn't with her, I'm afraid,' said Ben. 'I haven't seen it.'

'DCI Connell has, though.' Maiden frowned at his superior. 'This is awkward.'

'Awkward? Why?' asked Libby.

'He was off duty.'

'Does that matter?' Ben watched Ian deep in

8

conversation with his colleagues. 'He didn't know the – er – deceased.'

'No.' Maiden smiled again. 'I'm afraid we shall have to ask you some questions, though. Is there anywhere we can go?'

'The Manor,' suggested Ben. 'My office. You've been there before.'

Maiden nodded and went across to where Ian was talking to the other officers. By this time, a blue-suited scientist had headed to the back of the stage, followed by lesser blue-suited minions. Ian came back and joined them.

'I'm relegated.' He sighed. 'Not that I particularly want to be involved. Come on, we've been told to report to your office.'

He said nothing as the three of them walked across the field to the drive. Hetty was waiting anxiously at the heavy oak door of the Manor.

'Another one, is it?'

Ben sighed and nodded. 'Yes, Mum. Go back in the kitchen. We'll come and see you in a little while.'

Fran emerged from the hall behind Hetty.

'What's going on?'

Ben told her.

'I don't believe it.' She shook her head. 'No one would.'

'No.' Libby smiled grimly. 'Ben and I have to go and be grilled. We'll see you later.'

'What about Ian?'

'Yes. I have to be grilled, too,' Ian said with a smile. 'I'm going to ask if you can go and keep an eye out for guests or bands arriving this morning.

9

Who's coming, can you remember?'

'Oh yes.' Libby pulled a face. 'Can't you?'

'No.' Ian frowned.

'I can,' said Ben. 'The two founder members of Ellis doing an acoustic set.'

Ian and Fran looked shocked beyond belief.

Guy came out onto the forecourt. 'Sophie's coming over this morning,' he said. 'She was – is – a great fan of Ellis. Especially the original two.'

'Should we tell them?' asked Libby.

'I will.' Ian sighed, and led the way into the Manor.

The inquisition, as Libby called it, didn't take long, and after warning them all not to say anything to anyone, and in particular the other members of Ellis, Inspector Maiden let them go.

'Where, though?' said Libby. 'What are we supposed to do?'

'We'll go and see what they've said to Tim and Harry,' said Ben. 'They'll know what the public have been told to do.'

Tim and Harry were sitting disconsolately on upturned crates in front of their respective businesses.

'They aren't letting anyone in,' said Harry. 'They're questioning everyone who stayed in the camping part overnight and sending them home.'

'What about the guests in the Manor?' asked Libby. 'And Ron Stewart. They were all here last night.'

'Was the victim, though?' said Ian.

Four pairs of eyes looked at him in surprise.

'He must have been,' said Libby. 'Where else would he be? He was killed here!'

'Actually,' said Ian with a sigh, 'I think he was here last night. I'm pretty sure he was here.'

'Why did you ask if he was, then?' said Libby.

'Because, like all witnesses, I can't be absolutely sure.' He turned and looked over his shoulder. 'I suppose I ought to tell Maiden.'

'You're always telling us -'

'I know.' Ian sighed again. 'I won't be long.'

'Well!' said Harry, as they watched him stride over to the knot of policemen in front of the stage. 'What happens now?'

'No idea,' said Ben. 'He's been told not to get involved.'

'He said Ron Stewart was here last night,' said Libby. 'But we saw him leave.'

'I expected he meant during the evening,' said Ben. 'Look, here come Fran and Guy. At least they haven't sent them home.'

'We sent the other two band members in to Sergeant Maiden,' said Fran.

'Inspector,' corrected Libby.

'What do we do now?' asked Guy.

'Wait, I suppose,' said Ben. 'Tim and Harry, you might as well go home.'

Harry stood up and stretched. 'Why won't they let the festival carry on?'

'The stage is a crime scene,' said Guy. 'I suppose they could let people use the bar.'

'If anybody asks,' said Tim, 'send them into the pub.'

'I doubt if they will,' said Fran. 'They're clearing the car park. There won't be room on the high street.'

11

Tim and Harry vanished into their back doors just as a yellow-jacketed police officer approached them, looking irritable.

'Someone over there says he's supposed to be working here today.' He waved a hand towards the gate.

'My son,' explained Libby. 'May I speak to him?'

'Well...'

'Yes, Libby. Go on.' Ian materialised and fixed the officer with a minatory glare. 'In fact, I'll come over myself.'

The officer opened his mouth, took one look at Ian's face and shut it again.

'Adam?' Libby stuck two fingers through the fencing. 'Why didn't you come through the back gate?'

'Dom and I went to collect Bel.' Adam indicated his brother standing behind him.

'Where is she, then?'

'When we got here we found out and she went up to see Hetty.' Dominic looked pale. 'What happened, Mum? Who is it?'

'One of Ellis,' said Libby and held up a hand, 'but I don't think it's one of your friends.'

If possible, Dominic turned even paler.

'If I were you,' said Ian, 'I'd go up and join Belinda in Hetty's kitchen. We've only met briefly, but I'm Ian.' He held out his hand. Dominic took it gingerly.

'The policeman, right?'

'Yes, but I'm off duty today.'

'You're never off duty,' said Adam glumly.

'Go on, Dom,' said Libby. 'As soon as we can we'll come up. Go on, Ad, you go too.'

12

'What was Ad doing after the stall closed?' asked Ian as they walked back to where the others waited.

'He was in the audience. Then he went home via the back gate.'

'Would he have seen anything?' said Ian.

'I doubt it. When was he killed?'

'I've no idea, but last night, I would think.'

'What now?' asked Fran, as Libby came to a halt beside her.

'I don't know.' They all looked at Ian.

'I don't know either.' He looked round the field at various groups of officers, crime scene tapes and photographers. 'As far as I can see, they're questioning everyone in the car park field, then letting them go. I can't see why they wouldn't let you go, too.'

'But we've got to clear up and get the fencing and gates ready for the hire company to pick up,' said Ben.

'And the staging,' said Libby. 'Although Ron Stewart organised that. Someone ought to tell him.'

'Have you got a list of the people involved?' asked Ian.

'Yes – on my computer,' said Libby.

'Ah.' Ian stared at the floor for a moment. 'OK – wait here.'

'Where's he gone?' asked Libby, as Ian was lost behind a knot of blue-suited individuals.

'On stage,' said Fran. 'Do you suppose they'll throw him off?'

'I don't understand why they aren't letting him be part of the investigation,' said Guy. 'He knows us, the village, even the field. And a lot of the people.'

'That's why, I expect,' said Ben. 'He's been warned in the past about keeping us – or Libby, anyway – out of investigations. They probably think he'd hide things.'

'Then they don't know Ian,' snapped Libby.

'All right, all right.' Ben patted her arm.

Inspector Maiden emerged from the backstage area and started purposefully towards them.

'Mrs Sarjeant, DCI Connell tells me you have a list of people concerned in this – ah – event – at home. Would it be possible for us to send someone to fetch it?'

Libby raised her eyebrows. 'Fetch it? I'll go and collect it, if you like.'

'Um – well, it would be better...' Maiden eyed her warily.

'No.' Libby's cheerful face rarely looked stormy, but when it did...

'Send somebody with Mrs Sarjeant.' Ian came up behind Maiden. 'She's hardly likely to run away with it, is she?'

Libby turned a fulminating eye on Maiden. 'Do you really imagine I would let someone into my house alone to search my computer?'

'If they had a warrant you'd have to, Lib,' said Ian mildly. 'As it is, I'm sure you can fetch it yourself.'

'Hmph,' said Libby and turned on her heel towards Allhallow's Lane. Maiden, caught unawares, cast round for an officer to send with her, and finding no one, set off after her at a trot.

Libby left the door open for him.

'I'm afraid,' she said, opening up her laptop, 'that I shall have to send it to the Manor Estate Office. That's

14

where the printer is.'

'Oh.' Maiden hovered uncertainly by the door. 'Can we send someone to collect that? Or should Mr Wilde...?'

Libby, bad temper forgotten, beamed. 'I'll ring him.' Before Maiden could protest, she'd pressed speed dial on her phone.

'There,' she said, and turned the screen to face him. 'That's the list of bands and suppliers. Luckily, it's only a tiny festival. All the licenses are listed there, too.'

Maiden bent down to look at the screen.

'It looks very clear,' he said, straightening up. 'And you're sending that to the printer at the Manor?'

'I've already done it.'

'And you have to let all these people know when you've finished with – with -'

'Their services, or the bands. In fact, the bands that were due to play this lunchtime and early afternoon will be here already, I should think. The two members of Ellis, the band the – er – well, they're here, aren't they?'

'They've been interviewed,' said Maiden. Libby nodded and shut down the computer.

'Come on. Ben will be back with your printout by now,' she said, and led the way out of the front door.

Ben was waiting by the stage, the printout in his hand.

'The other two bands have both arrived,' he said. 'Can we tell them to go home?'

'I suppose so,' said Maiden. 'I'll just check.' He vanished behind the stage.

'Is there someone else in charge now?' asked Libby in a whisper.

'No, but Ian keeps getting called in.' Ben looked

15

amused. 'I don't think they're going to be able to keep him out of it. They've asked his advice three times since you've been gone.'

'Well,' said Libby, her eyes fixed on the low black car that had drawn up in the drive, 'I think that's just about to change.'

Chapter Three

Ben followed her gaze.

'Is that -?' he whispered.

'Certainly is,' said Libby. 'Good morning, Superintendent Bertram.'

The woman came to a halt ten feet from the stage.

'Mrs Sarjeant,' she grated out.

Superintendent Bertram hadn't changed much since Libby had last seen her several years ago. Her face was a little more lined, but her skirt was still as short, her hair still as bright and her expression still as vicious.

'Where is Inspector Connell?'

'Detective Chief Inspector Connell is helping the police with their enquiries,' said Ben helpfully. 'We'll be at the Manor if we're needed.'

'Where's that?' Bertram snapped.

'Behind you,' chorused Ben and Libby, and set off towards the drive.

'I expect we've upset her,' murmured Libby as the officer on duty let them out through the temporary gates.

'Good,' said Ben.

A further officer was stationed by the huge oak front door.

'I'm afraid you can't go in here, sir.' He eyed Ben belligerently.

17

'You've only just arrived, haven't you?' said Ben. 'Well?'

'If you'd been here ten minutes ago you would have seen me leave this building.' Ben thrust a pugnacious jaw towards the officer. 'I live here.'

The officer cast nervous eyes to left and right. 'I – er – '

'Thank you, officer.' Ian's voice sounded comfortingly from behind Libby. She beamed at the officer and stepped past him.

'What happened?' Ben asked, as Ian shut the door behind them.

'Madam is trying to pull rank. She's only here because I'm on leave and there's no one else available. She's trying to tell me I can't speak to any of you or stay here.'

'Oh, how ridiculous,' said Libby.

'It's not entirely ridiculous,' said Ian, with a slightly crooked smile. 'I could completely mess up the investigation. I should think she'll be over here as soon as she can, so I'd better ask any questions I want to fairly quickly.' He opened the door to the large sitting room, which had been designated an equipment store for the duration of the weekend. Inside, various musicians sat or stood, looking disconsolate.

'Ladies and gentlemen,' said Ian, 'just a few questions to start with.'

'What happened?' asked a small, scruffy-haired man from behind a stack of speakers. 'Is Clive dead?'

Libby looked towards the two founder members of Ellis, who sat nursing their guitars alongside Belinda and Dominic.

18

'Yes, sorry.' One of them, long fair hair hanging over his face, nodded. 'Didn't know it was a secret.'

'Clive Eddington?' asked Ian. 'Can I ask how many people here knew him?'

A murmur rippled through the room.

'None of us knew him well.' Another member of Ellis spoke up.

'Where did he come from?' asked Ian.

'Up north somewhere. He only came to London a few weeks before we met him.'

'And nobody here had met him before then?'

Another murmur, this time definitely denial, rippled round the room.

The door behind them opened.

'DCI Connell,' said a sharp voice. 'A word, please.'

'Excuse me,' said Ian politely to the room in general, and went out. Ben reached behind him and shut the door.

'Who's that?' asked one of the members of Ellis.

'The local superintendent,' said Libby. 'I doubt if she'll be around for long.'

'Good.' Belinda patted the armchair beside her. 'Come and sit down, Mum.'

'I'm going to see Hetty,' said Ben. 'I'll be back in a minute.'

As soon as Libby sat down, she was surrounded by musicians.

'What's going on?'

'Was he really killed?'

'What happened?'

'When was it?'

'I don't know.' Libby shook her head. 'I found him this morning.'

'I wondered why he wasn't in his tent,' came a voice from somewhere behind more equipment.

'Terry,' said Dominic, 'when did you last see him?'

A young man with sleepy eyes emerged. 'Last night, I think. When Jonah Fludde came off stage. I'd had enough by then, and he said he'd be along in a minute.' He shrugged. 'But I didn't see him.'

'You weren't in the same tent?' said Libby.

'God, no! We'd never fit.'

'And we were over here,' said the fair-haired guitarist. He held out his hand to Libby. 'We didn't meet yesterday, did we? I'm George Poole.'

Libby shook hands.

'And I'm Kyle Rayner.' The other member of Ellis also stuck out his hand and smiled shyly. Very dark, he was sitting as close to Belinda as he could. Dominic regarded him with amusement.

'I'm pleased to meet you,' said Libby, 'but very sorry it's under such awful circumstances.'

'You might have known, Mum,' said Belinda. 'Everything you do –'

'That's not fair, Bel,' said Dominic. 'Not *everything*.'

'When will they let us go?' asked the scruffy man. 'I've got another gig this afternoon.'

'Oh, heavens, I don't know.' Libby frowned. 'I can't see why they need to keep everyone if they didn't know – Clive, did you say?'

'Can't you ask Ian?' Dominic raised his eyebrows. 'He's here as a friend this weekend, isn't he?'

20

'Yes, that's the trouble,' said Libby, frowning.

'Who's Ian?' asked Kyle.

'DCI Connell. The bloke who was asking questions just now,' said Belinda. 'I told you before.'

'Oh – the bloke who thought the whole thing up?'

'And I bet he wishes he hadn't,' said Libby. 'He's been banned from the investigation, now.'

'What was he doing asking us questions, then?' asked the scruffy one, somewhat belligerently.

'Helping,' said Libby, scowling at him.

Ben came back into the room, followed immediately by Ian.

'I'm afraid someone will be over here to take your statements,' Ian said. 'After that you will be able to leave. I can only say I'm sorry, on behalf of the festival, that this has happened.'

'I thought you were a copper?' said the scruffy one.

'He is,' said Ben, 'but even the police have private lives, and this was to have been part of DCI Connell's.'

'We're not getting that cow who just came in, are we?' The scruffy one's belligerence was mounting.

'Superintendent Bertram will be overseeing the investigation from her office,' said Ian. 'Libby? Fran, Guy? We can go now.'

Outside the sitting room, he ushered them silently into the kitchen. Hetty stood up and moved towards the kettle.

'What's going on?' asked Libby.

'She's trying to throw her weight around,' said Ian. 'No idea why – it isn't her territory – and luckily, Maiden has got the backing of our own superintendent, and he stood his ground. Trying to get me banned from not only

21

the investigation but the whole scene was going a bit far.'

'She's never forgiven us all for that business over at Creekmarsh,' said Libby.

'And she's been promoted sideways, hasn't she?' said Fran.

'She has, and she's likely to be suspended shortly,' said Ian, 'but I can't say anything about that. I doubt she'll be with us for long.'

'And now I'm dying to know why,' grumbled Libby.

'Tea or coffee?' asked Hetty.

Half an hour later, Ian suggested they walk down to the pub to see what the mood of the villagers was.

'And if any of the people who bought tickets have ended up in there,' said Guy.

'There won't be anywhere to park,' said Ben. 'The police were evacuating our car park and camping field.'

'Will you have to refund for today?' asked Fran.

'I don't know,' said Libby. 'It's something I've always dreaded at the theatre.'

'And let's face it, we've had enough near-disasters there,' said Ben.

The five of them walked down the drive, trying to ignore the lines of uniformed officers doing what appeared to be a fingertip search of the festival field.

'Have they got any ideas at all?' asked Libby.

'I don't know. It must have been someone who knew their way around backstage,' said Ian.

'Why, though?' said Ben. 'Anyone could have walked up on stage and gone round to the back.'

'And it must have been after everyone left last night. Fran and I didn't see anyone while we were clearing up,

22

did we?' said Libby.

'Well, we did. We saw the members of Jonah Fludde clearing up.'

'Yes, but they were legit.'

'Who else was here when you left?' asked Ian.

'We were last to leave,' said Libby. 'Ben and me. You'd gone with Fran and Guy, Ron Stewart had taken his lot off in their minibus and the earlier band had cleared their instruments into the Manor. It was some of them who were in the sitting room just now. Lots of the villagers – pub regulars, mostly – helped Fran and me clear up the rubbish and plastic glasses.'

'Shall we see if any of them are in the pub now?' suggested Ian.

Ben frowned. 'Are you interfering, DCI Connell?'

Ian grinned. 'You bet I am!'

On the way past The Pink Geranium, Libby put her head round the door and explained the current situation to Harry and his partner Peter, Ben's cousin.

'Adam's sulking in the flat,' said Harry, casting his eyes upwards. 'Despite what he said, he actually enjoyed running the food stall.'

'If he makes an appearance tell him we're in the pub,' said Ben.

'I'll join you in a bit,' said Peter, patting Harry's shoulder. 'Sorry, love.'

The pub was packed. Tim hailed them over the heads of the regulars, who turned avid eyes on them.

'What happened?'

'Who was it?'

'Was it really murder?'

Tim held up one hand and rang the bell with the other.

'Quiet folks! Let the dog see the rabbit. What'll it be, Ian?'

Ian placed the order for all five of them and prepared both to answer and ask questions.

'First,' he said, turning and leaning an elbow on the bar, 'I want to know who was here clearing up with Libby and Fran.'

'And what they saw,' said Libby.

A tentative hand went up from the back of the crowd.

'I saw someone. Just as I was leaving.'

'What was that, Dick?' Tim peered over the sea of heads.

'I saw one of those blokes from that band the night before. What was it called? Ellis – that's right. On stage, he was.'

The man at the back of the crowd looked startled as all eyes turned on him.

'Wh-wh-wh-?' he stammered.

'It was a member of Ellis who was found dead,' said Libby. 'Sorry.'

Ian frowned at her.

'Sorry,' she said unrepentantly, 'but you did ask.'

Tim leant across the bar. 'There were quite a few of us clearing up.' He beamed round at his customers. 'Good lot, they are.'

The regulars shuffled their feet and mumbled. Libby grinned.

'Well, we know that,' she said. 'We've known them a long time.'

'That put me in my place,' said Tim.

Everyone laughed and the atmosphere lightened.

'You're that copper who was here when that runner got killed, aren't you?' said someone.

'I am,' said Ian. 'So does anyone apart from this gentleman remember seeing anything last night?'

'Nothing what you might call suspicious,' piped up another voice. 'That Screwball Stewart and his lot packin' away.'

'Yes, we know about that,' said Ian. 'Only you saw the Ellis band member then, Mr – ?' He turned back to the original speaker.

'I dunno.' He shrugged. 'I'm Dick Fowler. I've got the photography shop over the road.'

'No one else, then?' Ian looked round the company, who all shook their heads.

'Dick was one of the last to leave,' said Tim. 'You'd gone, Libby, and you'd gone back to the Manor, Ian, with Fran and Guy.'

Guy grinned and winked at Ian. 'Can't pin it on us, guv.'

'All right, just getting it clear.' Ian grinned at him and turned back to Dick Fowler. 'You couldn't give me an idea of who was left – or what the field looked like when you left, could you, Mr Fowler?'

Dick, still looking slightly bewildered, nodded. Ian led him over to a small table in the corner of the lounge bar, followed by Fran, Guy, Ben and Libby.

'Well,' said Dick, after he'd been settled with a fresh pint by the attentive Tim. 'There were quite a few of us clearing up.' He turned to Libby and Fran. 'Weren't there?'

25

'Quite a few,' agreed Fran.

'And after Screwball Stewart had got his lot off the stage, a couple of the band who'd played before them went up to collect stuff. I didn't see them leave.'

'Oh, I didn't see them,' said Libby.

'They took their equipment to the Manor to leave in the sitting room with the others. They had tents in the other field,' said Ben.

'And there were all the Regionals. They were in the field.'

Everyone looked blankly at Dick

'Regionals? What do you mean?' asked Libby.

Guy snorted. 'The Nether Regionals.'

'The what?'

'The local biker group,' said Ian, with amusement. 'I'd forgotten them.'

'Bikers?' said Fran.

'The least trouble of any group of people I've known,' said Ian. 'Any festival, especially with music and beer, they'll be there, especially if there are camping facilities.'

'How did I not know?' Libby said, surprised.

'Because I took the group booking,' said Ben, looking embarrassed. 'I forgot.'

'You purposely didn't tell me,' accused Libby.

'He mentioned them to me,' said Ian. 'I put his mind at rest.'

'Where are they now?' Libby looked round nervously.

'Some of them are in the bar next door,' said Dick. 'They're all right.'

'I hope they aren't going to drive home, then,' said Ian, getting to his feet. 'I'll just have a friendly word.'

'They do a lot for charity,' said Guy, as they heard a ragged cheer go up in the next door bar at Ian's entrance. 'They organise their own events for Cancer Research every year, and a Toy Run at Christmas.'

'And an Easter Egg run at Easter,' put in Dick.

'How come I didn't know any of this?' said Fran.

'It just hadn't crossed your path yet,' said Guy. 'Until Sophie joined the Harriers you didn't know anything about them or running, did you?'

'Neither did I,' said Libby gloomily, 'and I rather wish I still didn't. '

Ian reappeared from the other bar accompanied by a diminutive woman in leathers.

'This is Edna,' he said. 'She's got something to tell us.'

'Call me Ed.' The woman beamed round at them all, her face dissolving into a thousand tiny lines. 'I saw that bloke – the one what got murdered.'

'Oh? When?' Libby looked from Edna to Ian.

'Late last night,' said Ian. 'Go on, Ed.'

'See, he was in the tent sort of next door to me. With his mate the other side. And I gets up to go and take a leak, and there he is coming out of his tent, too. I thought he was going for a leak, too. But he wasn't. He didn't come anywhere near the loos.' She shrugged. 'Didn't really think about it at all at the time, if you know what I mean. Just thought of it this morning.'

'He was definitely coming out of his tent, was he?' asked Ian. 'Not going back in?'

Ed shook her head. 'Oh no. Coming out, like. He went off towards the other field.'

27

'You mean the music field?' asked Guy.

'And the stage,' said Ed. 'And there was somebody waiting for him.'

Chapter Four

A mixture of gasps and exclamations greeted this extraordinary statement.

'Who?' asked Libby, eventually overcoming all the other voices.

'She doesn't know,' said Ian.

'But you saw him?' said Ben.

'Not really. I saw him speak to someone.'

'Where?' asked Fran.

'On the stage. Look,' said Ed, her patience obviously wearing thin, 'I weren't paying attention, was I? Just saw him go up to the stage, speak to someone and that was it. I was in a hurry.' She raised her chin defiantly.

'Sorry, Ed, of course you were,' said Libby.

Ian patted her on the shoulder. 'Thanks, Ed. You get back to your pint, now.'

Ed sent a wary smile round the group, paused and looked at Ian. 'Great little festival, by the way. Bands were awesome.'

Dick Fowler watched her go and cleared his throat. 'Is that all? Can I go now?'

'Of course,' said Ian. 'It was kind of you to talk to us.'

Dick gave them a nervous smile. 'Anything I can do to help. She was right, though. Great bands. Hope we can do it again.' He slid out of his seat and went back to the bar.

'I haven't come across him before,' said Ian, when he was out of earshot. 'Photography shop, did he say? I didn't think Steeple Martin was big enough to have a photography shop.'

'He sells cameras and tripods and stuff,' said Libby. 'And frames. But his main business is wedding photography.'

'He was here taking official photos for us,' said Ben. 'We thought we might need publicity.' He sighed. 'Looks as though we'll get more than we wanted, now.'

'Would he show us the photos?' asked Ian. 'That could be useful.'

'To identify someone?' said Fran. 'But how would we know who? He wouldn't be taking a picture when the victim went to meet his murderer, would he? And earlier, no one would know who it was.'

'If he took any pictures with Clive Eddington in and we could identify who he was talking to,' said Ian, 'that might help.'

'But it wouldn't help Superintendent Bertram, I suppose,' said Libby innocently.

Ian grinned at her. 'Possibly not.'

'So what's your position in all this, Ian?' asked Guy. 'Can they really keep you out of it?'

'Oh, yes.' Ian leant back in his chair. 'I was off duty and part of the organisational set-up of the festival. So I'm too close to the enquiry. It's the same as close friends or family members not being allowed on cases, or, in the case of doctors, to treat or operate on friends or family members.'

'But you're going to investigate anyway,' said Fran

30

shrewdly. 'Just as we do.'

Ian looked embarrassed. 'Maybe.'

'You already are,' said Libby. 'Don't you dare moan at us in future.'

'But you aren't members of the police force, Lib,' said Ben. 'Ian actually is.'

'It must be discretionary, this ban?' said Guy. 'It surely isn't in the rules.'

'Yes, it's discretionary,' said Ian. 'If they get very short-staffed or – well, they could ask me in.'

'Or in a muddle,' said Libby helpfully. 'Which Bertram is likely to do.'

'You said she was likely to be suspended shortly,' said Fran.

'I also said I couldn't say anything about that,' said Ian, 'so don't ask me.'

'Even if Maiden has your own superintendent's backing, she could put a serious spoke in his wheel, couldn't she?' said Libby.

'But probably not in mine,' said Ian. 'People in this village know me and who I am, don't they? Unless it's broadcast that I'm off the enquiry, people will be inclined to talk to me.'

'Maybe,' said Libby doubtfully.

'But not all the visitors were from Steeple Martin,' said Ben. 'In fact, there were more people from outside than locals. That's why we had the camping field. And by the way, what are the bikers going to do? I thought the police were clearing the campers?'

'Some of them were camping in a field up New Barn Lane,' said Ian.

'Farmer Giles!' said Libby.

'No – really?' Fran's eyes were wide.

'Actually, yes.' Libby laughed. 'Poor bloke's suffered all his life. When he was younger he never told anyone he was a farmer.'

'They've all gone there now, and apparently told all the other campers to go, too,' said Ian. 'Farmer Giles is going to be doing a roaring business.'

'Does he need a licence or anything?' asked Fran.

'I wasn't asked to get one,' said Ben.

'What about the portaloos?' asked Libby. 'When will they be collected? Could they be relocated?'

'Tomorrow morning, so no help really,' said Ben. 'Will it help the investigation to have the visitors still here, Ian?'

' It might. Meanwhile,' said Ian, standing up, I'm going to ask our helpful friend Dick the photographer if I can see his pictures of last night.'

The four friends sat in silence for a few moments, each contemplating the events of the morning. Libby realised she had overcome the shock of finding the body in the flurry of activity, and was quite ashamed to have done so. She noticed the time on the pub clock with surprise.

'It's almost two!' she said. 'What will happen to the other bands?'

'I expect they'll be turned back by the police,' said Guy.

'And they might come and look for us in here,' said Ben.

'What do we say to them, though?' Libby frowned into her glass. 'Will they expect to be paid?'

32

'We'll deal with that when we come to it.' Ben patted her arm. 'Let's just concentrate on the murder for the time being.'

'I never thought I'd hear you say that,' said Libby.

Tim appeared round the side of the bar.

'I've been thinking,' he said. 'I've got all those craft beers to shift. What am I going to do with them?' Guy and Ben exchanged glances. 'And no funny suggestions, please!'

'What can you do with them?' asked Libby. 'Can you give them back?'

Tim, Guy and Ben all laughed.

'They've been tapped, Lib,' said Ben.

'How long will they keep?' asked Fran.

'Varies, but over a month,' said Tim. 'What I was thinking was, could we keep the bar set-up out the back and use it as an extension of the garden?'

'You mean put a few seats and tables out there?' Ben looked thoughtful. 'I don't see why not. But what about the licence?'

'Not sure. But would it be all right with you?'

'Certainly,' said Ben. 'In fact, you could go and tell all the punters that have transferred from the festival now, couldn't you?'

'The police are keeping the field sealed off, aren't they?' Tim sighed. 'Never mind. I'll put it about that the beers are still there. We'll do a social media campaign.'

'The old owner would never have done that,' said Libby, watching Tim cheerfully collecting glasses and chatting to customers.

'No.' Ben smiled. 'Altogether a different sort of

landlord.' He stood up and went over to Tim. 'You could still sell the stuff from here, couldn't you?'

Tim handed over a collection of glasses. 'You take these back and I'll go and get the list.'

Ian reappeared and watched Ben with surprise.

'Ben suggested selling the beers over the counter in here,' explained Libby. 'And when the police have cleared the back field for use, Tim's going to keep the little bar on to sell the rest. How did you get on with Dick?'

'Fine. He let me see what he's got on the camera, but I've only had a quick flick through, so he's put them on a memory stick for me.'

'You'll need a computer then,' said Fran slyly. 'The estate office or number seventeen?'

Ian resumed his seat. 'Believe it or not, I came equipped.' He reached into the backpack at his feet and brought out a top of the range laptop. 'My personal one.' He grinned at Fran. 'Just in case.'

'Are we allowed to look?' asked Libby, as Ben came back to the table.

'As I'm not official, yes.' Ian raised an eyebrow. 'And don't spread it around.'

They gathered round Ian and peered at the screen as the series of images flashed past.

'They're good,' said Ben, 'but they're mainly of the stage.'

'There are some of the audience,' said Fran. 'Those from the Friday night – there are quite a lot.'

'And that was when Ellis was playing,' said Ian, 'so probably just as useful.'

34

'Those two crop up on both nights,' said Libby, pointing.

Two young women, both with long fair hair, waved plastic beer mugs at the camera.

'Is there one of them watching Ellis?' asked Fran.

Ian pushed the laptop towards her. 'You find the pictures of Ellis and we'll see.'

Fran gave a smug little smile and sat down on the other side of the table. Libby went round to watch.

'Yes,' said Fran eventually. 'Here we are, but they're simply watching, nothing more. I'll see if there's anything for Saturday.'

Libby sat back and looked at the others, eyebrows raised. 'I think someone's enjoying this.'

'They're in a lot,' said Fran, after a few minutes. 'Should we try and find out who they are? Dick might know, as he took so many of them.'

'Who's we, Tonto?' asked Libby.

'Well, Ian is sharing with us,' said Fran serenely, and pushed the laptop back towards him.

He smiled at her. 'I am, indeed, and it's a good idea.' He stood up and took the laptop back to the bar.

'I like this being involved business,' said Libby. 'So much easier.'

It was Fran's turn to raise her eyebrows. 'Easier? We aren't investigating.'

'Oh, aren't we?' said Libby innocently. 'We're *involved*, though, aren't we?'

Ben sighed. 'Look, you two, we're involved on the periphery. You are *not* investigating. Leave it to Ian.'

'But he's not supposed to be investigating, either,' said

Libby. 'We're just helping.'

'No use, Ben,' said Guy. 'I'd give up, if I were you.'

Ian came back.

'No, he doesn't know them. He took photos because they were pretty and strikingly alike – and around a lot. He said a lot of people were taking notice of them.'

'I didn't notice them,' said Libby.

'Neither did I,' said Ben.

'Nor me,' said Ian.

'In that case, they can't have been around all that much,' said Fran.

'I expect,' said Libby thoughtfully, 'they were at the front of the crowd. We were always at the back.'

'Do you think they're still here?' said Fran.

'Haven't seen them in here,' said Libby.

'Show the bikers,' said Ben.

'Good idea,' said Guy. 'Go on, Ian.'

Ian sighed, picked up the laptop again and went off to the other bar. When he came back, Edna was with him.

'Ed says they were staying overnight, too, and she thinks they followed the others to Farmer Giles's field.'

'Yeah, I noticed them.' Ed nodded wisely. 'Their tent was near me.'

'So near Clive Eddington's, too, then?' said Fran.

'Who? Oh, the boy what was killed – yeah. Bit further away, though.'

'Could he have known them?' asked Libby.

Ed shrugged. 'How do I know? Didn't see 'em together.'

'Thanks, Ed,' said Ian. 'Can I get you a drink?'

He and Edna moved off together. Fran watched them.

'He's made a hit there.'

Libby gave her a warning look. 'No dog in the manger stuff.'

Fran laughed. 'As if! Now, don't you think we should go and see if the toothsome twins are up at Farmer Giles's field?'

'If they are,' said Guy, 'why haven't they come here? There isn't anything else to do.'

'Give us the laptop again, Ian,' said Libby suddenly as Ian came back from the bar. He handed it over and Libby began scrolling through pictures.

'There!' she said. 'At least three pictures of them eating Harry's food.'

'What? He took them eating?' Fran pulled the laptop towards her.

'No, they're pictures focusing on other people, but they're in the background.'

'What of it?' asked Ben.

Ian grinned. 'I think we might go and pay Harry a visit, don't you?' he said, standing up.

'He won't remember, and anyway, he wasn't there – Adam was serving,' said Guy.

'Come on, Libby and Fran,' said Ian. 'Let's see if we're right.'

Chapter Five

The Pink Geranium, as always at Sunday lunchtimes, was full. The current waiter, supplemented by a grumpy-looking Adam, both in long Victorian aprons, edged between tables crammed in more tightly than usual. On the sofa and armchairs in the left-hand window, people waited with drinks.

'Ma – you know we won't have room for you!' A harassed Adam skirted two tables bearing a loaded tray above the diners' heads.

'Not eating, Ad.' Libby tried to whisper, but already, customers were turning curious heads towards the door. A tug on her sleeve made her turn towards Fran.

'Found them,' she said.

Sure enough, Ian was already bending towards the two young women on the sofa, one perched on the arm next to her friend.

'But we're in the queue,' said the one on the sofa. 'We'll lose our place.'

Libby turned back to Adam. He rolled up his eyes and nodded. Libby suppressed a grin.

'I can assure you that won't happen,' said Ian. 'Even if the closed sign is up.'

'Absolutely,' said Libby. 'I'll bring you back myself.'

Looking as though they didn't know whether to take

38

this as a recommendation or not, the two girls stood up and allowed themselves to be led out of the restaurant and into the pub. Tim, spotting them as they came in, bustled forward.

'Would you care to come into the office?' he said.

Libby and Fran exchanged glances and followed Ian and the girls.

'Who are they?' asked the slightly taller of the two, as Libby and Fran went to stand behind Ian. 'You said you were a policeman. They don't look like police.'

'The organisers of the festival,' said Ian. 'They are as keen as we are to get to the bottom of this crime.'

The girls looked alarmed. 'We haven't got anything to do with it,' the shorter one said. 'Why are you talking to us?'

Ian hesitated and Libby leapt in.

'Because you were seen to be very close to the stage when Ellis were playing on Friday night, and we wondered if you knew the band.'

The girls relaxed.

'We're fans, that's all.' The taller one looked at Libby with interest. 'Hey, if you're an organiser, are you Bel and Dom's mum?'

Might have known, thought Libby, and nodded.

'Do sit down,' said Ian, indicating the two chairs at the other side of Tim's desk. 'First of all, may I have your names?' He pulled out a notebook and picked up a pen from the desk. *Unprepared*, thought Libby.

'Fiona Dawson,' said the taller girl.

'Tracey Field,' said the other.

'Thank you. And that was how you heard about the

39

festival? From Bel and Dom?'

'Yes, sort of,' said Fiona. 'We went to see Ellis play at a gig in Camden and Bel was there giving out leaflets. She said we could camp in a field next to the pub, so…'

'You've known Ellis for a long time?' continued Ian.

'George and Kyle, yes,' said Tracey. 'The other two have only joined in the last year.'

'Eighteen months, more like,' said Fiona.

'And was that an improvement?' asked Libby. Ian frowned at her.

'In a way,' said Fiona, considering, her head on one side. 'Made a fuller sound. But I always liked it when it was just the two of them. We were looking forward to that this afternoon, weren't we?' Tracey nodded.

'Oh, dear, I'm sorry,' said Libby.

'So you didn't see Clive near the stage yesterday evening? Or see anyone talking to him?' Ian regained control of the conversation.

Fiona and Tracey exchanged glances.

'N-no,' said Tracey. 'I don't think so. Did we, Fi?'

'No,' said Fiona, more definitely. 'We saw George and Kyle watching Jonah Fludde.'

'And not Terry or Clive?'

Fiona shook her head.

'Well, never mind.' Ian closed the notebook. 'If you do think of anything, just let the police know.'

'I'll take you back to the restaurant,' said Libby, and led the way out of the pub and back to The Pink Geranium, where Adam installed the girls at the now vacant table in the right hand window. 'Told you it would be all right,' she said. 'Enjoy your meal.'

Adam saw her out.

'You're remarkably cheerful for someone who found a body only a couple of hours ago.'

'I am, aren't I?' Libby frowned. 'I've been so busy since then. I think once I stop I might fall apart.'

Back in the pub she was surprised to find Belinda, Dominic, George, Kyle and Terry surrounding Ian in the lounge bar, while Fran, Guy and Ben looked on.

'They want to go and play to everyone up in Farmer Giles's field,' explained Fran. 'Ian's trying to decide whether they should or not.'

'Why shouldn't they?'

'I think the superintendent might object,' Ian spoke over the top of his petitioners.

'She hasn't kept them all at the festival, has she?' asked Libby. 'She's let them go. Surely they can do what they want? At least she'd know where they are.'

Tim reappeared with a tray of drinks. 'I think they ought to play here,' he said, unloading bottles and glasses onto a table. 'What about the function room upstairs?'

All eyes turned to him.

'Function room?' said Ben. 'What function room?'

Tim looked surprised. 'I thought you'd know. It was stuffed with junk when we arrived. Didn't they ever use it?'

'I've never known it used,' said Ben, 'and I've lived here most of my life. Well, my family have.'

'Have you cleared it now?' asked Fran.

Tim nodded. 'And given it a lick of paint. No chairs up there, but we could carry some up.'

'Are you licensed?' asked Ian, and was shouted

41

down by nine people.

'All we need to do is go down to Farmer Giles's field to tell the people there,' said Terry. 'I'll go – I'm not playing. Shall we say a time?'

Tim cast a speculative look at Ian. 'Three? Half past. It's almost three now.'

Ian sighed. 'Half past three it is. You'd better spread the word in the other bars, Tim.'

'Do you really think Big Bertha would try and stop it?' asked Libby.

'I'm sure she'd have a damn good try.' Ian stood up. 'We'd better try and find something to eat.'

Tim and Betty supplied them all with sandwiches, while the young people set about recruiting an audience for their impromptu performance, including sending Dominic into The Pink Geranium to spread the word there.

'Although it isn't exactly impromptu,' said George. 'Just a different venue.'

'Probably better here,' said Kyle. 'More intimate.'

'Just as well, the equipment's still up in the Manor,' said Ben. 'What about your guitars and so on?'

'We'll have to go and get those,' said George. 'Will we run into any trouble?'

'You could go with them, Ian,' said Fran.

'I'd make things worse,' said Ian, with a grin.

The performance was, in fact, a huge success. The remaining festival-goers had crowded into the function room and down the stairs, despite Betty fluttering up and down and worrying about health and safety. George and Kyle had dedicated it to Clive, and invited Terry to join them halfway through on his bongos, thoughtfully brought down along with the guitars. The only sour note was the arrival of Superintendent Bertram with a miserable-looking Inspector Maiden in tow. After she'd pushed her way through the crowds at the back of the room, Ian quietly took hold of her arm and guided her back downstairs.

'What did you say to her?' whispered Libby, when he reappeared.

'Simply that no one was contravening any orders, and in fact everyone connected with the investigation was helpfully in one place. I also mentioned that my own superintendent would be in touch in the morning.'

'And will he?' whispered Fran from his other side.

'I've no idea.' Ian kept his eyes fixed on the musicians.

By the time the performance – and resulting encores – had come to an end, the original crowd had been augmented by the remaining diners and staff of The Pink Geranium, including Peter and Harry, the few musicians left at the Manor, and Ron Stewart and the members of Jonah Fludde who had been staying with him.

'How did you know?' Libby asked him, as the crowd began to disperse.

'Your Ben rang – didn't he tell you?' Ron was peering interestedly at the guitars still propped on their stands while George and Kyle talked to enthusiastic fans.

'Did he tell you about the murder?'

'We already knew about that. The police were on the doorstep at the crack of noon.'

'Oh, yes, I suppose they would be.' Libby sat down abruptly on an amplifier. 'I'm still a bit shaky.'

'Are you? Why?' Ron turned his attention to Libby. 'You do look a bit pale.'

'I found – him.'

'Oh, f –f –f ... good God.' Ron crouched down in front of her. 'You do manage to get mixed up in things, don't you. Can I get Ben?'

'No, thanks.' Libby took a deep breath. 'I don't think I've had a chance to sit down and think about it since... been too busy.'

'You ought to go home.' Ron stood up and looked round the room.

Libby gave him a crooked smile. 'Too much to do. We've got to clear the site and the field and wait for the people to come and dismantle the stage.'

Ron frowned. 'You know, I don't think the police are going to let you do that today.'

Libby looked up, startled. 'Really? Oh –' Understanding dawned. 'Of course they won't. I didn't think of that.'

'Maria said you're welcome to come and stay at the house if you need to get out of the way for a few days.' Ron stared studiously at the stage.

Libby gaped.

'Well, might be a bit – you know – for a while,' he continued.

Libby recovered. 'That's incredibly generous of her, and I would have loved to, but I've got all my kids here at the moment. Do say thank you, though.'

Ron nodded, gave her an absent-minded pat on the shoulder and strode off towards the stairs.

'What did he want?' Ben appeared at her side.

'You'll never guess!' Libby turned to him enthusiastically. 'Maria – you know, his wife – offered to have me to stay if I wanted a refuge!'

'Really?' Ben frowned. 'Why would you want that?'

'Because of all the hullabaloo that's bound to go on over the next few days.'

'Oh.' Ben was still frowning. 'Are you going?'

'Course not, silly. Apart from anything else, the kids are here.'

Ben's brow cleared. 'Right.'

'Also, Ron reminded me we won't be allowed to clear the site or the stage yet.'

'No, I realised that. I called the stage hire people earlier, and Tim says he'll be here to oversee them when they're allowed in. I only hope they don't decide to charge us extra.'

Ian, who had been missing over the last hour, came through the door from the stairs. 'Are you going home?' he asked.

'I don't know. I suppose really we should go back to the Manor and check on Hetty.'

'And see if the police have let the other musicians go,' added Ben.

'Good idea,' said Ian. 'And we can sit down and have a chat about what we've learnt so far.'

Libby's and Ben's faces were a study, and Ian laughed. 'I'm not officially on the police team, am I? So I can join in your usual case conference.'

'That's usually just her and Fran,' said Ben. 'We don't often come into it.'

'You do!' said Libby indignantly.

45

'Usually protesting.' Guy had come up silently behind them. 'Now – what's going on?'

Chapter Six

Back at the Manor they found Hetty at her ease in her private sitting room in front of her favourite gas fire.

'All gone,' she informed them succinctly. 'Even that woman.'

'Can we make tea, Mum?' asked Ben. 'We'll bring you a cup. We've got a few of the musicians coming back here – the ones the police don't want to leave yet.'

Hetty shrugged. 'Gettin' used to it, aren't I?'

Ben pulled a face at Libby as they made their way to the kitchen. 'I wish I hadn't got Mum involved.'

'It wasn't your fault someone got himself murdered,' said Libby. She thought for a moment. 'Any more than all the other times.'

'Exactly,' said Ben. 'Let's not get involved in anything else.'

Libby looked at him over her shoulder as she pushed open the kitchen door. 'No theatre?' she said dubiously. 'I'll believe that when I see it.'

They found Guy, Fran, Belinda, Adam, Dominic and the remaining musicians from Ellis sitting round the huge scrubbed pine table.

'Where's Ian?' asked Libby, as Ben went to fill the electric kettle.

47

'The big kettle's already heating on the Aga,' said Fran, 'and Ian put it on. He's gone into the study. He said you wouldn't mind.'

Ben sat down. 'No point in minding. He always uses it if he needs to, and Big Bertha was in there earlier on.'

'Perhaps he's hoping she left something behind,' said Guy.

'Big Bertha?' Kyle looked round the table. 'Who's that?'

'Superintendent Bertram,' said Libby. 'That's what we called her when we came across her before.'

'Unpleasant woman,' said Terry, wrinkling his nose. 'Wish it was your mate in charge. He's human.'

'You may be just about to get your wish.'

Ian appeared in the doorway and they all turned to look at him. He smiled wryly.

'Yes, indeed. Apparently your favourite superintendent has been pulled off the case, which she had no right to have interfered with anyway, and the wheels are in motion for me to take over.'

'Oh.' Libby looked round the table. 'That means no case conference.'

George, Kyle and Terry all looked puzzled but the others sighed and looked downhearted.

'In which case,' said Ian, moving to the Aga and collecting the big brown teapot on the way, 'you'd better make the most of this afternoon. Once it's stamped and sealed I'll have to maintain my usual inscrutable demeanour.'

'We know,' said Fran. 'The satanic brows over the piercing eyes.'

Ian grinned over his shoulder as he poured water onto tea leaves.

'Can somebody explain what this is all about?' George demanded. 'We don't know what's going on.'

'It's my mother, George,' said Dominic wearily. 'This is her hobby.'

'Eh?' Libby spluttered a little and Ben patted her arm.

'Ian – or Detective Chief Inspector Connell – is a friend of ours, and has been since Libby and Fran first got mixed up in murder. He also suggested this beer festival and took the weekend off to come and help. Now, instead of simply being a punter and possibly a suspect –' Ben glanced mischievously at his friend, 'it looks as if he's been recalled to duty. So instead of being able to discuss the case with us freely, he'll have to abide by his rules and regulations. Is that right, Ian?'

'Succinctly put.' Ian placed the teapot on the table and Fran went to fetch milk from the fridge, while Libby collected mugs.

'And in case Bel and Dom haven't told you, this is Ben's mother's house, and he and she own the theatre next door –'

Ben interrupted her. 'And Libby and my cousin Peter are directors of the theatre. There. Potted history.'

'So who runs the B&B?' asked Kyle.

'We started it,' said Libby, 'after Ben's dad died, and we wanted to run painting and writing courses.'

'But they failed,' said Adam, 'after one of the guests was murdered.'

'Surprisingly,' said Belinda.

'No, I don't believe it either,' said Dominic,

49

intercepting a disbelieving look between the three members of Ellis, 'but it's all true.'

'You didn't warn us,' said George.

'Would it have made any difference?' asked Libby. 'Just because you come to Steeple Martin doesn't automatically mean a ticket to the graveyard. Anyway, you met Ron Stewart and Jonah Fludde.'

'It might have made a difference to Clive Eddington, though,' said Ian.

They all looked at him.

'I'm going to take Mum's tea in,' said Ben. 'Don't start without me.'

He left the room as Libby stood up and went to fetch the large cake tin. 'Has anyone had lunch?' she asked.

No one had, and the cake was gratefully accepted.

'This is terrific,' said Terry through a mouthful of crumbs. 'Did Ben's mum make it?'

'No, it came from some friends who run a lovely cafe near Whitstable,' said Libby. 'It's lavender and zucchini.'

Eyebrows were once more raised, but Ben came in and demanded tea.

'Carry on, Ian,' he said. 'What did you mean, made a difference to Clive Eddington?'

Ian was silent for a moment, gazing down at his mug. 'Supposing,' he said eventually, 'he'd known police were involved in this little festival. That Steeple Martin tended to be a place the police were very familiar with. Would he have come?'

George, Kyle and Terry looked bewildered.

'Why?' said Terry. 'Are you suggesting he was a criminal?'

'How well did you know him?' countered Ian. 'He was new to the group, wasn't he?'

Kyle frowned. 'Not that new. A year? Eighteen months?'

'June last year,' said George. 'You recommended him, Terry, didn't you?'

'Well, I was new myself,' said Terry defensively. 'You got me, and said you wanted...'

'Yes, I know,' said George, 'but we'd seen you around for years. We hadn't seen Clive.'

'He'd just moved down from Manchester,' said Terry. 'I met him in my local at an Open Mic night.'

'And you don't know anything else about him?'

'No, not really. Only that he got into blues in Manchester. He talked about some of the guys up there, but I'd never heard of any of them.'

Ian sat back in his chair and looked across at Fran and Libby. 'Well?'

'He could have come from anywhere,' said Fran, after a moment's thought. 'You didn't take up references, did you?' She looked at George and Kyle.

'No. We auditioned him, then we heard him play in Terry's local. That was enough for us. He was good.' Kyle looked at George. 'Perhaps we should have?'

'Why?' George shrugged. 'We haven't had any trouble with him, have we? We've had no suspicious thefts or...' he frowned.

'Or any drugs knocking about,' said Terry. 'He was very against drugs.'

Libby attempted to look cool and knowing. Adam shot her an amused look.

'The other musicians who were here this morning,' said Ian. 'They said they didn't know him. Did you know any of them?'

Kyle, George and Terry looked at each other.

'Not really,' said George. 'They were all local.'

'So it's unlikely they would have known him.' Ian looked at Libby. 'Did you know any of them?'

Libby shook her head.

'I wasn't here,' said Adam. 'Who were they? I might know them.'

'There was a scruffy one who was getting belligerent,' said Belinda. 'He was with one of the bands who played earlier yesterday.'

'He was complaining about you questioning us,' said Kyle. 'And he didn't seem to much like that woman. The superintendent.'

Ian raised his eyebrows. 'Did he know her?'

'No, he just called her "that cow".'

'Right.' Ian consulted a notebook which had suddenly appeared in his hand. 'Nobody knows which band he was with?'

'All the musicians who were here this morning were people who'd played on Saturday and camped overnight,' said George. 'We all left our instruments here because they were safer.'

'And the scruffy one said he had another gig this afternoon,' said Belinda.

'So we look for a band who had a gig today and who played here yesterday,' said Ian, pulling a sheet of paper from his back pocket.

'Why are you interested in him?' asked Libby. 'He

didn't seem any different from the others to me.'

'None of the others were belligerent.' Ian smiled. 'I'm being intuitive.'

Ben snorted.

'How do we find out who had a gig today?' asked Fran.

'Gig guide,' said all the young people together.

'Ah,' said their bewildered elders.

Dominic took out his phone as Adam began scrolling through his.

'Fat Dragon,' said Adam. 'That's who it was.'

'Yeah, he's on their website,' said Dominic, eyes fixed to his screen. 'It gives you a good plug.'

'What's his name?' asked Ian.

'Hold on –' Dominic scrolled some more. 'Here – Danny Coleman.' He handed his phone to Ian.

'Were any others from that group here this morning?' asked Fran.

'I don't know – I wasn't here,' said Adam. 'Ian's got Dom's phone – Bel, have a look on yours.'

'It's a different world,' said Libby admiringly, as she watched Adam, Ian, and Belinda, with Dominic leaning over her shoulder, concentrating on the tiny screens. Kyle, George and Terry were doing the same.

George looked up, amused. 'It's how we live now,' he said.

'Like the runners,' said Libby. 'Surgically attached to their phones, they were.'

'Runners?'

'Mum and Fran's last sortie into crime-fighting,' said Belinda. 'Don't worry about it.'

53

Kyle, George and Terry shared another look. Dominic sighed.

'Look, we'll tell you all about it later,' he said. 'You won't believe it, but it's all true. Carry on, Ian.'

Ian looked amused. 'Thank you, Dominic. Well – do any of you know where we might find this Danny Coleman?'

'Where was the gig this afternoon?' asked Adam.

All attention returned to the small screens again.

'Canterbury,' said Ian. 'But it finished at six.' He looked at his watch. 'It's after that now.'

'Somebody must know him,' said Adam. 'What about Ron Stewart, Ma?'

'Doubt if he'd know anyone like that,' said Libby. 'Oh, come on, you must have friends who are into local bands? Mog might, don't you think?'

'Mog?' chorused George, Kyle and Terry.

'Adam's boss,' said Belinda.

George frowned. 'I thought his boss was the restaurant owner?'

'Oh, dear,' said Libby. 'We do seem to live complicated lives. Adam lives in a flat above the restaurant and helps out on occasions, but during the week he works for a garden designer.'

'Quite a good one,' said Adam. 'We work mainly at Creekmarsh.'

The members of Ellis looked even more confused.

'Have you heard of Lewis Osbourne-Walker?' asked Guy, who had been silently entertained by the conversation.

'Bloke off TV?' said Terry.

'That's him. Well, he has a big house near here, over towards the marshes, called Creekmarsh, and the gardens are gradually being restored for a programme of Lewis's.'

The Ellis members turned fascinated eyes on Adam.

'You on the telly, then?' asked Kyle.

'Sometimes,' said Adam, turning pink.

'Anyway, what about Mog knowing Fat Dragon or Danny Coleman?' said Libby, dragging the conversation back to the matter in hand.

'I don't suppose so, but I'll ask him,' said Adam, retrieving his phone from Ian.

'Nothing else you can think of to help, then?' said Ian, leaning back in his chair and surveying the table. Everyone shook their heads.

'I can think of one thing,' said Libby, standing up. 'Food. No one's eaten, have they?'

Now everyone looked confused, but one by one shook their heads.

'Well, there are too many of us to descend on the pub, Harry's closed and my house isn't big enough. So I'm going to ask Hetty if I can borrow her kitchen and rustle up an enormous bowl of pasta and some sort of sauce.'

'Excellent idea,' said Ben. 'Will she have pasta?'

'Oh, yes,' said Libby with a grin. 'I make sure she's got all the basics in case we get sudden overnight guests. There's sacks of mince in the freezer and bottles and bottles of passata in the larder, so we should be able to create some sort of sauce. Is that all right for everyone?'

There was an enthusiastic response and Libby went off to ask Hetty for permission, which was granted on the condition that no one asked her to join them and they left her alone with her Sunday evening television.

Ben and Guy were dispatched to select wines, while Libby set the young people to chopping onions and garlic and she set a huge pan of water on to boil. Fran oversaw the creation of the sauce and Ian disappeared to the office. Eventually they all sat down to the impromptu meal, the members of Ellis still looking dazed and confused.

'This is very kind of you,' said Terry.

Libby grinned. 'Couldn't let you starve.'

'And now,' said George, 'you promised to tell us all about the crime-fighting, Dom. So, come on!'

Chapter Seven

Monday morning was a miserable experience. Ian left to go straight to Canterbury, Fran and Guy drove back to Nethergate to open Guy's gallery/shop, and the members of Ellis and Belinda and Dominic sat in the big sitting room at the Manor waiting to be told if they could return to London.

'You could,' said Libby to her daughter. 'You aren't material witnesses, or whatever it is.'

'We couldn't desert the boys, though,' said Belinda, and Kyle put an arm round her shoulders. 'We brought them here.'

'What about work, though?' asked Libby, and received a "Mothers!" sort of look from Dominic and Belinda.

'We weren't going in today, either of us,' said Dominic. 'We were always going to stay over until today, you know that. Anyway, you'll need us to help clear the site, if Ian gives permission.'

'They're out there going over it with a fingertip search – again,' said Ben, coming away from the window. 'Ian said he thought we'd be all right to let the stage people come to take everything away this afternoon.'

'Has he found Danny Coleman?' asked George.

'No idea,' said Ben. 'Adam was going to ask Mog, but I haven't heard anything.'

57

'I can't actually see why he's important,' said Dominic.

'I don't either,' said Libby, 'but I think it was simply Ian trying to find someone who was here yesterday morning to talk to. And Danny Coleman was noticeable because he was belligerent.'

'I expect the police will talk to everyone again – especially all the various bands,' said Ben. 'They can't afford to leave any stone unturned.'

'Think of the outcry,' said Libby. 'Can't you just imagine all the naysayers? "Bound to happen – all those long-haired layabouts – bet it was drugs" – ' She shook her head. 'It'll all have to be done by the book. Especially as Ian himself was involved with the organisation.'

'I can't see us getting permission to have another one,' said Ben. 'Even if Tim got all the right licences, I bet the locals would stop it. A lot of them were against it in the first place.'

'Why? Because of what Mum said? Long-haired layabouts and drugs?' asked Belinda.

'And noise,' said Libby. 'Though there were sound limiters and a midnight deadline.'

'Oh, well, it was a lot of work, wasn't it?' said Dominic. 'You could always have a mini music festival for local bands in the theatre, couldn't you? That would be easier.'

'Not the same as a beer festival,' said Ben. 'But you're right.'

'I'm going home for a bit,' said Libby. 'There isn't anything I can do here until all the equipment's cleared, so I might as well go and do something useful at home.'

58

'I'll go into the office then,' said Ben. 'Will you all be all right?'

'We'll be fine,' said Belinda. 'We'll show the boys the village. Pity Harry isn't open on a Monday.'

Libby walked slowly down the Manor drive towards the high street, one eye on the swarm of uniforms and white boiler suits on the field. It wasn't the first time murder had come close to the theatre, but this time it seemed as if the whole village was involved. She sighed and turned the corner into the high street.

'Danny! It is Danny Coleman, isn't it?' She stopped short in front of the scruffy-looking man who had just crossed the road right in front of her. He hesitated, looking hunted.

'Hello, er...' he managed.

'Libby, Libby Sarjeant – with a J,' said Libby helpfully. 'Up at the Manor. How are you? Did you get to your gig all right yesterday?'

Coleman gave a small smile. 'Oh, yeah, ta. No problem. They let us go.'

'Actually, DCI Connell wanted to have another word with you, but couldn't get hold of you.' Libby looked hopeful. 'Can I tell him you're here?'

'What does he want? Not with that woman, is he?'

'No, it's only the policeman who was with us yesterday. He's in charge now.'

'I don't know.' Coleman looked sideways at Libby. 'I was just off...'

'Why are you here?' Libby risked the direct question.

Coleman looked surprised. 'Pick up the stuff I left at the house. The old lady said it was OK.'

'Oh – I didn't know. OK, then, I'll let you get on,' said Libby. 'The members of Ellis are still there at the moment.'

'Oh, right.' Coleman moved from one foot to another. 'I'll get off.'

Libby looked after him thoughtfully. What was he uneasy about? She pulled out her phone and sent a text to Ian's official phone, then, after a moment's thought copied it to his private number. Within a minute, the phone rang.

'He's there?' Ian sounded incredulous. 'Why?'

'He says to pick up stuff from the Manor. Hetty said it was OK, apparently.'

'Can you keep him there?'

'No, Ian! I'm not there, I met him in the high street.'

'The high street? Why was he there? Why hadn't he driven straight up to the Manor?'

'I don't know!' said Libby, exasperated. 'I just thought you ought to know as you said yesterday you wanted to speak to him.'

'Any of his damned band,' said Ian. 'Haven't been able to track them down. OK – I'll get one of the search team to go and talk to him until I can get there. Thanks.'

Libby found herself staring at the silent phone. 'Honestly!' she muttered to herself, and continued on her way down the high street, almost getting run down by an old Volvo estate.

Back at number seventeen Allhallow's Lane, Libby did her best to placate Sidney and began restoring the cottage to its normal state after several days of neglect. She hadn't got very far when her mobile rang.

'Ian says we can clear the site now, and the hire people

are on their way,' said Ben. 'Are you coming back?'

Libby pulled a face. 'Do you need me?'

'What?' Ben sounded surprised.

'Well, the kids are there, aren't they? And we aren't needed to take down the stage. And we said we'd get in that cleaning company Ian suggested, didn't we?'

'Oh, all right.' Ben sounded disappointed and reluctant. Libby sighed.

'OK, OK. I'll come, although I don't see why. Shall I bring a sandwich?'

'No, it's fine. I'm sure we can persuade Tim to find us some sandwiches.' Ben sounded brighter but hesitant. 'Sure you're all right?'

'Yes, yes, I'm fine. I'll see you in a bit.' Libby ended the call and sighed again. All she really wanted to do was sit down with Sidney on her lap and doze over a book.

After putting a load of washing in the machine, she picked up her trusty basket and made for the Manor once more. She was surprised to see Danny Coleman emerge from the Manor drive ahead of her as she turned the corner into the high street. He barely looked as he darted across the road and disappeared, to her acute puzzlement, into Maltby Close towards the church.

By the time she drew level with the close there was no sign of him.

'Perhaps,' she mused to herself, 'he's got an elderly aunt or granny who lives there. I wonder if Ian's caught up with him?'

She found Ben, Adam, Belinda and Dominic sitting on folding chairs by Tim's outside bar watching a diverse crew of operatives dismantling the stage. The people who had come to remove the sound equipment were obviously getting frustrated and irritated. One of them broke away and walked purposefully towards them.

'Can you do something about them, mate?' he asked Ben. 'Bloody cowboys! They're wrecking our wiring.'

'Don't you work with them regularly?' asked Ben warily.

'The company, yes. Not this bunch of wa –' he glanced at Libby, 'buggers. You sure they're kosher?'

Ben frowned. 'Well, they turned up and said they'd come to take the stage.' He stood up and sighed. 'I suppose I'd better go and check.'

'I'll come too,' said Libby, linking her arm with his.

The representative of the sound system dismantling team led the way to where two men were attempting to dismantle some scaffolding in a desultory fashion.

'Do you have something for me to sign?' asked Ben in a mild voice as they looked up. The two men exchanged confused looks.

'Sign?' said one.

'Yes, sign. To show that you are entitled to take this equipment away. That I won't be charged for it, or accused of losing it.'

More confused looks. Then one of them got to his feet.

'I better go and ask Woody,' he said and went off towards what had been the backstage area. It appeared to be a signal for all the other workmen to stop work and stand around looking at one another.

'I'm going to see if Ian or Inspector Maiden are up at the Manor,' murmured Libby. 'I think we might need them.'

'Really?' Ben looked at her sharply. 'Why?'

'Just a feeling.' Libby dug him in the ribs. 'Don't let anyone leave.'

She found Ian just leaving through the Manor's impressive oak door.

'I think we might have a situation, Ian,' she said, stopping in front of him. 'Can you come?'

He scowled. 'What situation? I've just had a singularly unfruitful conversation with young Coleman...'

'Not my fault,' said Libby. 'Please come. It's the stage.'

Ian's expressive eyebrows shot into his hairline. 'Come on then.'

They arrived back at Ben's side to find neither the operative nor the "Woody" he had gone to find had materialised. The remaining member of the stage crew was fidgeting and looking worried. His colleagues lolled around on the half-dismantled stage.

Ian fished his phone from his pocket and murmured into it, then asked, 'Where's your boss?' of the hapless man in front of him.

'Dunno. Dunc went to get him.'

'Name?' barked Ian.

'Sc – Scotty.' The man now looked not just worried but scared.

'Boss's name.'

'Woody.'

'Where's Woody?' Ian's raised voice penetrated to everyone in the field, and Libby suddenly realised that uniformed officers were converging on them. There was a scuffling noise and from behind the stage emerged two grinning officers, one holding a ruffled Dunc, the other escorting a small, sandy individual with an impressive scowl.

'Trying to do a bunk, sir,' said the officer holding Dunc.

'Are you Woody?' asked Ben. Ian frowned at him.

Woody maintained a sullen silence.

'Can you show me your authority for removing this stage?' asked Ian. 'I'm the hirer, so I need a receipt.'

Woody rolled his eyes. 'Bloody cop. Mighta known.'

'Known what? Who told you to remove it?'

'Not saying' nothin',' said Woody.

'And you?' Ian turned to the sound specialist, who was watching proceedings with an appreciative grin.

'Oh, me – I've already seen the guvnor here –' he indicated Ben. 'I'm legit.'

'Right – I've got this.' Ian turned to Woody and Dunc. 'We'll go and have a chat, shall we? And your friends can come too.' He signalled to the other officers who closed in on the stage and encouraged the remaining crew to climb down.

'Use the theatre foyer,' said Ben. 'The door's open and it would be easier to keep them all together than in the manor.'

'Thanks, Ben.' Ian gave him and Libby a quick smile. 'And thanks for tipping me off. I believe we've heard of this lot before.'

'It wasn't us,' said Libby. 'It was – ' she stopped. 'I don't know your name.'

'Barry Cunliffe.' He held out a hand. 'Happy to help.'

'Well, thank you, Mr Cunliffe,' said Ian. 'I'll be in

64

touch. You can carry on now.'

When Ian, the officers and the stage crew had left, Libby turned again to Barry Cunliffe.

'Did you realise what was going on?' she asked.

'I had a bloody good idea. That's what I said. We know the company. Not this bunch.' He grinned at Libby. 'Well, you know what I think.'

'Do they get away with it?'

'They have done. Has to be a one-off, like. Not someone who'd know.'

'We were ideal, then,' said Ben. 'First-time festival, inexperienced bookers.'

'Now, I didn't say that.' Barry was still grinning.

'But how do they get onto it?' asked Libby, frowning.

'Inside job, isn't it? One of the bands.'

'Really? Who?'

'Dunno for sure, but I reckon it's one of the members of that Fat Dragon.'

Chapter Eight

Libby and Ben stared.

'Really?' said Libby eventually. 'How do you make that out?'

'They've been on the bill every time it's happened.' Barry shrugged. 'Like I said, I dunno for sure. It's often...' He paused, looking thoughtful. 'Actually, that's right. It's when the take-down has been moved.'

'Ah!' said Ben, enlightened. 'You mean when it's been delayed? Not the time you were booked for?'

'That's it. Makes sense, don't it?'

'You mean – because the original crew aren't available?' Libby was frowning in an effort to piece it all together.

'Something like that, I reckon.' Barry grinned at them. 'You can tell your copper friend. I doubt that Woody will!'

'Shall we?' Libby asked Ben, as they moved away from the stage area.

'I suppose we ought to, but he'll probably insist on speaking to Barry.'

'And he might not want to say anything – I expect all these people know one another. He might meet someone up a dark alley one night.' Libby sighed. 'Doesn't it get complicated?'

Ben linked his arm with hers. 'It does, but let's go and tell our copper friend.'

To their surprise, they were stopped at the outer doors of the theatre by a uniformed officer.

'But it's our theatre!' said Libby. 'We offered it to DCI Connell.'

The officer looked concerned. 'Wait a moment, sir,' he said at last and moved slightly away, unhooking his radio as he went. A couple of minutes later he was back, and without speaking, stood aside and held the door open.

'Thank you,' said Libby, smiling sweetly.

The foyer/bar area was full of officers talking to uncomfortable looking crew members. Inspector Maiden left his table and came across to them, grinning cheerfully.

'Sorry about the hold-up,' he said. 'They don't know you.'

'That's OK,' said Libby. 'But we've just been given some information which might be useful.'

'Oh?' Maiden looked interested. 'Just let me sort out what I was dealing with and I'll be with you.'

He went back to his table and his interviewee and quickly returned to usher Ben and Libby over to a corner of the bar area.

'Now, what is this information?'

Libby and Ben between them repeated what Barry Cunliffe had told them. Maiden's frown deepened as he listened.

'It sounds highly unlikely,' he said when they'd finished.

'But it's exactly why you're questioning all these

people,' said Ben. 'They weren't supposed to pick up the equipment, it was supposed to be another crew. Only the time was changed because of the murder.'

'But how would they know?'

'Barry Cunliffe – the one who told us about this – said he thought it was a member of Fat Dragon.' Libby looked at him hopefully. 'Danny Coleman, perhaps?'

'No – what I meant was, how would they get the OK to go to the site without bumping into a genuine crew?'

'Oh.' Libby and Ben exchanged looks. Neither had thought of that.

Maiden pursed his lips. 'I'll go and interrupt the DCI. Wait here.' He disappeared through the double doors to the auditorium.

'Do you think it has anything to do with the murder?' said Ben, idly wandering behind the bar and starting to check the optics.

'Can't see how,' said Libby. 'Just a complication.'

Maiden came back and smiled.

'I think he knew,' he said. 'I told him and he just grinned and said thank you. Oh – and could he speak to you later this afternoon?'

Libby and Ben sighed in unison.

'Of course,' said Ben. 'He can ring us. I don't know whether we'll still be at the field or at home.'

'I'll tell him. And nice to see you both.' Maiden hurried back to his table and his disgruntled interviewee.

'What shall we do now?' asked Libby, as they left the theatre.

'Go home?' suggested Ben. 'Do some normal stuff?'

'Like what, though? We'll still have to come back here

when someone – whoever it is – clears the field. And you ought to be here to sign off the audio people.'

'I suppose so,' said Ben gloomily. 'Well, you go and see if Tim will give us something to eat, and we'll sit at one of his little tables.'

But before Libby had reached the temporary bar and the back door of the pub, Harry appeared from his back yard.

'I'm doing lunch for me and Pete. Want some? Only soup, and I've got some nice soda bread just out of the oven.'

'Oh, yes please! I was just going to ask Tim to rustle us up a sandwich.'

'No need. Come and talk to me while I finish it off, and you can tell me what all the activity's been this morning.' He held open the back gate for her.

Watching while Harry finished off his soup with cream and chilli oil, Libby filled him in on everything that had happened since she had last seen him.

'What does Ian think?' Harry lifted the soup tureen onto a tray. 'Fetch the bread, will you? We'll have it at Tim's tables.'

Libby obediently carried the board with bread and butter out behind Harry. 'I don't really know. Now he's in professional mode he can't really tell us. When we went to tell him about what Barry Cunliffe had said, Maiden told us he already knew. So goodness knows what he's learnt since he carted the stage people off to be interviewed.'

'And you really think they're fake? They're trying to nick the equipment?'

'I'm not sure.' Libby frowned and found a space to put the bread board down. 'It seems so very unlikely. It's so large-scale. And how could they know they wouldn't be interrupted by the real crew?'

'Bullion robberies are large-scale, petal. And I would imagine they've been told by someone that the original – real – crew can't come. So they weasel in.'

'So someone who knew who the stage hire people were....'

'I expect most of the bands knew. They all do these festivals all summer, don't they?'

'Yes. But someone must have known who to get in touch with...'

'At the company? Maybe.'

'And perhaps,' said Libby, a theory forming, 'Woody or someone is a legit member of the team, so he's actually told about the delay and can come in with his rogue crew?'

'Sounds feasible. I'm going to fetch Pete. Can you call Ben?'

Ben came over to the table and Libby told him about the latest theory.

'It sounds like a daft plot from an old detective story,' said Ben dubiously.

Peter came up behind him. 'I tend to agree, cuz. We should get Libby's friend Rosie onto it.'

Rosie was the novelist Amanda George, from whom Fran had once taken a creative writing course, and who had herself been involved in a couple of the weirdest of Fran and Libby's adventures.

'That really would be a mistake,' said Libby. 'She's

even flakier than I am.'

'Come on, then,' said Harry, advancing with bowls and a bottle. 'Someone fetch the glasses from the kitchen for me.'

The subject of the possibly kidnapped stage was dropped while they enjoyed Harry's soup. Eventually, Peter sat back in his chair and sighed.

'Very good, my love. Is it going on the menu?'

Harry grinned mischievously. 'Not unless I have loads of leftovers every day.'

'Best sort of soup, leftovers,' said Ben. 'Due to closing early yesterday?'

'Not quite – don't forget loads of the punters came to be fed after you'd closed down here. But yes, I had over-catered.'

'What happens now?' asked Peter, waving a languid hand towards the half dismantled stage.

'No idea,' said Ben. 'I suppose we wait to be told.'

They helped Harry clear up, then went back to find Belinda and Dominic.

'We've been told we can go,' said Dominic. 'I was just going to collect my stuff from the flat and Bel was going back to Allhallow's Lane.'

'All right, we'll see you back here,' said Libby indicating the Manor. 'Have you seen Ian?'

'In passing,' said Bel. 'Inspector Maiden told us we could go.'

'You don't know any more, then?' said Ben.

'Nothing.' Dominic shook his head.

Libby and Ben went into the Manor and found Hetty in the kitchen.

'That Ian's still in your office,' she grumbled. 'I said why didn't he go over to the theatre with all the rest of 'em, but he said there's nowhere private.'

Ben sighed. 'I just hope they don't want to set up an incident room here. We've got a touring company coming in.'

'Beth might let them have the village hall,' said Libby. 'Carpenter's would be too small and too overrun with pensioners.'

Carpenter's Hall was a community space belonging to the small complex of converted barns in Maltby Close. The residents, all over 55 and mostly over 65, owned their properties leasehold, except for Flo Carpenter, relict of the late Frank Carpenter, who owned Carpenter's Hall and the land. Flo, Hetty's best childhood friend, with whom she had originally come down to Kent hop-picking, had married Carpenter, the farmer, while Hetty had married the son and heir of the Manor estate and hop gardens, Greg, who had died only a few years ago.

'Will you ask Beth?' Ben looked hopefully at his other half.

'Not my job. I'll suggest it to Ian – or you can.'

Ben sighed again. 'If he ever comes out of my office.'

However, Ian appeared just as Dominic and Belinda arrived back at the Manor.

'You're going back to London, are you?' he said affably. 'What about your friends from Ellis?'

'I think Inspector Maiden said they could go too,' said Dominic. 'Is that all right?'

'Yes, as long as we know where to get in touch with you.'

72

George, Kyle and Terry now came out of the Manor loaded with bags and instrument cases.

'Thanks for everything,' said George, holding his hand out to Ian. 'I mean, for the festival...' he trailed off, looking uncomfortable.

Ian smiled. 'Don't mention it. I'm only sorry it ended the way it has. Don't forget to ring, any time, if you remember anything you think I ought to know about.'

In a flurry of hugs and goodbyes, Dominic and Belinda climbed into Dom's car, and Ellis into their minivan. Ian, Libby and Ben waved them off down the drive.

'I came to tell you I'm going to give you back your office,' said Ian, turning to Ben, 'but we'll need an incident room. Any suggestions? I know we can't use the theatre.'

'We were just talking about that,' said Libby. 'I thought Beth might let you have the village hall.'

'Beth? Oh, Bethany the vicar? Yes, that would do nicely. But don't they have toddlers' groups and so on there?'

'I think so, but I'm sure something could be worked out.' Libby fished for her phone. 'I've got her number here...'

Ian punched it into his own phone, then strolled a little way away to conduct his conversation.

'Doesn't want us to hear how much he'll pay for it,' said Libby.

'Don't be a cynic,' said Ben.

Ian came back. 'All settled,' he said. 'Now I have to arrange for it to be set up tomorrow as early as possible, so I'll go and retrieve all the bodies in the theatre and I'll see you tomorrow.'

'Now,' said Ben, as they watched him disappear through the theatre doors, 'what are you going to cook me for dinner, woman?'

Chapter Nine

Life returned to normal for the village, other than the continued presence of the police in the village hall. The various groups that used it grumbled, but most of them were generously accommodated in Carpenter's Hall, by kind permission of Flo.

The genuine crews had arrived to collect staging equipment, Tim had set up his "pop-up" beer garden properly and Ben had got his office back, but on Tuesday afternoon Libby received a phone call from him.

'Guess what!' he said. 'Ian's booked back in with Hetty. He says he needs to be on the spot.'

'He's never needed that before,' said Libby dubiously. 'Do you suppose he wants us to feed him?'

'Of course not! Hetty offered, apparently, but he declined, saying he would eat at the pub or at Harry's.'

'Oh.' Libby frowned. 'We've never had an incident room, either, even for the Pendle murder. Or the running one.'

'Or the ukulele one.' Ben sounded amused. 'Have you got names for them all?'

'I don't know,' said Libby, surprised. 'I've never thought about it.' She thought for a moment. 'Anyway, I'd better ask Ian, just for form's sake.'

'He might not want to be associating with us under the

circumstances,' said Ben, 'but you can try.'

But before Libby could ring Ian, her mobile warbled.

'Libby, could I pop in and see you this afternoon?'

'Of course. When? I was going to ring and see if you wanted to eat with us this evening, but Ben thought it might be inappropriate.'

'It might be, but I'd love to, thank you. And I want to talk to you about ... well, an aspect of...'

'The case?' Libby suggested.

'Yes, but it's off the wall, and at present off the record. I'd like Fran's opinion, too, but I'll try and see her tomorrow.'

'You don't want me to ask them up here for dinner?'

'You can't keep dragging them up here,' said Ian. 'I think Guy gets a bit fed up.'

'I think you're right,' said Libby. 'OK. What time do you want to come over? What time shall we eat?'

'I'll come about six, shall I? Then we can have a drink while I tell you about...well, about *it*.'

Libby reviewed her plans for dinner and the contents of her fridge, and then phoned Fran.

'And I have no idea what it's about,' she concluded, 'but he wants your opinion, too. He says he'll see you tomorrow.'

'He doesn't want me to come this evening?'

'He said it wasn't fair to drag you up here. It can't be urgent, whatever it is. What am I going to feed him?'

'Don't ask me! Don't forget to ring me if you think it will help.'

Libby rang off and sighed. The sausages she had been going to present to Ben for dinner no longer seemed adequate.

By six o'clock, Libby was seething with curiosity. When Ian didn't turn up on the dot, she began fidgeting, and by the time his knock came on the door at a quarter past, Ben was getting worried about her blood pressure.

'Sorry I'm late,' he said, presenting Ben with two bottles of wine. 'This is why I'm not married.'

'Huh?' said Libby.

'And why so many police marriages fail. Policemen are never on time.' He grinned. 'Never met anyone who would put up with me.'

'You did,' Libby said to herself, 'only she chose someone else.' Aloud, she said 'So what on earth do you want my opinion on? I just couldn't think.'

'Can we sit down?' He and Libby sat, while Ben opened wine. 'Now, this is going to seem odd, but it's to do with the inquest.'

'The inquest?' Ben handed glasses.

'This morning.' Ian held up his glass. 'Cheers.'

'Well?' said Libby impatiently. 'What happened? Were there any surprises?'

'Not about the body. Normal young man, mid-twenties, non-smoker, well-nourished. No sign of drug misuse, now or historically.'

'So – what?'

'This was tucked into the top of his T-shirt.' Ian pulled a clear evidence bag from his pocket. Libby took it.

'What is it?'

'A piece of paper with a – what is that?' asked Ben.

'A symbol. This is a copy. I've left the original with the evidence at the incident room. The original piece of

77

paper looks as though it was torn from something else and is very creased. Looks as if it has been kept somewhere for some time.'

Libby frowned down at the symbol. It looked like a figure of eight, surmounted by a capital I with two cross bars.

'Is it astrological?'

'Not quite. Have you ever seen it before?'

Libby shook her head. 'Ben?'

'It seems vaguely familiar,' said Ben. 'Why have you brought it to us?'

'It's a sigil.'

'Occult!' gasped Libby.

'It's actually the sign for Alchemy, but used to represent Satanism.'

'Alchemy!' Libby handed back the bag and sat back in her corner of the sofa. 'Clive Eddington was into Alchemy?'

'Either that, or someone wanted us to think he was.'

'I still don't understand why you wanted to ask us,' persisted Ben.

'Because you – or rather, Libby – have had dealings with local covens before. I wondered if there was anybody you could think of with links to them.' Ian sighed. 'I'm afraid the pathologist and Inspector Maiden both rather dismissed the idea, but this was put there for a reason.' He frowned down at the strange symbol. 'So I thought I'd ask you. And Fran.'

'Actually,' said Libby, 'Fran's had more to do with this whole business than I have. You remember the Black Masses out at the Tyne Chapel?'

'Of course, but then there was the May Day business –'

'That wasn't really witchcraft,' said Libby uncomfortably.

'Really? Dead cockerels?'

'We – ell,' said Libby.

'And of course the business at St Aldeberge's.' Ian sat back triumphantly. 'Ordinary people involved in very odd goings-on. Have you heard of anyone round here?'

'No!' Libby was shocked. 'And no one's likely to confide in me, anyway!'

'Would Belinda and Dominic know if Clive was into anything like that?'

'No, of course not! They didn't know him really – they only knew George and Kyle properly.'

'Would you ask them?'

Libby looked at Ben. 'They'll think it's odd. Can I tell them why?'

'Just say it's come to our attention that he might have a link.'

Ben shook his head. 'I don't like it.'

Ian sighed. 'I've got to pursue it, you must see that.'

Libby nodded slowly. 'I suppose so. But couldn't it just be a ploy to divert suspicion?'

'It could, but from whom? If we were already looking at a suspect, I'd agree, but we haven't got a clue.'

'But it could be just to send you haring off in the witchcraft direction rather than concentrating on – well, I don't know, but people at the festival.' Ben looked hopeful.

'Maybe,' said Ian, 'but either way, I need to find out. If you can ask around, I can concentrate on the normal routine.'

79

Libby sighed. 'All right.' She thought for a moment. 'I don't know if I'm right, but haven't I heard somewhere that some bikers have a link to witches?'

'I think I've heard something like that,' said Ian. 'Perhaps you should ask Edna.'

'I don't know how to get in touch with her,' said Libby. 'But I expect I could find out.'

After dinner Ian excused himself to go back to the incident room, Ben and Libby loaded the dishwasher, and Libby phoned Fran.

'Well,' said Fran when Libby had finished reporting Ian's requests, 'I can see we're going to be busy. What do you want to do first?'

'We do it?' Libby was surprised. She didn't think Fran would be that keen.

'Of course. Ian has asked us, we have a legitimate reason to go poking our noses in. And don't tell me you don't want to.'

Libby grinned at the phone. 'OK, of course I want to. What do you think of my idea of the bikers?'

'Actually,' Fran sounded thoughtful, 'I think it's a good one. I'm sure I've heard something of the sort, although it may be an urban myth. I'm sure there's a small-budget cult film about it...I'll ask Guy. He might know.'

'We can look the Nether Regionals up on the net, can't we? I bet they've got a site. I'd like to talk to Edna.'

'Yes, good idea. And what about asking Bel and Dom?'

'Well, I was thinking...' Libby cast a quick eye at Ben, who apparently was taking no notice, head buried in a book. 'Could we perhaps go to London?'

'London? What for?'

'I thought we could meet the kids socially – and perhaps the members of Ellis. Even your Lucy. She's still in London, isn't she?'

'I think we'd better talk about this,' said Fran firmly. 'Why don't you come over here tomorrow and if we've found any links to the Nether Regionals we can maybe see Edna, if she's not at work, and discuss other ideas.'

'OK.' Libby beamed. 'I'll see you in the morning, then.'

'What was that all about?' said Ben. 'London.'

Libby made a face. 'I just thought...'

Ben looked up and grinned. 'Ian's given you the perfect excuse, hasn't he?'

Libby went and sat next to him. 'You don't mind, do you?'

Ben slipped an arm round her shoulders. 'You'll have to make it up to me, you know...'

The following morning was bright, warm and sunny, with just a hint of autumn in the air. Libby drove along the Nethergate Road, past the turning to Steeple Mount and the Tyne Chapel, singing along to the radio and reviewing what she'd found on the internet. The Nether Regionals had a page on a biking website, and a Facebook page. Libby hadn't left a message, deciding she should talk to Fran first, but Edna was given as a contact on both.

Fran was in the shop with both Guy and Sophie.

'Sophie knows a bit about it,' Fran said. 'It shouldn't surprise me, but it did!'

Sophie grinned. 'There's a film — Step-mama was quite right — about a group of bikers who kill themselves to become the Undead. But better than that, there are actually a couple of women's biker groups who openly say they promote witchcraft.'

'How do you know this stuff?' asked Libby in awe.

'I knew about the film because it was a choice in the film club at uni, but I looked up the bikers on the internet.'

'I looked them up, too, but that didn't come up.'

'Search parameters,' said Sophie succinctly. 'I've given Fran the link.'

She turned and disappeared up the stairs to the flat.

Libby shook her head. 'I thought I'd got quite good at all this new technology and stuff, but the young have me floored.'

Fran laughed. 'I know. And now, even Guy has started using graphics technology to make artwork. It's scary.'

Libby looked at him, horrified. 'You haven't!'

'Yes, I have! It all adds to the portfolio. And I've been talking to a group of artists who use it all the time. They're having a show in London I thought I might go up and see.' He watched Libby carefully as he imparted this nugget.

'London? When?' She took the bait.

Guy looked at his wife in triumph. 'See! Told you so.'

'What?' Libby looked from one to the other.

'He said you'd leap at the suggestion of going to London,' said Fran.

'Well, yes. I suggested that yesterday...'

'So we've found a great new excuse for us to go

without making it pointed that we want to ask about the murder.'

'All of us?'

'All of us. Sophie's going to mind the shop. And believe it or not, Ellis have a gig tonight at a pub in Camden.'

Chapter Ten

'OK,' said Libby, sitting at Fran's big table with a cup of tea, 'now we've sorted out our visit to London, what about the bikers?'

'You said Edna was given as the contact for the Nether Regionals. Why don't we phone her?'

'There's only an email address,' said Libby. 'I wonder if anyone else would know?'

'If we knew one of their regular meeting points we could go there and ask.'

'Meeting points?'

'You know, like that famous cafe on the A3 in the fifties. Or sixties. Or something.'

'You mean the Ace of Spades. Actually, it burned down in the fifties, and the roundabout was called the Ace of Spades. Its association with bikers was because they used to do a ton through the new Hook underpass... Gosh, I didn't realise I remembered all that. Comes from being a Sarf Londoner.'

'Anyway, you know what I mean,' said Fran. 'There must be pubs or cafes where they meet.'

'Ian would have her number,' said Libby thoughtfully.

'And –' said Fran suddenly, 'so would Ben!'

'Eh?' Libby was startled.

'He said he'd taken the booking for the group! There

would have to have been a contact number. Even if it wasn't Edna, whoever it was would have her number.'

'Oh, bother.' Libby took out her phone. 'Why didn't I think of that before I left home?'

Luckily, Ben was in the estate office when Libby called, and was able to look up the booking for the Nethergate Regionals. Sure enough, it was Edna's phone number on the form.

'I expect we'll be contravening all sorts of data protection regulations using this,' Libby told Fran, as she keyed in Edna's number.

Fran raised her eyebrows. 'I doubt if Edna will tell anyone.'

'No – oh! Hello – is that Edna? Do you remember me? Libby Sarjeant – with a J – from the festival.'

She nodded at Fran and held up a thumb.

'I hope you don't mind, but Fran and I – do you remember Fran? – Yes, that's the one – well, she and I have been asked to look into the possibility of, um, witchcraft... No, no! Nothing like that!' She made a face at Fran. 'No, what I mean is, Ian – I mean the police – have heard there is sometimes a connection. None of us knows anything about it, but we thought you might. Not,' she added hastily, 'that we thought you had anything to do with it, just that because you're a biker, and in that world so to speak... You have? Really? I don't suppose we could talk to you about it, could we? Oh, yes, we're both in Nethergate... No, just us, off the record. Where?' She gestured madly to Fran, who picked up a pencil and paper. 'Oh – Cliff Terrace? Yes, I know. We've got a friend living there. Right. Yes, we'll be there in – what? Fifteen minutes?'

She switched off the phone and heaved a sigh of relief. 'Gosh, that was a bit tricky.'

'Was she suspicious?'

'A bit, at first, but she actually suggested meeting this morning, so she can't be that worried.'

'Cliff Terrace? Are we going to walk?'

Libby looked surprised. 'Well, of course, unless we park in the car park, which is a bit daft when we're only five minutes' walk away.'

'Which number?' Fran was collecting her mobile and bag.

'Melbourne,' she said. 'Is that number one? On the end?'

'Yes. It's got some land behind it.' Fran paused, looking thoughtful. 'Wonder if that's where she keeps her bike?'

'Doesn't seem very likely place for a biker chick,' said Libby. 'Bit genteel.'

'Ageing biker chick,' corrected Fran.

Cliff Terrace, originally called Victoria Place until the new promenade was built and became Victoria Place, was a terrace of tall, mid-Victorian townhouses named after prime ministers. It overlooked that end of town and The Alexandria, the Edwardian Pavilion, former home of The Alexandrians Concert Party and now summer home of the Oast House Theatre Company.

It was a very different Edna who opened the door of Melbourne House. Her wispy hair was drawn back from her face, and instead of leathers, she wore a long skirt, floaty top and a heavy silver necklace.

'Come in,' she said, obviously amused by their

surprise. 'I don't always look like an overaged groupie, y'know.'

'Oh, "Stage Door Jenny"!' said Libby. 'Neil Sedaka. I loved that song.'

Edna beamed. 'Glad y'know yer music. Come in the front room.'

The room was painted a light duck egg blue, and tastefully furnished with what looked like some antique pieces.

'What a lovely room!' said Fran. Libby scrutinised her friend's face for any sign of uncomfortable "moments" but could detect none.

'Good, innit?' Edna took a seat by the window and waved Fran and Libby to a squashy sofa on the other side of the fireplace. 'The old man's taught me a lot. He's in the business.'

'Antiques?' said Libby.

'Well, junk shop to start with, love. But he had what they call an "eye" or a "nose". So we moved up to better things. Tell you what – we've got a friend in common.' She leaned forward.

'Lewis?' suggested Fran.

Libby looked startled. 'How – '

'Well, o'course!' said Edna. 'Same background, innit? Course he's younger than us.'

'Oh,' said Libby, and looked cautiously at Fran, who was sitting, quite relaxed, at her end of the sofa.

'So you wanted to ask about bikers and witches.' Edna now leaned back and surveyed the other two women carefully. 'Course, you got mixed up in that lot out at Willoughby Oak, din't yer?'

'Er – yes.'

'That prat of TV director got mixed up, too.'

'Tim Bolton? He wasn't really mixed up in it,' said Libby. 'He was just trying to interfere.'

'Too much interference. Tried to get a programme out o'me, once.' Her mouth shut with a snap.

'Us, too,' said Fran.

'You, I bet,' said Edna shrewdly.

'Well, yes,' said Fran.

'That's the only reason I'm talkin' to yer,' said Edna surprisingly. 'Reckon yer might understand.'

'Oh?' Libby tried to sound unintrusive.

'And I reckon *you're* the nosy one,' said Edna, wagging a finger. Libby went bright red. Edna grinned. 'See, the whole connection started with the Hell's Angels thing.'

'Oh!' said Fran with an air of enlightenment. 'Of course! I didn't think of that! And the Grateful Dead.'

'An' I dunno where the witchcraft thing started, except it was just *there*, know what I mean?'

Fran nodded. Libby didn't dare do anything.

'There was this film see – '

'The bikers' suicides one?' suggested Fran.

'Psychomania, that's it!' Edna nodded vigorously. 'Anyway, there was a few feelers put out.' For the first time, she looked uncomfortable. 'And then it started.'

'You're part of it?' said Fran, surprised.

'Oh, we just muck about.' Edna gave a little laugh. 'We got a slogan, see. "We raise hell and support witches." We got branches all over England. Not witches, really.'

'So you don't know what this is?' Libby fished a copy of the sigil out of her pocket.

Edna peered warily at the piece of paper, then sat back in obvious relief. 'Never seen it before. Looks a bit like some o'those witchy symbols – is that what it is?'

'We think so,' said Libby, equally warily. 'Anyway, you don't know anything about real witches or covens?'

'I didn't say that, now, did I?' The older woman sat forward in her chair, elbows resting on her knees.

They stared at her in silence. She sat back again and smiled.

'All right. Our witches are just biker chicks. Bloody awful name, that. Anyway, we're all women, maintain the bikes ourselves, no trikes, no pink paintwork – you know the sorta thing. We do what we say – raise merry hell. Just what the blokes do.'

'So why witches?' asked Libby.

'Seemed like a good name,' said Edna with a shrug. 'But then this – y'know – coven got in touch. Said we was takin' the piss. An', as I say, it started. They started gettin' at some o' the younger kids. They got all woo-woo, if yer know what I mean. We still got some, although I got rid o' some, too. Silly cows. It don't mean anything.'

'So you've got nothing to do with real witches?' said Fran.

'They ain't REAL,' said Edna with fervour. 'Witches ain't real!'

'A lot of them believe they are,' said Libby. 'We've met some.'

'Load o' nonsense.'

'Yes, but they use these covens as covers – sorry! – for

all sorts of... er... behaviour,' said Fran.

'Oh, yeah.' Edna nodded wisely. 'Bikers get blamed for all o'that, witches or not.'

'Well,' said Libby, 'that's about it. There was some sort of suggestion that the young musician had a, well – a connection.'

'To witches?' Edna laughed. 'Don't be daft. Course 'e didn't.'

'How do you know?'

'He weren't the type. 'E weren't no goth. If they got any interest in witches they're all goth and black make-up.'

'So none of your Nether Regionals have any links with real witches,' said Fran.

'I didn't say that,' said Edna, looking sideways at them. 'Couple o'them – I think they got interested.'

'And you didn't get rid of them?' asked Libby.

'No, I said we still got some, didn't I?'

'Would they talk to us?' asked Fran.

'Course they wouldn't.' Edna held out her hand. 'Tell you what, though. Gimme that sign, whatever it is, and I'll show it around – careful-like. See what I turn up.'

'I'll copy it for you,' said Libby. 'Got any paper?'

Edna got up and went to a side table holding a laptop and printer. 'Use it for Regionals stuff,' she said, taking a piece of printer paper from the printer tray. She presented it and a black marker pen to Libby, who carefully copied out the sigil.

'There now. You can tell your policeman you've talked to us naughty bikers.' She sat down again by the window.

90

Libby felt the blush creeping up again.

Fran laughed. 'Come on, Edna. You're a perfectly respectable member of Nethergate society. And tell your Desmond Guy's got a couple of things he'd really like him to see.'

It was Edna's turn to go pink.

'I'll tell him,' she said, and shut the front door hurriedly behind them.

'Desmond?' Libby turned to Fran as they stood on the front steps of Melbourne House.

'I suddenly twigged who she was.' Fran grinned as she started down the steps. 'Her husband's Desmond Hawker. He's got that antique shop at the top of the town. You know the one with practically nothing in the window?'

'Oh, I know! The one with the one chair and the picture on an easel?'

'That's it. Very expensive. No wonder they live here.'

'Is Desmond a biker, too?' asked Libby, as they strolled back along Cliff Terrace.

'Good Lord, no, I shouldn't think so! He and Guy do the occasional bit of business together – Desmond asks Guy to value a painting and Guy asks him to look at the odd thing he's picked up with a picture.'

'And no dodgy antiques?'

'Definitely not. I believe the local force regard Desmond as a consultant. So Edna wouldn't get into anything – odd. If I'd realised who she was to start with...'

'Still, we've got some information about witches and bikers,' said Libby. 'Even if it isn't much use.'

'Is it worth investigating that line of enquiry any further, do you think?' asked Fran. 'If Edna doesn't think there's anything in it?'

'She said there are still members of the Regionals who are into it properly,' said Libby. 'But to be honest, I don't think they'd talk to us. Look how difficult we've found it in the past.'

'In that case,' said Fran, 'are we ever going to find anything out? I can't see any of the musicians talking to us about it, either, even if they knew what we were talking about.'

'There must be something,' said Libby. 'And we want to see if we can find anything out about Clive before he came to London, don't we? I think it's time we went up to London. Guy must be champing at the bit.'

'I don't see what we can find out that Ian and the police can't,' grumbled Fran, following Libby across the square towards Harbour Street and home. 'But I don't suppose I have a choice.'

Chapter Eleven

'So we're off to a gig?' said Ben. 'Are you sure about this?'

'Guy's idea, not mine. There's a show he wants to see, and Ellis have a gig tonight. So we can go there while he looks at weird pictures.'

'I think I'd rather go with Guy,' said Ben. 'Have you spoken to Dom and Bel?'

'No,' said Libby guiltily. 'I'll do that now.'

As it happened, Dom wasn't able to attend the gig that evening, but Belinda was going as Kyle's guest.

'It's only a pub, Mum,' said Bel. 'I'm sure the boys will get you in. You want to talk to them, I suppose?'

'Well, that was the idea,' said Libby. 'Will they mind?'

Libby heard a sigh. 'I don't expect so. Are you all coming?'

'Well, Guy's going to an exhibition or something, but I suppose he'll join us. Ben's said he'll drive up, and we'll come back this evening rather than find somewhere to stay.'

'Poor Ben won't be able to have a drink,' said Bel.

'No, but he says that's just as well at London prices. So where exactly is this pub?'

By the time they arrived at the venue somewhere in

Camden Town Libby was feeling stressed. London, her home town, had changed so much she barely recognised it.

'It's the atmosphere,' she said to Fran. 'It's foreign, somehow.'

'Don't start going racist on us,' said Fran, with a worried glance.

'I don't mean that, stupid. I mean London itself – it's alien.'

'I've lived here more recently than you,' said Fran, 'and it isn't really any different underneath. And I bet that pub's the same inside.'

The Craven Castle was a large, decoratively tiled Victorian pub on a corner. It was the twin of a dozen or more pubs of the same era dotted around the capital, and sure enough it still was the same inside. There was a large back room where Libby could see instruments set up.

'There they are,' said Ben, waving. Fran and Libby turned to see the three members of Ellis, together with Bel and a girl they didn't know, at a table in the corner.

'Hello, Ma.' Belinda stood up. 'This is Jenny.'

Jenny, small, fair and shy-looking, smiled up tentatively. Terry shifted his chair slightly closer to hers.

Ben offered drinks, then, accompanied by George, went off to buy them.

'So what did you want to ask us, Mrs S?' asked Kyle. 'I thought the police asked us everything on Sunday.'

'Libby, please,' said Libby. 'And this is Fran.'

'It's actually something that's emerged since then,' said Fran, edging her chair forward.

'Emerged? A clue?' said Terry.

'In a way,' said Libby. 'It's probably a vain hope that you might know anything.'

'Well, we've told you, we knew nothing about Clive before he came here,' said Kyle.

Ben and George returned with drinks.

'Mrs S – Libby – wants to ask us something else about Clive,' said Kyle.

'But we don't know anything about him,' said George.

'It's a long shot, I know,' said Fran, 'but did you ever hear him talk about witchcraft?'

A shocked silence fell. Then:

'*Witch*craft?' said Terry.

'Didn't some punk or goth bands go in for it years ago?' asked Libby nervously. 'Sorry if I'm showing my ignorance.'

The three band members exchanged glances.

'Well, yes,' said George eventually. 'There still are. All started, more or less, with Black Sabbath.'

'And there's a whole sub-culture of them these days. A lot in the States,' said Terry.

'There, see!' said Libby. 'I knew it.'

'But we don't know that Clive had any connections to the – er – movement,' said Kyle.

'What about Whitby?' said Terry. 'That's in the North.'

'That's like saying we're in the South and so is Weymouth,' said George.

'Then there's the Pendle Witches,' said Kyle.

Libby, Fran and Ben cleared throats and looked at their feet.

'Sensitive subject,' said Bel.

'Oh?' said Jenny, revealing that she had a voice. 'Why?'

That everyone else felt this was an intrusive question was left in no question, when everyone tried to shush her. She went bright red and retreated into her shell.

'Anyway,' said Terry, placing a hand over one of Jenny's, 'why do you ask? Something emerged since Sunday?'

Fran and Libby exchanged glances and at a nod from Fran, Libby spoke.

'The police found a piece of paper on Clive. It had a sigil on it.'

'A sigil?'

'A what?'

'What's that?'

'It's a sort of occult symbol,' said Fran.

'What of?' asked Kyle.

'You mean like a pentagram?' said George.

'A bit,' said Libby. 'This one is the sign for Alchemy.'

Ben opened his mouth and Fran trod on his foot.

'Where was it?' asked Terry. 'In his pocket?'

'On his body,' said Fran. 'That's all we know.'

'On paper, though?' said George. 'Not a tattoo?'

'No, paper,' said Libby. 'So none of you had heard of any connections of his with this sort of thing?'

Terry was frowning.

'Terry?' said Ben. 'What are you thinking?'

'We – ell,' said Terry slowly, 'I was just remembering one of the bands he said he played with in Manchester.'

Everyone turned to look at him.

'Don't you remember?' He looked at the other two

members of the band. 'Devil something?'

'Oh!' George clicked his fingers. 'Yes, of course! No, not Devil – Satan, or something like that.'

'Lucifer's Maiden,' said Jenny, in a small voice.

Attention was once more focused on her.

'You know them?' said Libby.

Jenny nodded.

'And you knew Clive was with them?' said Fran.

Jenny cleared her throat and looked at a corner of the ceiling.

'Come on, Jen,' said Terry, clasping her hand more strongly. 'You were up there, too, weren't you?' He turned to the others. 'That's how we met Jen. She used to live in Manchester, and came along to a gig down here after Clive joined us.'

'Great! So you know he was with them,' said Libby. 'How well did you know him – or them?'

Jenny cleared her throat again. 'I was with them, too,' she whispered.

A stunned silence spread over the company.

'You what?' said George.

'Singer,' said Jenny.

'*Singer*?' Terry looked astonished.

'Oh, I get it!' Kyle was scrolling through sites on his phone. 'Here we are!' He turned the screen to face the others. 'This is you, isn't it, Jen? You were the original Maiden!'

'But they were quite big, weren't they?' said George, looking over Kyle's shoulder. 'He didn't tell us that.'

'Only locally,' said Jenny.'

'What happened, then?' asked Terry. 'If you and he

97

both came down here?'

'Oh, it broke up.' Jenny was looking at her hands in her lap.

They all waited to see if she would say any more. When she didn't, Libby said 'Was there a reason?'

'Not sure. The bloke who started it – well, he wanted to stop...' Jenny trailed off, and Libby made a mental note to do some research.

'So you actually knew Clive,' said Ben. 'And do you know if he was interested in witchcraft? Or –' he looked at Libby and Fran, 'Satanism?'

'*Satanism*?' echoed the rest of the company.

Fran shook her head and Libby sighed.

'Bit brutal,' she said, 'but yes. That's what the sigil meant. What the police want to know is if he had any connection to – er – that sort of thing at any time.'

Jenny's face was now tomato-coloured.

'Come on, Jen,' said Terry gently. 'You know something.'

Jenny stuttered for a few moments, took a drink, cleared her throat and looked at the floor.

'They were...' she began and took a deep breath. 'They *said* they were Satanists.' She looked up at Libby, almost imploringly. 'I wasn't – I was just the singer - but they were always going on about... about... stuff. But Clive didn't. He kept himself to himself. Like I did.'

' Did you make friends because you were both – I don't know – outsiders?' asked Fran.

Jenny shook her head. 'We were only together for gigs or rehearsals, and we never travelled far. No touring or anything like that. I used to take my own car as much as possible. So did he.'

'But there's a connection,' said Belinda. She smiled at her mother. 'You were right to come up here and talk to the boys.' She turned to Jenny. 'Even if it wasn't them who told you anything.'

Jenny, colour now returned to normal, smiled. 'I hated it. I'd already decided to leave. Clive went first, and I thought I would stick out more now he wasn't there, if you know what I mean, so I left. And...' she looked round cautiously, 'they started threatening me.'

'*Threatening* you?' said seven people together.

'Well, sort of.' Jenny's colour was returning. 'Saying they'd do things – or the – the devil would.'

'I hope you didn't take any notice?' said Libby, her voice shaking with outrage.

'I tried not to, but it was scary. My mum suggested I come down here and stay with my Auntie Lilian.' She shrugged. 'So I did.'

'And you didn't know Clive was here?' asked Ben.

Jenny shook her head. 'I came to a gig here with my cousin and there he was. And I met the others.' She cast a shy look at Terry, who went nearly as pink as she was.

Libby sighed and sat back in her chair. 'Well, it helps.'

'Of course it does,' said Fran briskly. 'Jenny, if our friendly policeman wants to talk to you, would you mind? I don't suppose he'd ask you anything more than we have, but it would be useful, I think. Clive seems to have been a very private person and the more we can learn the better.'

'I suppose so.' Jenny looked at Terry again, who nodded encouragingly.

'No one knew anything,' said Libby, frowning into

99

her glass. 'It's unnatural.'

'Maybe not,' said Ben quietly. She looked at him, frowning, but he shook his head. 'Now anyone for another drink? We've got to wait until Guy gets here, anyway.'

'We're going to finish getting set up now,' said George, standing up. 'Will we see you later?'

'We've got to drive back to Kent,' said Fran, 'so maybe not. But I'm sure we'll see you all soon.'

The room at the back of the pub was filling up now.

'Jen and I will go and sit down by the stage, if you don't mind, Mum,' said Belinda. 'Being a groupie's such hard work.' She grinned amiably at the other girl.

'All right, darling, and thank you for persuading them to talk to us.' Libby gave her daughter a kiss.

'They didn't mind, and it seems an awful long way just for half an hour's chat,' said Belinda.

'But valuable,' said Ben, kissing her other cheek.

'Very,' said Fran. 'Now, off you go and enjoy yourselves.'

Guy arrived when Ellis were about ten minutes into their first set and suggested they ate something before leaving to drive home. The other three decided they'd rather get home, and pick up a takeaway on the way. Waving to the band, Belinda and Jenny, they followed Ben out to where he'd managed to park the car.

'No wonder no one drives into London anymore,' he said as he unlocked it. 'So bloody expensive, what with the congestion charge.'

'Now tell me if you found anything out,' said Guy when they were settled inside.

Between them they related Jenny's story as Ben made

his way out of south-east London.

'And does it help?' Guy asked, as they crossed Blackheath.

'It's not our problem if it doesn't,' said Fran. 'We just turn the information over to Ian.'

Libby made a face at her friend.

'There's one thing that he'll have to do,' said Ben.

'What's that?' asked Libby.

'Find out if Clive was in the Witness Protection Scheme.'

Chapter Twelve

'Eh?' They all turned to look at him.

'Well, doesn't it make sense? There's no record of him anywhere before he appeared in Manchester.'

'We don't actually know that,' said Guy, 'unless I've missed something.'

'I think it would already have come up,' said Libby. 'As far as I know from the TV, if the police try to find out something about a person who's in the UKPPS (is that it?) the computer says no. Or "Access Denied" or something.'

'So Ian would already know?' Ben frowned. 'Why hasn't he said anything, then?'

'Perhaps because there's a very valid reason for Clive's real identity to be kept secret?' suggested Guy.

'But it could be the motive for his murder,' said Fran.

'I expect Ian's thought of that,' said Libby.

'Is he staying at the Manor tonight?' asked Guy. 'We won't be back late. You could ask him.'

'Oh, I don't know,' said Fran. 'Seems a bit of a cheek.'

'He did ask us to find stuff out,' said Libby.

But Ian had gone home.

Once again, Ian stood at the tall window of his sitting room and looked out at the moonlit lake. The silver slice across the black surface was as theatrical a spotlight on

102

the flagged terrace below, as it had been a few short days ago.

'Well,' he said to himself, 'that'll teach you to get involved in Steeple Martin schemes.'

Somebody came out of the apartment below his and called. A barely defined shape slid across the terrace and disappeared. A door closed. For a moment Ian regretted not having a pet to keep him company during his rare times at home, but immediately dismissed the idea as selfish. He turned away from the window and went to pour himself a large Scotch. If he couldn't commit to an animal, how did he ever think he could commit to a human being? The image of Fran Castle, as she had been then, drifted across his mind and he remembered with fondness the few – the very few – moments of intimacy they had shared. He sighed.

But that was a long time ago, and these days he saw more of Libby than he did of Fran, and that was a good thing. But he was missing something.

He went back to the window and reflected on what he had learnt that day. And wondered what his unofficial investigators had managed to unearth. He smiled and finished his Scotch. He'd find out tomorrow.

Libby and Ben were discussing when to call Ian over breakfast the following morning when the doorbell rang.

'Ian!' said Ben, on opening it. 'We were just talking about you.'

Libby got up from the kitchen table to fetch another mug. 'Tea or coffee?'

'Is there tea in the pot?'

Libby grinned. 'There is. You know I'm the only person who makes it in a pot.'

'Except Hetty,' said Ian.

'So what do you want to talk about?' asked Ben, pulling out a chair for Ian.

'You first. Or rather, Libby. Did you go on your fishing trips yesterday?'

'Yes, we did. We even went all the way to London.' Libby pushed Ian's tea towards him and leant her elbows on the table. 'It was all quite interesting.'

Between them, she and Ben related the previous day's activities.

'And finally,' she concluded, 'although I don't suppose you'll tell us, Ben thought Clive Eddington might have been in the Witness Protection Scheme, or whatever it is now – the UKPPS is it? – as there was no information available about him. And this Jenny we met last night didn't know anything about him even though she was in a band with him.'

'Did she follow him down? Was there a relationship?' asked Ian, not answering the question.

Libby looked at Ben. 'It didn't sound like it, did it?' she said.

'We'll have to interview her.' Ian pulled out a notebook. 'What's her name?'

'Oh! She was just introduced as Jenny.' Libby got up and fetched her laptop. 'If we put in *Lucifer's Maiden* she'll come up, won't she?'

'Doing it now,' said Ian, waving his phone at her. 'And she has. Jennifer Dean. But no information about her. Would Belinda tell me?'

'I expect so. Do you want me to ask?'

'Is it likely to create mother-daughter conflict?'

'I don't think so, but it might create Belinda-Jenny conflict. Jenny might think Bel has betrayed her.'

'Why?'

'I got the impression she didn't really want to remember her days with the band.'

'She said she hated it,' said Ben.

'She told you about it,' said Ian. 'She could have kept quiet.'

Libby shrugged. 'Well, I'll try. I'll ask Bel to ask Jenny. Then I'll tell you what she says.'

'And there was very little from Edna?' Ian closed the notebook.

Libby shook her head. 'I told you, she said there were a couple in their group who maintained contact with a coven, but they won't talk to us. Or you. And did you know she's Desmond Hawker's partner?'

'I do now.' Ian smiled. 'Singularly appropriate name, isn't it?'

'Stands to reason she wouldn't get involved in anything – well, dodgy.'

'I agree. Edna is a good upstanding citizen. But it's definitely worth talking to Jenny.' He finished his tea and stood up. 'You'll let me know as soon as you have her contact details?'

'Yes, of course.' Libby stood up as Ben followed Ian to the door. 'But – what about...?'

'He didn't answer the question.' Ben came back, grinning. 'I thought he wouldn't.'

'Which means,' said Libby, sitting down again, 'that

he was. In the UKPPS.'

'It might, I suppose.' Ben picked up his mug and peered into it. 'Cold. But it doesn't mean he knows the real identity, does it? When they ask about somebody it just comes back "Access Denied", doesn't it? Didn't Guy say that yesterday?'

'But surely there'd be some kind of method of finding out? I mean, wouldn't the police want to know if the protected person had been murdered?'

'I expect it's already been flagged up,' said Ben. 'The minute the name was punched into the computer. Or HOLMES, or whatever it is these days.'

'Oh, yes.' Libby looked despondent. 'And they won't tell us, will they?'

'Unlikely.' Ben stood up and moved the big kettle back onto the hob of the Rayburn. 'What are you going to do today?'

'First, tell Fran what Ian said – or didn't say. Then I'll think about it. What about you?'

'The touring company's coming in this morning. Once I've seen them in they can more or less be left on their own as long as they can get hold of me, you or Pete fairly quickly. And I'm having a chat with someone about reviving the hop garden this afternoon.'

'Oh?' Libby looked up. 'You didn't tell me.'

'Well, it's only a vague idea as yet.' Ben looked embarrassed. 'Someone suggested it over the weekend.'

'The beer festival?' Libby's eyebrows hit her hairline. 'How come?'

'You know we were talking about the craft beers the other day?'

106

'Yes, and how long they kept.'

'Well, Tim was talking to one of the brewers the following day apparently, and mentioned me...'

'Just happening to drop into the conversation that there used to be a hop garden here.'

'And this bloke suggested...' Ben shrugged helplessly. 'I thought it couldn't hurt to talk to him.'

Libby laughed. 'It's not my business, but actually, I think it would be rather a nice idea. What would you grow? Fuggles?'

'They've been subject to wilt over the past few years, but I think someone has developed a resistant strain, and it is the traditional Kentish hop.'

'Have you got enough time to spend on it?'

'What do I do, these days? I go and sit in the office and pretend to work.'

Libby frowned. 'That's not what you tell me.'

'Well, obviously I do more than that, but yes, I've got time. And there are always people in the village who can help at harvest time. Practically everyone's involved in one way or another, aren't they? Field crops, soft fruit, apples, pears...'

'Yes, I'll give you that.' Libby was getting interested. 'What about the other end of the business? You know, twiddling the bines, or whatever?'

Ben grinned. 'I don't think you get the handsome young pole-pullers, these days.'

'They were the other end of the season,' said Libby. 'Even I know that.'

'You probably know more about it than I do,' said Ben. 'After you and Peter wrote the play.'

107

'Peter wrote the play,' said Libby, 'and he hasn't got over it yet.'

'Well, I shall have to steer warily round him, won't I?' Ben leant over and gave his best beloved a kiss. 'Be good.'

'I thought you were going to make more tea?'

'Haven't got time, now,' said Ben, with another grin. 'Make your own.'

Libby sighed, finished her own tea and went upstairs to dress.

By the time she had gone back downstairs and loaded the dishwasher, she'd decided to call Fran, then go and see Harry for an early lunch.

'You're not going to do anything else, then?' said Fran.

'There's nothing else to do. Ian's got it all in hand, and we're not going to be told anything else, despite having trailed all the way up to London yesterday.'

'I suppose not.' Libby heard Fran sigh. 'It's a shame though, after all that effort yesterday.'

'Think of the effort the police have to go through during an investigation with no results,' said Libby.

'But they get paid for it.'

'That's very true.' Libby giggled. 'Perhaps we should ask Ian for expenses.'

'OK, you try! But seriously, if we're not going any further with this, I might as well get down to some work here.'

'Work? There? You mean in the shop?'

'Not exactly. Now the season's over we're not busy enough until Saturday and Sunday.'

'What, then?' asked Libby after a pause.

Fran sighed again. 'I knew I shouldn't have said anything. I'm going to try writing again.'

'Writing?'

'Well, don't sound as if it's the most outlandish thing in the world. I was getting quite good at it.'

'But what?' said Libby. 'You don't take classes anymore.'

'Most writers don't,' said Fran. 'And you didn't, when you were writing panto scripts, did you? You learnt by doing panto.'

'Yes,' conceded Libby doubtfully. 'But you don't "do" books. You read them.'

'Precisely!' said Fran triumphantly. 'I read a lot. So I'm going to have a go. If I don't succeed at first, I'll keep plugging away. I want to be able to earn at least some of my own money.'

'Most writers I know barely cover enough to pay for printer paper,' said Libby.

'Thank you, cheerful. Anyway, I've started.'

'So you'll finish, all right. Shall I let you know if anything happens? You know – about the investigation?'

'Of course,' said Fran promptly. 'Good research.'

Libby ended the call and sat back in her chair and glowered at the ceiling. Fran didn't want her, Ian didn't want her and even Ben was now off on a solo project. She tried to shake off a feeling of desolation, peered out at the weather, decided to take a jacket, then collected her basket and left the house.

As she turned the corner into the high street, a car hooted its horn, and looking up she saw Peter pulling into the kerb. The passenger window slid down and he leaned forward.

'Being a good little hussif?'

'Haven't got anything else to do. I thought I might pop into the caff and con Harry out of some lunch.'

'You'll be lucky.' Peter grinned at her. 'He's shut up shop and gone off to see a new organic producer on the Sussex border. Adam's gone with him, would you believe.'

Libby stared at him.

'I'd say you could come with me, but I'm doing a feature on prisons and you haven't got clearance.' He sat back behind the wheel. 'Ciao. See you later.' The car slid away from the kerb.

Resisting an instinct to burst into tears, Libby stood, irresolute, on the pavement outside the vicarage, and wondered what on earth to do next.

Chapter Thirteen

'Libby! Mrs S!'

Salvation had arrived in the shape of Dick Fowler. He stood waving outside his little shop. When she lifted a hand to wave back, he beckoned. She crossed the road and came to a halt beside him.

'Morning, Dick. What can I do for you?'

'Well, it's these photographs, see. I developed them all to see what I could use for the local paper and the *Kent Illustrated*.'

'Oh, they're using some, are they?'

'They like photographs of county events. I write a little bit about them and they write them up properly.'

'Good for you,' said Libby. 'I didn't realise they had to be developed. I thought they were all digital.'

'They are, but they have to be converted into the right format. And different print publications require different dpi, so...'

'What?'

'Dots per inch,' said Dick, frowning at her. 'Well, never mind. I've got them all in the studio, and there were a couple of things I'd like you to see. I didn't know if I should tell the policeman, so I thought I'd show you.'

'Oh, OK.' Libby nodded brightly and followed him into the shop and through the door at the back. 'Will you hear if anyone comes in?'

'Oh, the "closed" sign's up,' said Dick, pulling up a stool by the work bench. 'The shop doesn't do much business, to be honest.'

'Oh.' Libby perched on the stool and dumped her basket on the floor. 'It's mostly this sort of work, is it?'

'And weddings. You'd never believe marriage is supposed to be going out of fashion. Some of the sights I've seen...' He shook his head. 'Now, here we are.' He started scrolling through photographs on the computer in front of them. 'These are the Friday night, just before his band was going to play.'

'You mean, the dead boy? His band, Ellis?'

Dick nodded. The photograph on the screen showed Clive Eddington standing at the side of the stage turned away from the audience, an angry expression on his face. He moved on to the next frame. Libby sat forward and peered.

'It looks as if he's having an argument with someone off-stage.'

'But there wasn't anywhere at the sides,' said Dick. 'Only at the back.'

'Then it was right off the stage. Didn't you get any shots of that?'

Dick shook his head. 'I was focusing on the bands.'

'Well, it's interesting, but without the other person I can't see it would be any interest to the police.'

'There's more.' Dick whizzed through more frames until he slowed down at some Libby recognised.

'That's the two girls, Fiona and Tracey,' she said. 'But what are they doing?'

'That's what I wondered.' Dick leant forward and poked a finger at the screen. 'Look, they're talking to someone behind the stage.'

'Well, Clive wouldn't have been there, would he? Not if this was Saturday.'

'But he was, wasn't he? Later?'

'But not while the gig was still running,' said Libby, sitting back and looking at him.

Dick frowned. 'Anyway, do you think I ought to show them to that policeman?'

Libby frowned back. 'I don't see that it wouldn't help. He can always get some hapless constable to trawl through them all. Who knows what he might pick up.'

'I'll put them on another memory stick, then.' Dick slid off his stool and rummaged in a drawer. 'Don't let them use any, though, will you?'

'Me? Why me?'

Dick looked surprised. 'I thought you'd take them to him.'

'Why can't you do it?'

'I – er – I don't know. I suppose I could.' He made a face. 'I'd feel silly.'

'And I wouldn't?'

'You're used to it.'

'All right.' Libby watched him copy all the files onto the memory stick. 'And they can get hold of you here if they need to?'

Dick nodded, handed her the stick and ushered her out of the shop. 'Thanks, Libby. I've been worrying about that.'

Libby grinned at him. 'Don't worry. I'm sure this will

113

help. I don't know where they've got to at the moment.'

'Really?' Dick raised his eyebrows. 'I thought you...'

Libby shook her head. 'No. We're simply bystanders.' She smiled and patted his arm. 'If I can, I'll let you know how things go.'

Well, she said to herself as she walked along towards Maltby Close, now what? I've got something to do, but I don't know how to go about it. She stood on the corner by the doctor's house and thought. Go up to the hall and see if the police were there? Ring Ian?

'What's up, gal? Lorst sixpence and found a ha'penny?'

Flo Carpenter stood behind her, cigarette between her fingers, duster in her other hand.

'Hello, Flo. No, I've been given some information for Ian and I don't know what to do with it.'

Flo's artistically drawn eyebrows rose. 'Give it to 'im, o'course.'

'I don't know where he is.'

'Well, 'is mates are all up at the Hall. Thought you'd know that.'

'We're being kept out of this one,' said Libby. 'A bit too close for comfort.'

'Rubbish!' Flo snorted. 'You bin closer'n this before!'

'But Ian hasn't. He wasn't going to be allowed on the team, so now he's got to be really careful.'

'Daft, I call it. Cuttin' off their noses, they are.'

'Yes, well...' Libby looked doubtful. 'If they're up at the hall I'd better take this stuff up there.' She heaved a sigh. 'Thanks, Flo.'

Flo put her head on one side. 'Sure you're all right?

Want a drop o' something?'

Libby smiled. 'I'm fine. Everyone's off doing something else and I'm here on my own. Well, I was until now.'

'You watch the Devil don't find work,' said Flo. 'Welcome to come back here and have a bit o' lunch.'

'Thanks, Flo, but I've got to pop in on Hetty anyway. See you Sunday for lunch!'

As she walked up Maltby Close drive a patrol car passed her, the driver peering interestedly out at her. She beamed at him.

Inspector Maiden, bent over a long trestle table inside the hall with two uniformed colleagues, looked up and saw her.

'Mrs Sarjeant!' He came towards her. 'What can we do for you? I'm afraid...'

'No, no!' said Libby hastily. 'I was asked to deliver these. They're photographs taken over last weekend.'

Maiden took them, frowning. 'But we already saw these, didn't we?'

'These are different ones. Quite a lot of them, and some quite interesting. At least, the photographer thought so.'

Maiden looked doubtful. 'Same photographer?'

'Yes, Dick Fowler. Can you give them to whoever wants to see them?' She turned to go.

'DCI Connell will be back soon – shall I get him to give you a call?'

'No, don't bother.' Libby smiled over her shoulder. 'He'll be busy.'

Maiden opened his mouth, as if he was going to say

that it hadn't ever bothered her before, but shut it again with a frown. Libby smiled again and left the building.

She found Hetty in her kitchen making a pie.

'Apple?' she asked.

'And blackberry.'

'Did you pick them?'

Hetty cocked an eye at her. 'Course I did. Do one fer you, shall I?'

'Ooh, yes please.' Libby sat at the table. 'Did they come from the edge of the wood?'

'Yes. Wouldn't take yer a minute to go up there of an evening.'

'I know, I know. I never think about it.' Libby rested her chin on her hands. 'What do you think about Ben's latest idea?'

'Which one?'

Too late, Libby realised that Ben might not have told his mother about the nebulous hop growing idea.

'Oh, about the hops,' she muttered.

'Startin' up the old garden? Yeah, he told me.' Hetty sounded amused. 'Was you worried in case I was upset?'

Relieved, Libby nodded.

'Good idea, if you ask me. All these micro-breweries and craft beers, as well as the little special places – like the smokeries and them.'

'Smokeries?'

'You not keepin' up, gal? They're all out there. Private smokehouses – fer bacon an' that. Like the one in Whitstable.'

'Really?'

'An' all these cake places. You got some friends who

do cakes, ain't yer?'

'I have. So it's quite a movement, then, is it?'

'Thought you would've known, bein' young. Young Hal knows.' Hetty pulled a pie dish filled with fruit towards her. "'E's gone orf to see some producer today, ain't 'e?'

'Yes. Peter told me.' Libby eyed her mother-in-law-elect as she carefully laid pastry over the fruit. 'I don't know how you get to hear these things.'

Hetty shrugged. 'Bin 'ere a long time. Friends all over.' She turned and carried the pie to the Aga.

'I suppose so, but I thought I'd been here a long time too.'

'Not as long as me. And I'd moved 'ere permanent by the time you was born. You lived in London until you got married. Longer'n me.'

'And then I wasn't exactly here, was I?' Libby sighed. 'I've probably still got a lot to learn.'

'You've talked to a lot of my old mates. That's 'ow you learn.' Hetty closed the Aga door. 'Cuppa?'

By the time Libby left the Manor, she was restored to good humour, and decided to walk home across the fields and see if she could see blackberries at the edge of the wood.

'Libby!'

Startled, she turned round just as she came level with the hoppers' huts. Ian was waving to her from the theatre. Scowling, she stood there and waited to see if he would come after her, feeling disinclined to traipse back across the field. After a second's indecision, he did.

'Sorry I wasn't there,' he said, as he came up to her.

117

'I didn't expect you to be. I was simply asked to deliver them.'

'Oh.' Ian sounded surprised. 'Who by?'

'Didn't Maiden tell you? Dick Fowler. Who else would it be?'

'All right, don't snap. Why couldn't he do it himself?'

'He said he'd feel silly.' Libby couldn't suppress a giggle. 'So as I was coming up to see Hetty –' almost true - 'I said I'd bring them.'

'Well, thank you.' Ian frowned at the ground for a moment. 'Have you seen them? Are they any different to the ones he showed us the other day?'

'There's just a lot more of them. A few that might bear looking into, I suppose, but I don't know that they'll be much use.'

'What do you mean? What are they?'

'There are a couple which look as if Clive Eddington's having an argument with someone, and another couple where those two girls seem to be talking to someone behind the stage.' She shrugged. 'None of them looked worth it to me, but maybe you or one of your specially trained chaps will spot something.'

'They're more likely to complain. This ranks with checking CCTV footage in a town centre on Saturday night.' Ian sighed. 'All right, thanks, Libby. There wasn't anything else?'

Libby widened her eyes at him. 'No, nothing.'

In contrast, Ian narrowed his eyes at her. 'Why don't I believe you?'

'I've no idea. I'm simply spending a blameless day in the village, going shopping –' She stopped short. 'Oh, bother. I got distracted and forgot the shopping.'

Ian grinned. 'Dinner, was it?'

Libby nodded sadly. 'Ben won't be pleased.'

Ian patted her arm. 'Don't be daft – he won't care. Especially when he hears I'm taking you to dinner at Hal's.'

Chapter Fourteen

'You are?'

'It's Wednesday, isn't it? Patti and Anne will be there. I'll give Harry a call.'

'He might be out, still.' Libby explained where Harry had gone. 'But you could leave a message.'

Feeling a good deal more cheerful, Libby continued her way across the field towards home, being met by Sidney stealthily stalking her through the long grass.

'Come on, cat,' she said. 'Race you home.'

Ben was delighted to be told he was being taken out to dinner. The touring company in the theatre had everything under control for their opening night on Saturday, so Libby called Patti to tell her they would not only see her and Anne in the pub after dinner, but actually in The Pink Geranium first.

Patti Pearson, the vicar of St Aldeberge's church, a few miles north down the coast from Nethergate, came to Steeple Martin every Wednesday to see her friend Anne Douglas, who lived round the corner from Libby. Their invariable habit was to dine with Harry in the caff and join Libby, Ben and whoever else happened to be around in the pub afterwards. Ian often joined them, although even Libby hadn't yet discovered if he was on his way home when he did so, and if so, where he was on his way home to.

She wasn't surprised when she and Ben arrived at the caff to find Fran and Guy also ensconced in the left-hand window with Ian. Patti and Anne waved from a table further down the room.

'We decided you probably needed to talk amongst yourselves,' said Anne. 'What with this latest murder and all.'

'Ridiculous, isn't it?' said Libby with a sigh. 'No one would believe it if you read it in a book.'

'You should have got your Rosie to write up your adventures,' said Patti.

'Actually, Fran's going to have a go at writing something,' said Libby. 'You know she took classes from Rosie? That's how we met her.'

'There you are, then. Fran can write them up. Turn them into best-sellers,' said Anne.

'Oh, no, I couldn't bear it,' said Libby.

'You could change the names,' said Patti. 'I don't think I'd particularly like to feature in a book with my real name.'

'Would anyone?' Libby made a face. 'Now I'd better go and sit down before they drink all the wine.'

'Right,' said Ian as she joined the others, 'now tell me what's been happening today?'

'Nothing much,' said Libby. 'I told you earlier when I saw you.'

'What?' asked Fran. 'You haven't told me.'

Libby repeated Dick Fowler's story and explained about the photographs. 'So did you look at them, Ian? Was there anything in them?'

Ian frowned. 'Possibly. Fowler was quite right when he said they were a bit worrying. Eddington is seen talking to somebody off camera several times, and at no time does he look pleased.'

'But Dick doesn't catch whoever it is? And what about the two girls?'

'I don't think they would have had anything to do with it,' said Ian.

'Except that they knew the band in London,' said Fran.

'You mean they could have recognised another London fan in the audience?' said Guy.

'Maybe.'

'Did you find anything out about Jenny Dean and Lucifer's Maiden?' asked Ben.

'Only what you told me.' Ian played with the stem of his wine glass.

'There's something else, isn't there?' said Libby.

'Possibly.' Ian looked up. 'There's an "Access Denied" on Eddington's name.'

'See!' Libby looked round the table in triumph. 'We were right. Witness Protection scheme – or whatever it is.'

'UK Protected Persons Service,' said Ian, 'and not necessarily. And even if I find out, I probably won't be able to tell you anything about it.'

'So why are you telling us now?' asked Fran shrewdly.

Ian smiled. 'Why do you think?'

Ben and Guy looked at each other and shrugged. Libby looked bewildered. Fran smiled back.

'So that we look into it ourselves,' she said.

'Oh!' said Libby.

'Not that I can sanction anything.' Ian picked up the bottle and topped up their glasses.

'Of course not.' Libby nodded vigorously.

'But you'll have to give us some pointers,' said Fran. 'We can't start blind.'

'Find out what he was doing in Manchester.'

'How do we do that?' asked Libby. 'We don't know anyone in Manchester.'

'You know Jenny Dean.'

'We met her last night. We know nothing about her,' said Libby.

'Musicians have a network,' said Ian. 'And don't tell me you won't go immediately to all the social media sites. And there'll be a link to someone you know.'

'How do you know?' Fran narrowed her eyes at him.

'I'm guessing.' He grinned. 'Come on – that's Harry telling us our table's ready.'

Despite Libby's impatience, the conversation stayed away from the murder while they ate. Anne and Patti finished their meal and left for the pub, Adam cleared away their plates, and Harry came out bearing a bottle of brandy.

'Pete'll be here in a minute,' he said, turning a chair round and straddling it. 'So tell me what's been going on.'

'Nothing really,' said Libby. 'What's been going on here?'

Peter emerged from the kitchen. 'Not a lot,' he said.

123

'What did you do with yourself after all this morning, Lib?'

'I went to visit Dick Fowler and look at his photos.'

Harry nudged Ben. 'Other men's etchings, mate. Watch it.' Ben rammed the chef's hat down over his eyes.

'So you aren't investigating our murder, then?' Peter pulled up another chair and poured himself a brandy.

'Unofficially,' said Ian, 'but word isn't to get round. The official investigation is going on, and, as it happens, Dick Fowler's photographs are very useful, but there are other aspects which Libby and Fran might be able to help with.'

'Until they crash into the official investigation,' said Peter. 'What do you think, cuz?'

'If Ian thinks they can help then it's up to them. We've never been able to stop them yet,' said Ben. 'Have we, Guy?'

'Even when we go on holiday,' said Guy, with a sigh. 'Let them get on with it.'

'You mentioned Dick Fowler's photographs,' said Peter. 'Do you mean the ones he showed us on Sunday?'

'Some of those,' said Ian, 'but a lot more. Taken over the whole weekend.'

'Ah.' Peter nodded. 'Only I just wondered because of the old ones he found.'

'What old ones?' asked Fran.

'The shop had been a photographic studio before Dick took over. There were loads of old negatives and other stuff upstairs when he moved in.'

'I didn't realise you knew him,' said Harry, squinting under his chef's hat.

'Not well, and only since he took over the shop.'

'Has everyone had all they want?' asked Ian. 'Only I can then pay the bill and we can go to the pub to see your friends.'

'And you want to see if Dick Fowler's in there,' said Libby.

Ian grinned. 'I might.'

Patti and Anne had saved their usual large round table, and Libby and Fran sat down while Ben and Guy went to buy drinks. Ian disappeared into the other bar.

Patti raised her eyebrows.

'Where's he gone?'

'To find Dick Fowler, I imagine,' said Fran.

'Dick Fowler?' repeated Anne.

'He owns the photographic shop over the road,' said Libby. 'Not something I'd ever taken much notice of, but he was the sort of "official" photographer for the weekend.'

'Did he take some pictures with clues in?' Anne's eyes were bright with interest.

'He thinks so. He showed me this morning.'

'Can we know what's been happening?' asked a diffident Patti. 'I'm sure we're not really supposed to.'

Between them Fran and Libby described the events of the last couple of days. The men arrived with the drinks, but Ian was still missing.

'So basically you need to know if there was anything in this boy's background that would make

125

him a victim?' said Anne. 'Whether it's a long way back or more recent.'

'That's about it.' Libby nodded.

'And the sigil,' said Patti. 'I saw some of those when we had all that trouble before.'

'This one means Alchemy, but it's used to represent Satanism as a whole.' Fran frowned down at her glass. 'We asked someone about it.'

'Who?' asked Patti warily. 'Not more witches?'

Libby explained.

'Oh, Edna! I know her.' Patti beamed. 'Desmond Hawker's wife. They often turn up at events locally. I think they know Ron Stewart.'

'That would make sense,' said Fran. 'Anyway, no one seems to know anything about the boy, even in London, although we haven't been able to find out much up there. But even his own band don't know anything about him.'

'Or his former band,' put in Libby, 'which makes it even weirder. And sadder, too,' she added thoughtfully.

'It is sad,' said Patti. 'Fancy being that lonely. Do you think he came to London to find more friends than he had up north?'

'I don't know. Everyone who knew him seems to say he didn't welcome attempts to get close.' Libby turned round. 'Here's Ian.'

Ian picked up his customary coffee and sat down.

'Has he found anything else in the shop?' asked Libby. 'You were a long time.'

'I was asking about the photographs he took at first,' said Ian. 'Then I asked if he'd found anything in the rooms upstairs. He says he hasn't really been through them.'

'Really?' Fran's eyebrows shot up. 'I couldn't have resisted going through them in – what was it? – six years?'

Libby, Patti and Anne all offered fervent agreement, and the men laughed.

'Doesn't he live up there?' asked Anne.

'Apparently not. He's got a house in Lendle Lane.'

'Which backs on to the high street. Convenient,' said Libby.

'Did he say anything about the photographs he took over the weekend?' asked Guy.

'Not a lot, except that he thought they might be significant. As he said, if he'd known what was going to happen he would have acted differently.'

'Would he let us go through the rooms upstairs and anything we might find?' asked Libby.

'He might, but I should think he'd be very wary,' said Ian. 'You scare him, rather.'

'Me?' Libby was indignant. 'I'm not scary!'

'I can't see,' said Fran thoughtfully, 'what good looking at anything that had been in the shop for years would do. After all, this isn't a local murder, is it? The victim didn't come from here, and the clues are always in the personality of the victim, aren't they, Ian?'

'Sometimes.' He looked at her oddly for a moment. 'But sometimes the reasons are simply down to the murderer themselves. For instance, if they are seen stealing something they may lash out to protect themselves.'

'Do you think that's what happened in this case?'

127

asked Patti. 'The murderer was caught in the act?'

'Whatever "the act" was,' said Anne. 'It seems a bit over the top, though.'

'I can think of another reason,' said Libby, looking as if a star had burst over her head. 'Woohoo!'

Ben shook his head and groaned. Guy patted his shoulder in sympathy.

'Go on, then,' said Anne. 'What?'

'We said Clive was probably in the UKPP-whatever-it-is. Well – ' Libby took a deep breath ' – someone recognised him!'

'That's rather good,' said Patti.

'Except,' said Ian, 'surely then the victim would have been the murderer instead.'

Frowns all round the table indicated that the company was trying to work this one out.

'Oh, yes,' said Guy. 'He would have killed whoever recognised him to prevent his real identity from coming out.'

'Oh.' Libby's mouth turned down at the corners.

'But it was a very good theory.' Ian smiled and leant over to pat her hand. She glowered.

'Don't patronise.'

'What happened,' said Ben, unsubtly changing the subject, 'about Danny Coleman?'

'Danny Coleman?' echoed Patti and Anne together.

Ben explained.

'After I had that chat with him,' said Ian, ' nothing. I'm pretty sure he has something to do with the fake crew –'

'Fake crew?' said Anne.

128

'– but there was something else he wasn't telling me, I'm sure. And I couldn't work out what he was doing wandering round the village this morning.'

Chapter Fifteen

'Fake crew?' repeated Anne. 'I don't get it.'

Libby did her best to explain.

'But it doesn't seem to have anything to do with the other boy's murder,' said Patti.

'Well –' began Libby.

'We don't know that. As I said, I'm sure there was something he was holding back.' Ian smiled round at the company. 'And now, I'm going back to my room at the Manor. I have to be up early in the morning.'

'Thank you for our meal, Ian,' said Libby dutifully. 'What do you want us to do next?'

'Who said I wanted you to do anything?' Ian raised his eyebrows at her.

'You did. You said you wanted us to look into Clive's background ourselves.'

'That's true, you did,' said Guy. 'And on your own head be it.'

'But I also said I couldn't sanction it.' Ian grinned at her. 'See you tomorrow.'

'Well,' said Fran, when he had gone. 'What *do* we do now?'

'I really don't know,' said Libby helplessly. 'It's all very well...'

'I think you should try and find that boy who Ian thinks had something to do with the – what was it? –

fake crew,' said Anne.

'Why?' asked Ben.

'If Ian thinks he needs to be talked to,' said Anne, 'then he must think he's relevant.'

'He said he was holding something back,' said Patti. 'You should find out what.'

'But how?' asked Libby. 'Nobody seems to know him. Or Fat Dragon.'

'What about Ron Stewart?' said Guy.

'I've already said I doubt that he would know him – too small fry,' said Libby.

'He's your best bet,' said Anne. 'I wish I could do it.' She looked wistful, and the others looked uncomfortable. Anne didn't let her wheelchair hinder her most of the time, but there were some things she really couldn't do.

Libby shifted in her chair. 'OK, I'll ring him tomorrow. Or Maria.'

'His wife,' amplified Fran.

'Yes, I know,' said Patti, standing up. 'If you want any help, just ask. I know them both.'

'Are we going?' asked Anne.

'I think so.' Patti smiled down at her friend. 'Too much excitement.'

'We must go, too,' said Fran. 'Two late nights on the trot aren't good for us old people.'

'What are we going to do, though?' asked Libby, finishing her drink. 'I can phone Ron, but I don't think that'll be much help.'

The following morning, while Ben went up to check on the touring company in the theatre, Libby gloomily contemplated her neglected housework, and finally, after changing the spare bed where Belinda had stayed over the weekend, she sighed and found the Stewarts's telephone number.

'Maria! Remember me? Libby Sarjeant?'

'Of course I do, Libby. Do you want to come and stay after all? Bit of time out?'

'No, no – it's lovely of you, but I'd better stay here. We've got hirers in the theatre, and... well, what I actually wanted to ask was, do you and Ron know the band Fat Dragon?'

'Fat Dragon... oh, hang on, yes, I think Ron's come across them. Played at your festival, didn't they?'

'That's right. Ian – the policeman, you know – he thinks one of them might – well – he thinks –'

'One of them might be up to something?' Maria sounded amused. 'Wouldn't surprise me. At least by the look of them. But that may be prejudice on my part.'

'Prejudice? You?'

'Don't forget we were in the thick of the sex, drugs and rock and roll movement. Well, just after it, I suppose, so I may be judging by appearances. And there was all that business with the ukulele group.'

'How could I forget?' Libby sighed heavily. 'But you don't actually know them?'

'Afraid not. I'll ask Ron – he's still got a lot of contacts. But as you know, they do very few gigs these days, and mainly the big festivals.'

'I know, that's why it was such a coup for us to get them to play at ours,' said Libby. 'Although I doubt if we'll be doing it again. Every time we try anything someone seems to get murdered. The concert with the ukulele group, our writing weekends, the ballet...'

'That was excellent,' said Maria. 'We were very privileged to see it down here first.'

'I know.' Libby sighed again. 'But you see what I mean.'

'I do. But cheer up. You'll be thinking about panto soon, won't you?'

After this non-event of a phone call Libby was at a loss. Maria's reminder of panto prompted her to get out her theatre file and review the progress made so far on the new season's offering, but it wasn't inspiring. She'd just decided she ought to get on with her latest painting for Guy's gallery when the landline rang.

'Mrs Sarjeant?'

'Yes?'

'Inspector Maiden here.' There was a pause. 'Are you at home?'

'Obviously, or I wouldn't be answering the phone.'

'No...' Maiden sounded confused. 'Ah – could I pop round?'

'Certainly. Why?'

Maiden cleared his throat. 'I'll explain when I see you.'

Libby made a hasty call to Fran to find out if she too had received a mysterious phone call, which she hadn't, and just as she was going to call Ben, there was a sharp knock on the door.

Inspector Maiden, accompanied by a very young uniformed constable, stood outside looking sheepish. Libby frowned at him.

'What on earth is the matter?'

'May we come in?'

'I suppose so.' Libby led the way into the sitting room and perched on the sofa, waving a hand at the chair opposite. The constable remained standing, looking acutely uncomfortable.

'Well?' She fixed Maiden with a militant eye.

'Mrs Sarjeant...' Maiden cleared his throat again. 'Did – um – did DCI Connell see you last night?'

'Yes.' Libby's stomach turned over. 'What's happened?'

'Well...did he mention Danny Coleman to you?'

'Yes, he did. I saw him the other morning, you know.'

'Yes, we know.' Maiden looked at the floor. 'This is awfully awkward, you know.'

'What is?' Libby was scowling now.

Maiden's complexion was by now a pretty shade of pink. 'Well, you see...we know DCI Connell suggested...' He dried up.

'That I tried to find out something about Danny Coleman and his band? Yes he did. Shouldn't he have done? We booked the band. It was perfectly sensible. Actually, it wasn't precisely his suggestion. Our friend Anne thought it was what he might want.'

'Yes, of course. But you see, the thing is... did you?'

'Did I?' Libby glanced at the constable who was by now looking as bewildered as she felt.

'See Danny Coleman?'

'No, of course not. How could I? I don't know where to find him. All I did was to call a friend to see if she knew anything about him.'

'And the friend is...?'

134

'Ron Stewart's wife, Maria. Why? For goodness' sake, get to the point, Inspector Maiden.'

'Well, you see...' Maiden's eyes slid sideways. 'We've found him.'

Libby felt a surge of relief. 'Is that all? Well, that's good isn't it? If DCI Connell thinks he knows something.'

'No, but you see – he's dead.'

Libby gasped. 'What?'

'Yes. And you see...' Maiden now looked as if he wanted to crawl under the carpet.

'No, I don't. You'll have to explain.' Libby was breathless. ' Is DCI Connell in trouble?'

Maiden's pink face was threatening to become puce. 'Not exactly, but – well, we wondered – um – we wondered if –'

'Ah.' Light dawned. 'If I had managed to track him down, jumped in with both flat feet and somehow precipitated his death?'

Maiden's colour receded and the constable let out an audible breath.

'Well – yes.' Maiden tried a hesitant smile.

'Honestly, Maiden. I know we don't know each other all that well, but you have known me for several years now. Couldn't you have come straight out with it? And why didn't Ian – DCI Connell – ask me himself?'

'He was – um – embarrassed.'

'Bloody hell!' Libby exploded. 'And you weren't?'

'But he's a friend of yours. It *was* embarrassing – I can see that.'

Libby regarded him quizzically. 'You did make a bit

of a meal of it. Tell me what happened.'

'I suppose it would be all right,' said Maiden doubtfully.

'Look – after thinking I had something to do with his death –'

'Oh, no!' interrupted Maiden hastily. 'We never – I mean – well, anyway. DCI Connell went back to the incident room last night and looked to see if the band –'

'Fat Dragon, yes.'

'– had a website.'

'Surely that had been done already?'

'I don't think it was given a very high priority,' said Maiden, beginning to go pink again.

'Someone'll be for the high jump, then.'

'It should have been done,' agreed Maiden, with a nod.

'Anyway – do they?'

'Do they what? Oh – have a website. Well, actually, no. I don't understand why not, everybody has a website these days, but eventually, this morning one of our IT support people found their social media page. And they had a gig last night.'

'What I don't understand,' said Libby, frowning, 'is that only yesterday you were all chasing down Jenny Dean and Lucifer's Maiden online. It should have been a simple leap.'

'Yes,' said Maiden with a sigh. 'I think it was because the beginning of the investigation was so confused.'

'With Superintendent Bertram trying to take over and DCI Connell being kept out?'

He nodded.

'OK, so they found out Fat Dragon had a gig last night. Where?'

'A pub in Canterbury. We know it.'

Libby noticed the constable grinning.

'*That* sort of pub. I see.'

'The upstairs rooms are run as a club. We've had a fair amount of trouble from there.'

'And that's where Fat Dragon played last night?'

'Anyway, we had some of the names and addresses of the other members of the band, so we rang up the one who was given as the contact.'

'But why on earth wasn't this done before?' Libby was astonished. 'If it was so important to find this Danny Coleman?'

'As I said, it wasn't given the highest priority. It was only DCI Connell who felt it was important.'

'But he's the SIO.'

'I know.' Maiden looked miserable and the constable looked nervous.

'So, as I said before, someone'll be for the high jump.' She heaved an exasperated sigh. 'Well, go on then. This person was called, and then?'

'Gave us Coleman's address. Only he wasn't there.'

'And?' prompted Libby. 'This must have been quite early this morning.'

'And then his car was found. Still parked in Canterbury. And he was in the boot.'

Libby felt herself go pale.

'Well, that's about it.' Maiden stood up. 'I'm sorry to have bothered you, Mrs Sarjeant.'

'Oh, that's all right.' Libby also stood up. 'I suppose after having suggested Fran and I looked into Danny Coleman it was reasonable to wonder if we'd alerted someone to him – although quite how, I don't know.'

The constable, standing to attention by the door, beamed as Libby went past him.

'I'm sorry I didn't ask you to sit down, officer,' she said.

'That's fine, ma'am. Made a nice change.' He beamed again and Maiden shot him a look.

'What will happen now?' asked Libby. 'Where did he live, by the way?'

'In Canterbury.' Maiden, followed by the constable, went out of the front door. 'Thank you, Mrs Sarjeant.'

Libby flew to the phone and rang Fran.

'Well!' she said. 'I didn't see that coming.'

'No, neither did I, but just think of Ian suspecting us –
'

'No, that's logical,' said Fran. 'If we'd really been focusing on him we could have alerted someone to him.'

'But alerted them to what? The fact that he was ferreting round the village?'

'Well, yes. Because someone didn't want him to.'

'But we hadn't. Alerted them. Whoever they were.'

'No. It's rather odd, isn't it?'

'So what are we going to do?'

'Nothing,' said Fran. 'Ian said we could look into Danny Coleman, and now the police have found him and he's dead, so what else can we do?'

138

Chapter Fifteen

'You don't think we should carry on looking?' said Libby.

'What for?' said Fran. 'They've found him, and whatever he was doing in Steeple Martin, he isn't going to tell them now, is he?'

'Looking for a reason he was killed, I mean. He must have known something.'

'It could have nothing to do with Clive Eddington at all. It could be – oh, I don't know. Drugs? A woman?'

'Oh, come on. People round here don't kill over a woman.'

'They kill over many things, Lib, as you should know by now.'

'Hmm.' Libby thought for a moment. 'I suppose that's it, then. What a swizz.'

'Libby!' Fran sounded shocked. 'A man's dead! That's more than a swizz.'

'Oh, you know what I mean.' Libby heaved a sigh. 'Oh, well. We'll have to wait and see if Ian tells us anything.'

She had just gone back into the conservatory to make yet another start on the current painting when her mobile rang.

'Libby, it's Ron Stewart.'

'Oh, Ron! Thanks for ringing back'

'No problem. I was just saying to Maria, I was interested in two other bands over the weekend, Ellis – the band the guy who was murdered was in – and Fat Dragon. They're a local band, and my old manager wanted my opinion on them. Not my sort of thing, but they weren't bad.'

'Actually, the police wanted to track them down – or rather, one of the members, but they've found him now.'

'They have? Which one?'

'One of the guitarists. And they found him dead.'

'Oh, f... I don't believe it. Where?'

'I don't know. I just know they found him dead.'

'Bloody hell. Is it you? Are you a death magnet?'

'Ron!'

'Sorry – but you must admit it's a bit strange... Can't understand why that policeman mate of yours hasn't pulled you in.'

'Don't think he hasn't thought about it,' said Libby ruefully. 'Anyway, he's found what he was looking for, so I can stand down.'

'Did he ask you to ask me?'

'No, he just wondered if I knew anyone locally who knew the band. I didn't really. I don't even know how he was booked.'

'They're a Canterbury band,' said Ron musingly. 'Don't know where the various members come from, though. Could be anywhere. Why did your mate want to know?'

Libby thought for a moment. 'Actually, it was only because this bloke had been seen in the village after the festival. By me, actually. And as far as I know, he wasn't very forthcoming when Ian – that's our policeman – tried to talk to him. Not much, really, is it?'

'Enough, I'd have thought, if he turns up dead.'

'I suppose so. Anyway, I don't need to ask any more questions.'

Ron gave a snort of laughter. 'But you will.' He was quiet for a moment. 'But I'll tell you what. There's a bloke who lives near us who books a lot of local bands – sort of unofficial agent. More just putting people in touch with each other, if you know what I mean.'

'Really? And he knows Fat Dragon?'

'Oh, yeah. And I reckon that's how they were booked for your do.'

'Why didn't Ben know, then?'

'I don't know, do I? Ask him. Anyway, do you want this bloke's name or what?'

'Yes please,' said Libby meekly, resolving to get hold of her ever-loving as soon as possible.

She didn't have to wait long. Almost as soon as she'd finished her call with Ron Stewart, Ben burst through the door.

'What are they saying? Why were they questioning you?'

Libby regarded him, half way between amusement and resentment.

'Come to that, why didn't you give Ian the contact details for Fat Dragon when he wanted to get in touch with Danny Coleman?'

Ben stared, his mouth half open.

'As it happens, they wondered if I'd been asking about Danny and inadvertently poked an ants' nest.'

'And you hadn't? Or had you asked Ron Stewart?'

'No – not until I'd been told Coleman was dead. He's given me the name of a booker who knew the band. But you would already have had that. And I printed off that list of everybody for the police, didn't I? I had to come back here and then send it to you at the office.'

'So you did. So Ian has had contact details for all the bands all the time.' Ben frowned. 'Why does he want you poking around then?'

'Because Fran and I are likely to get the more personal stuff? Anyway, I don't quite see what else we can do now. Ian's got all the information we have, and more.'

'So what about this person Ron told you about?'

'He thought it would have been him whom you booked Fat Dragon through. You probably already have his details.'

Ben shook his head. 'It was Tim who got me the other bands, except Jonah Fludde and Ellis. What more do you want to know?'

'Well.' Libby sat down at the kitchen table. 'Personal stuff. I know we asked on Sunday morning if anyone knew Clive and everyone said no, but I want to find out if that's true.'

Ben frowned. 'But Clive came from Manchester. Nobody else came from Manchester.'

'Did he come from Manchester originally, though?'

'Has someone said he didn't?'

'No – no one's said anything. But suppose he didn't. Suppose I was right about someone recognising him.'

'But,' said Ben reasonably, 'Ian said it would be more likely that Clive would murder the other person, surely.'

142

'Unless,' said Libby triumphantly, 'the other person had a reason to kill Clive. Perhaps he'd been responsible for convicting their partner for murder or something.'

'Maybe,' said Ben doubtfully. 'Anyway, how would you find out?'

'I'm not sure. I'll talk to Fran.'

'Just don't get in the way of the police,' said Ben. 'After all, you can't blame them for wondering,' said Ben.

'I suppose not. But I don't even know where he was found, except it was in the boot of his car in Canterbury. You'd have thought they would have told me.'

'I should think that was the last thing they'd be likely to do,' said Ben. 'Right, I'm going back to the theatre. There's a problem with the lighting rig.'

'I thought this company had all their own technicians?'

'Not exactly used to a full theatre rig,' said Ben. 'They're supposed to be professional, but...'

'Anyone can call themselves professional,' said Libby. 'We could.'

'But we are,' said Ben.

'Some of us are ex-pro. But we do all this for love, which, in the strict sense of the word means we're amateur.'

'But we do often get paid,' said Ben.

'True, but...'

'Oh, don't let's argue.' Ben kissed her cheek. 'I'll see you later. And come up and watch them rehearsing, if you like.' He grinned. 'It's an education.'

After Ben had gone, Libby wandered out into the garden. The September weather was still pretending to be August, although there were a few leaves decorating the lounger underneath the cherry tree. Sidney strolled up and wandered between her legs.

'What shall we do now?' Libby asked him. 'Shall I call Fran? Or what?'

Sidney sat down and stuck his back leg in the air. Libby scowled at him. 'You're no help,' she said, and went back inside to fetch her phone.

'Look,' said Fran, sounding exasperated. 'I've already told you, the police have found him. There's no more to be done.'

'But Ben didn't book Fat Dragon, Tim did.'

'What difference does that make?' Fran heaved a sigh. 'Look, Lib. If Danny Coleman was killed as a result of Clive's murder it's up to the police to find the reason, not us. And it doesn't matter where he was found. If it's relevant, it will come out.'

Grumpily, Libby ended the call. Sidney, who had followed her back inside, was trying to hook up his food bowl with a delicate paw.

'Which means you want food,' said Libby. 'So I'd better go and buy some, hadn't I?'

A quick study of the kitchen cupboards revealed a sad lack of food for both humans and cat, so Libby decided to make one of her infrequent trips to a supermarket in Canterbury. At least, she thought, as she made herself a list, it would give her something to do.

Having decided which of the three major supermarkets to patronise, Libby quite enjoyed the drive to Canterbury. Although the road was a route to the seaside, Nethergate wasn't a hugely popular resort, and the new school term had started, so the traffic wasn't heavy. After the usual struggle to find a pound coin for the trolley, Libby finally found her way inside and began wandering through the fruit and vegetable aisles.

'Hello, Libby!'

She turned sharply, to find herself facing a small, trim woman of about her own age with a beaming smile.

'Janet!'

'Don't often see you in this neck of the woods,' said Janet Duncan, 'not since you moved to the depths of the country.'

'No, I know. I do most of my shopping in the village these days.'

'And do you have most of your dental work done there, as well?' Janet gave her a wicked grin.

'Oh, sorry!' Libby sighed. 'I'm really bad, aren't I? When did I last come and see you?'

'It's so long ago I can't remember,' said Janet. 'I expect when you get toothache you'll be along to see us again.'

Libby laughed. 'I expect I will.'

'Actually,' said Janet, her smile fading, 'I'm glad I've bumped into you.'

'Oh?'

Janet scowled into her trolley. 'It's a bit difficult, really. I don't suppose you've got time for a coffee, have you?'

Libby's eyebrows rose in surprise. She and Janet had known each other in a vague dental hygienist/patient way for at least fifteen years, but although they bumped into one another socially on the odd occasion, neither had ever sought the other out.

'Yes, as it happens, I have.. I haven't bought the frozen stuff yet, so I've got time.' Libby turned towards the coffee shop. 'Here?'

'That'll do.' Janet turned her trolley and followed Libby.

'Right,' said Libby, when they were seated. 'What can I do for you?'

Janet's smile was slightly crooked. 'Well, I don't actually know – but I thought if I told you...' She stirred her coffee. 'You could put me straight.'

'If you think I can.'

Janet looked up. 'You've got quite famous, you know. With all the murders.'

'Oh, Lord. I might have known.'

'I'm sorry. If you'd rather not...'

'No, no,' said Libby hastily. 'Go on.'

'Well...' Janet leant her elbows on the table. 'I saw the stuff about these murders.'

'Murders?' As far as Libby knew, Danny Coleman's murder wasn't public knowledge.

Janet looked up quickly. 'Oh, was I wrong?'

'I don't know. I mean – I don't know what it is you saw...'

'The thing about Clive Eddington and your festival,' said Janet.

'Yes.'

'And then this morning, there was a bit on social media about Danny Coleman...Was that wrong?'

Libby frowned. 'I didn't see it.'

'Oh.' Janet looked confused. 'I did get it wrong then.'

'Look, tell me what it was you saw,' said Libby.

146

'It was a bit about Danny Coleman, and it seemed to be linking it to the other murder. And I don't think it's got anything to do with it, but I just remembered.'

'*What* did you remember?' Libby was getting exasperated now.

'When Danny was at school, there was that murder.'

Libby gaped. 'Eh?'

'You would have lived here, then. I mean, before you – er – moved away.'

'Before Derek left, you mean.'

'Yes, well...'

'I don't remember any murders.'

'Don't you? It was quite a big thing.' Janet put her head on one side. 'It was a schoolboy. At Danny's school. I remember it because he was having trouble with his teeth and his mum used to bring him to me regularly.'

'Danny, or the other boy?'

'Danny, of course. I didn't know the other boy. Or boys, I should say. They were twins.'

Chapter Seventeen

'It was twins who were murdered?' gasped Libby.

'No, no.' Janet shook her head impatiently. 'Honestly, I can't believe you don't remember. It was huge.'

'Well, I don't.'

'No. I suppose you were single-handedly taking over the drama society at that time.' Janet gave her a slightly sour look.

Libby opened her mouth and shut it again.

'Anyway,' Janet went on, 'I didn't know anything about it until Danny went home from school with a letter from the headmistress for his mum and dad saying that one of the pupils had been taken away by the police.' She sighed and looked away. 'We didn't really hear much else. It was all kept under wraps until the trial, which was kept quiet, too, although there was a lot of speculation in the press. Not as much as there would be now – no social media, for a start – but enough.'

'And did Danny know the boy – boys?'

'They weren't friends, thank God, but yes, he knew them. As far as his mum knew. And there was a lot of talk – you know, rumours. Witchcraft, some were saying.'

Libby swallowed. 'Witchcraft? What – you mean like black magic?'

'Oh, I didn't take much notice, but yes. Even in the

148

local paper. I'm still surprised you didn't hear some of it. Weren't you quite pally with the *Times* editor?'

'Oh, yes!' Libby giggled. 'Sounds so grand, put like that, instead of the local rag. Samantha Potter you mean. Yes, I was, then.'

'Didn't she tell you?'

'Not that I remember. Anyway, so that was Danny. At school with murdering twins.'

'No, not murdering twins. One twin murdered the other.'

'Oh, God.' Libby stopped short. 'That's dreadful. It wasn't an accident?'

'No.' Janet stared down at the coffee. 'See why we remember it so well?'

'Yes, I do, and you're right, I shouldn't have forgotten. What happened to him?'

'He was put away, and his parents left the area. Not surprising, really.'

They both fell quiet. Eventually, Libby looked up. 'And what about Danny?'

'Oh, he just carried on as normal, as far as I could see. I think he went to college – he stopped coming to me when he was about fifteen – and the next I knew, he was playing gigs. I don't know if he had another job.'

'No, neither do I.' Libby shook her head. 'So when you heard about him being killed it reminded you of the old murder.'

'Well, yes. Wouldn't it have reminded you?'

'I suppose it would. What a horrible coincidence.'

'Anyway.' Janet took a deep breath and smiled. 'I just thought I'd mention it. In case... you know.'

149

'I know,' said Libby, smiling back, although she didn't really know what Janet expected her to say.

'What school was it?' she suddenly asked, just as Janet was about to go to the checkout.

'School? Oh, Danny's? Eastfields, I think.'

Libby stood staring at frozen peas for quite a long time after this. Surely that couldn't be the reason for Danny's death? She finally picked a packet of peas and made her way slowly towards the laundry aisle. No, it couldn't be. She remembered Eastfields – quite a large primary school in the middle of her former home town. None of her children had gone there, but it was conceivable that they could have known pupils from there, although they didn't seem to know Danny Coleman. But he wasn't the only pupil to have been at school with the twins – and why on earth would he have been murdered for that? No, it must be simply a coincidence. She shrugged and picked up a bottle of washing up liquid.

Outside, she called Fran and told her what Janet had said.

'What do you think? Anything to do with the murders? Janet seemed to think so.'

'Are you going home now? I'll see if I can find anything about it online and call me when you get home.'

'All right,' said Libby grudgingly. 'It is odd, though, isn't it?'

'Yes,' said Fran, sounding thoughtful. 'Leave it with me.'

I don't have much choice, said Libby to herself, heaving her shopping into the boot of the silver bullet. She left the supermarket car park and turned towards home.

150

By the time she was half way there, she'd come up with a theory. Clive Eddington had been one of the twins, the one who killed the other. Danny had recognised him and – what? Here she came to a halt, as she couldn't think why Danny would have been killed after Clive had been murdered. Unless he knew who had killed Clive and it was to protect the murderer. Yes, that must be it. Unless – she thought a bit more – he'd been killed because he recognised Clive. But that would mean someone else didn't want Clive recognised. And why?

She finally parked opposite number seventeen and dragged the shopping out of the car. She steeled herself to put the kettle on and put the shopping away before she called Fran, sat down at the kitchen table and pulled the laptop towards her.

'Is Clive Eddington the murdering twin?' she began.

Fran laughed. 'Honestly Libby! Give a girl a chance!'

'Well, I was thinking it all out on the way home, and if he was, and Danny recognised him, that would be a reason to murder Danny, wouldn't it?'

'For Clive to murder Danny, yes, but Clive was already dead.'

'Someone who didn't want Clive recognised, then.'

'But no one here knew him,' said Fran. 'So, why?'

'I don't know.' Libby sighed. 'Go on then, what did you find out?'

'Wayne and Stephen Fulmore were twins attending Eastfields Junior School. They were in the top year group – year six – and about to go to secondary school in September. We're talking about April, here. At least, Wayne was going to secondary school. Stephen was going

151

to one of the grammar schools.'

'Oooh, I bet that didn't go down well,' said Libby.

'Apparently not. As far as I can find out from the various reports, there had been a flurry of activity indicating an interest in witchcraft among some of the pupils, and when Stephen was found in rather a graphic pose it was automatically assumed that it was a witchcraft slaying.'

'I bet it wasn't as quick as that,' said Libby.

'Well, no. And all the details aren't there. But Wayne was arrested and went to trial.'

'And then what?'

'It all goes a bit quiet after that. In fact there isn't half as much online as I thought there'd be.'

'I bet that's the Witness Protection thing,' said Libby.

'They couldn't remove all the references,' said Fran.

'They could keep quiet before the trial, though. See that not much went out. Did they have D notices back then?'

'I thought D notices were only for politically sensitive material.'

'Anyway, there isn't much more,' said Libby. 'That's annoying.'

'Only from a curiosity point of view. Ian hasn't asked us to find out anything else.'

'Do you think he's being stymied by the Witness Protection thing?'

'I don't know,' said Fran. 'He might be. They don't let on about the people with new identities, so he might not have got any further.'

'Except,' said Libby, 'if there's an "access denied"

notice slapped on the name he'll know.'

'Wait a minute – access denied would only be on the original name, wouldn't it?' said Fran.

'Don't ask me – I don't know.' Libby finished her tea. 'We can't go any further, then.'

'No, frustrating as it is. So we'll have to wait until Ian decides to tell us what he can.'

'If he does,' said Libby gloomily.

Tonight was the opening night of the touring company's play, and Libby and Ben were going to watch. Ben would be holding a watching brief for the theatre and the technical side, and Libby would be overseeing the bar. After an early supper, they set off for the theatre, looking forward to seeing someone else's efforts instead of their own.

To their surprise, not only Peter was waiting in the foyer bar for them, which they expected, but so was Ian.

'Do you want to speak to us?' asked Ben, looking wary. 'Only I've got to go and do all the theatre checks and reassure the company.'

'No, thanks, Ben. I just decided to come and watch. I've been seeing the posters all week and I love farces.'

'Really?' Libby frowned. 'I wouldn't have thought they were at all your thing. I would have had you down as more of a Brecht man.'

'Brecht? Good Lord! Give me a good juicy Shakespeare or an old-fashioned farce and I'm happy.' Ian followed Peter up to the bar. 'What would you like to drink?'

Libby was able to stay on the audience side of the bar for the first fifteen minutes, but as more and more people came to order interval drinks, she was forced to go and help Peter, who was the official licensee for the theatre.

'Why is he really here?' Peter murmured, as he dispensed three gins and tonics at once.

'No idea. Perhaps he suspects one of the actors.' Libby handed change with a bright smile. 'Are you going to cope with all these interval drinks on your own, or do you want me to stay and help?'

'No, you go and watch. I'm happy here.'

The company, a small independent travelling band, were well-rehearsed and slick, the play a popular farce from several years ago, and the audience loved them and it. Libby joined Peter behind the bar in the interval and listened to the comments of the playgoers in order to pass them on to the actors later. Ben, watching from the lighting box, was deep in conversation with the company technical director and of Ian there was no sign.

'Where's he gone?' Libby muttered to Peter just before she went back to the auditorium for the second half.

'I'm here,' said a voice, and there was Ian, holding the double doors open for her.

'Oh.' Libby gave him a quizzical look and went inside.

'Don't worry,' he said, 'I'll see you at the end.'

She watched him go towards the back row, then, with a small sigh, turned towards her own seat.

The company, fizzing with success, wanted the bar kept open long enough for them to have a celebratory drink after the show, which Peter was happy to do, and Libby went to help him serve and put the bar to bed. Ben came back from a tour of the theatre, happy to leave it in the charge of the company manager, and they joined Ian at one of the little white garden tables in the foyer.

'I'm assuming you wanted to speak to us?' said Libby.

Ian sent her a quizzical look. 'Well, of course. You are my friends.'

'You know what I mean.'

He smiled. 'I told you. I've been here all week and I wanted to see the farce. I also wanted to know what you've been ferreting out since we last spoke.'

'Nothing, really.' Libby made a face. 'Only something I sort of found out by accident.'

'Really? Not something you went looking for?'

'No, she actually didn't,' said Ben. 'I can vouch for that.'

'Right. So what was it?'

Libby told him.

'So you see, it wasn't actually something I found out. More something that I – er – speculated on.'

Ian stood up. 'I'm going back to the Manor. Come back and have a nightcap.'

'OK.' Ben also stood, and went to say goodbye to the company manager.

The Manor was quiet. Hetty had long since retired to her little flatlet, and Ian led them into the huge kitchen.

'It feels a bit strange inviting you into your own home,' he said, placing gin and whisky bottles on the table. 'But better here than the theatre, I felt. Now, what will you have?'

Chapter Eighteen

'Strangely enough,' said Ian, after serving drinks and finding a packet of crisps at the back of one of Hetty's cupboards, 'we'd come to the same conclusion that you had. We knew that there was a question mark over Clive Eddington, and one of the bright boys in Canterbury remembered the Fulmore twins case.

'We haven't actually had it confirmed yet, because the hoops we have to go through with the UKPPS are many and complicated. We have to speak with his handler, but as it looks as though that's going to happen, I think we can safely assume that Clive Eddington was Wayne Fulmore.'

'It's a horrible story,' said Libby. 'Was witchcraft really involved?'

'As far as we can tell from the files it was a group who were using so-called witchcraft as a cover for other activities.'

'Nothing new there then,' muttered Ben.

'No, except that this lot included paedophilia in their unsavoury activities.'

'Oh, bloody hell,' said Libby.

Ian nodded. 'Indeed. And it at least had the effect of disbanding the coven, or whatever it called itself, and actually got some of them put away.'

'So was the Sigil you found on Clive's body supposed to draw attention to that?' asked Ben.

'It looks like it,' said Ian.

'But what about Danny?' said Libby. 'If he recognised Clive from schooldays, why was he killed *after* Clive was murdered?'

'No idea yet, but there's obviously a link of some sort. And, of course, I shouldn't be telling you any of this.'

'But we found it out ourselves. Not even by digging,' protested Libby.

'I know. Which is why I *am* telling you. And because there's every chance that, through your local contacts you might pick up more.'

'Is it the same murderer?' asked Ben.

'At the moment we're assuming so,' said Ian. 'Now we've more or less established the link between them, it would be very odd if it wasn't.'

'So,' said Libby, frowning into the remains of her whisky, 'someone who recognised Clive, and recognised someone who *knew* Clive.'

'And thought they would also recognise them. You see – it does make a convoluted sort of sense.'

'But who – ' began Libby, then stopped and shook her head.

'We don't know. Once we're allowed to talk to the UKPPS we can find out more about his background.'

'Well, if you work on the assumption that he was Wayne Fulmore you can check his parents, can't you?' said Ben.

'We can look them up, yes, but we'd get a severe rap on the knuckles if we went any further.' Ian waved the

157

whisky bottle at them. 'In any case, close relatives are frequently given new identities themselves.'

'I suppose so,' said Libby. 'You really wouldn't want the world and its wife staring at you for the rest of your life, would you?'

'No. If they aren't given an official new identity, they will often invent one for themselves. It's easy enough, after all.'

Libby sat back in her chair and raised her glass. 'Well, thanks, Ian. Now I shall be wondering about every single person I meet.'

Ian grinned. 'There are one or two oddities, here, though. An official new identity will take someone to a completely new area, where they have no previous connections. Clive was back here.'

'But that was an accident,' said Libby. 'He was in Manchester. I assume he was in prison? Or a young offenders' institution? So was he released into a new identity in Manchester?'

'We don't know. We're still trying to find out about his life in Manchester, but we're having difficulty tracing the former members of his band.'

'Lucifer's Maiden?'

'That's it. We've made contact with your Jenny, but to be honest, she hasn't been a lot of help.'

'I told you, she seemed scared,' said Libby.

'Yes.' Ian frowned. 'And that adds another complication. We can assume that the murderer – or the murders – have their roots here, in Clive's – or Wayne's – past, but what about his life in Manchester? And the possible link to witchcraft or Satanism with his band. Is that relevant? Could it be that his recent life is the clue? We don't know enough about it to look into it, and we won't until the UKPPS come across.'

'Will they, though?' said Ben.

'I hope so. They're a devious lot.'

'But they've nothing to hide, now Clive's been murdered. Surely it's in their interests to know how and who by.' Libby looked indignant.

'You'd think so.' Ian smiled. 'But it's quite on the cards that we won't be allowed to give away any of the details anyway.'

'What, you won't be able to question people from Wayne's past?'

'Quite possibly. There's still the problem of his parents to take into account.'

'Goodness, isn't it complicated.' Libby shook her head again.

'It is,' said Ian. 'So, unless another piece of information falls into your lap, I'd stay well clear.'

'But you said I might come across something with my local contacts...'

'And if you do, I'd be glad if you gave it to me, but unless that happens - well...'

'So no getting into trouble,' said Ben. 'Listen to the man.'

'I know, I know.' Libby sighed. 'Can I tell Fran?'

'You will anyway,' said Ian with another grin.

Sunday morning was wet.

'Well,' said Libby, as she looked out at the gloomy garden, 'it is autumn.'

159

'And I'm supposed to be visiting a hop garden,' said Ben. 'Oh, dear.'

'Oh, are you?' Libby looked interested. 'A proper one? Or a spanking new one?'

'A proper old-fashioned one.' Ben grinned at her. 'At least, more or less. Want to come?'

'Yes, please.' Libby turned to run up the stairs. 'I hope you weren't planning on keeping me out of it!'

The hop garden was, in fact, part tourist attraction. Not as large or commercialised as its big sister near Maidstone, it was, nevertheless, interesting and informative.

'Look, they've even got hoppers' huts,' said Libby, as she and Ben walked along the visitor trail towards the oast house.

'So have we,' said Ben.

'But what would we do about the oast house? We can't turn it back into a working one.'

'We aren't going for a heritage garden,' said Ben. 'We'll have mechanised picking and modern drying. I expect they do, except for display days.'

So it transpired. The owner of the garden gave them the behind-the-scenes tour and explained how the operation worked.

'We only manage to survive because we've got an arrangement with one of the craft brewers,' he told them when they got back to his office.

'That was what gave me the idea,' said Ben. 'We had several craft beers in for a festival last week.'

'Oh – the Roll Out The Barrel at Steeple Martin? Yes, Tim Stevens had some of ours.' The owner looked interested. 'That was the one with the murdered guitarist, wasn't it?'

'Oh, dear,' said Libby. 'I suppose that's how we'll always be remembered.'

'Oh, you were the organisers?'

'It was our land, and we were co-organisers with Tim and another friend of ours,' said Ben.

'Awful thing to happen.' The owner shook his head. 'And then you had another one – I saw it in the local rag. Well, in their online thing, you know?'

'Yes,' mumbled Libby.

'We don't know much about that,' said Ben, giving her a sharp look.

'Oh, we noticed because we knew the lad.' The owner sat back in his chair and crossed his legs.

'Oh, did you?' Libby and Ben both looked up.

'Oh yes. Came from near here. Went to school with my lad.'

'Really?' Libby was now on the edge of her chair. 'To Eastfields?'

'No, they went to the Grammar together. Young Danny used to come here weekends. Very shocked, we were.'

'I can imagine,' said Libby, wracking her brains to think of some way of keeping the conversation going. She didn't need to.

'Linked, were they? Did they know one another? Both guitarists?'

'We think they might have done,' said Libby, ignoring a warning glance from Ben. 'But again, when they were children. The other lad came from Manchester.'

161

'Manchester? Oh, not likely then, is it? Didn't have much luck, Danny, did he? There was that murder when he was little. The junior school one. That was the school you mentioned, Eastfields, wasn't it?'

'Er – yes. Well, we don't know much about that, either.' Libby gave a self-deprecating smile. 'We don't know much, actually.'

The owner narrowed his eyes. 'What did you say your name was?'

'Ben Wilde, from the Manor Farm Estate, Steeple Martin,' Ben hurried in.

'Oh, ah.' The owner looked disappointed. 'We was thinking about it, see, the missus and me. We had all that witchcraft stuff round about that time. We wondered if it was anything to do with that. Only you had some witchcraft shenanigans over your way, too, didn't you?'

Libby gulped and Ben made an exasperated sound. The owner's eyes widened in surprise. 'You did know about that, didn't you?' he said.

'Yes,' said Libby.

'Oh, wait a minute.' He put his head on one side and frowned. 'Manor Farm...got it. Oast Theatre. Wasn't you something to do with that witchcraft thing last year?'

Ben sighed. 'If you mean the ballet, yes. It wasn't really witchcraft though.'

'No – but there was quite a bit over that side of Kent, wasn't there? That church over near Felling? And those Black Masses at that chapel?' He shook his head. 'We never get any of that – not since the boys were little. That was a bit of a scandal if you like.'

'What happened?' asked Libby, grateful to be getting

162

away from the other side of Kent.

'Well, it all come out after that boy's murder. There was a group of 'em, like at those Black Masses. A bit like the Masons, they was. Only they got up to all sorts.'

'Oh. No, we didn't know anything about that,' said Ben. 'We're just very sorry about the two musicians.'

'Yeah – tragic. Well,' said the owner, standing up. 'If you've seen enough -?'

'Yes, thank you.' Ben also stood. 'Can I come back to you if there's anything else?'

'Course you can. Pleased to be a help. And watch the Fuggles.'

'Oh, yes!' Ben grinned. 'We know all about Fuggles.'

'So,' said Libby, as they made their way back to the car park. 'Even more witchcraft.'

'I don't think we need to tell Ian, though, do you? He's bound to know about it.'

'But it looks as though it might have something to do with both the boys' deaths.' Libby opened the car door.

'Only Clive's so far.' Ben started the engine.

'Hmm. but it looks as though it was very much more – what's the word? Prominent – in the case than we thought.'

'Well, if it is, I'm sure Ian will find out about it,' said Ben. 'Now, we'd better hope there isn't too much traffic or we'll be late for lunch.'

Libby was quiet on the way back to the Manor, trying to work out what, if anything, the new information had given her. Very little, if the truth be told, but she looked forward to telling Fran about it, and maybe Harry, when he had time off from the Pink Geranium.

The other regular Sunday guests were already sitting round the huge kitchen table: Flo Carpenter, Hetty's brother Lenny, Peter, his brother James and James's current girlfriend, whose name Libby didn't yet know - and, surprisingly, Ian Connell. Libby stopped dead when she walked into the kitchen and saw him.

'What are you doing here?'

There was a concerted protest round the table at this remark, but Ian laughed.

'Oh dear, Libby,' he said. 'I've put a stop to your speculation, haven't I? Come on – what have you been ferreting out now?'

Chapter Nineteen

'I haven't been ferreting!' said Libby indignantly. 'Ben and I had some more information thrown at us this morning.'

'Come and sit down, gal,' said Hetty. 'Ben, fetch the wine.'

'Yes, Mum,' said Ben with a grin. Libby went to sit at the table and glowered at Ian.

'What have you found out now?' asked Peter. 'And more importantly, does it help our poor beleaguered policemen?'

'I don't know,' said Libby. 'They've got people working round the clock, haven't they? And all those reports and detailed logs that they do. Our little bits of information have probably already been covered in detail.'

James turned to his girlfriend, who was sitting, mute, looking shell-shocked. 'Don't worry,' he said. 'They always go on like this. You'll get used to it. At least,' he added anxiously, 'I hope you will.'

Ben returned from raiding his late father's wine store.

'Nice little Neuchatel,' said Flo, peering at the labels. 'I got some o' that.'

Flo's late husband had been a connoisseur, and Flo had become almost as knowledgeable.

165

'Come on, then, Libby, tell me what happened.' Ian took one of the bottles from Ben, a bottle opener from the table and began to uncork the wine.

'Oh, nothing much,' said Libby with a shrug. 'And as I said, I expect you know all about it anyway.'

'Tell me anyway.'

Between them, Ben and Libby related what they had heard from the brewery owner.

'Yes,' said Ian when they'd finished. 'We did know.'

'Told you so,' said Libby to the table at large.

'Anything you can tell us about, Ian?' asked Peter. 'I shall have to undergo the third degree when I get back to the caff.'

'Very little.' Ian finished filling glasses, sat down and picked up his own. 'And to answer your earlier question, Libby, I'm here because, as you know, I'm staying with Hetty and she invited me.' He smiled at his hostess. 'Much easier than going home every night and sometimes not getting there until after midnight.'

'And having to get back here so early,' said Libby. 'Easier if you were going back to Canterbury, I suppose.'

Ian grinned at her. 'If that's a subtle enquiry as to my home address, yes, it probably is. This way, I can pop over to the incident room whenever I need to. I wish it was always as convenient as this.'

Libby opened her mouth and was offended to receive shushing noises from the assembled guests.

'I was only going to ask if there was any connection to Clive Eddington or Danny Cole,' she said, indignant once again. 'I mean, we know there's a school connection, but...'

166

'There might be to Eddington,' said Ian evasively. 'It's too soon to know.'

Libby bit her lip.

'So tell me about the hop garden, Ben,' said Ian. 'Craft beers, I take it?'

Libby sighed.

After lunch, Flo and Lenny went back home to Maltby Close, Peter took James and his girlfriend back to the cottage he shared with Harry, and Ian went back to his incident room in the church hall.

'Very Midsomer Murders,' said Libby, as she shut the heavy oak door behind him.

'What is?' asked Ben.

'Incident room in the church hall. Murder in the pub garden at a village event.' Libby went back to the kitchen. 'Hetty, go and sit down. We'll clear up.'

'I know, gal. I'll go and put me feet up.' Hetty gave them both a tired smile and retreated to her own little flat.

Libby began to load the dishwasher. 'So there might be a link to Eddington,' she said.

'We knew that anyway,' said Ben. 'If Eddington is Fulmore he killed his brother as part of a witchcraft ritual. We think.'

'Yes. But this looked like more of an organised group – he said "like the Masons" didn't he?'

'That's what they were like in the past, isn't it?'

'Well, not poor women like the Pendle Witches, or our poor Cunning Mary,' said Libby, scrubbing viciously at a roasting tin in the sink. Hetty had finally given in over her "pots", which she always used to insist on washing herself. 'It was the other people ganging up on them, wasn't it?'

'So do you think that's what it was when Clive and Danny were young?' Ben leant back against the draining board and folded his arms. 'Persecution?'

'No idea.' Libby shook her head. 'I just can't believe we've got ourselves mixed up with witchcraft again. We'll be getting a reputation.'

'What do you mean, "getting"?' said Ben, amused. 'Come on, you've nearly worn a hole in that tin. It's time we went and joined the others at Pete and Harry's.'

The second half of the Sunday ritual was to join their friends once Harry had finished at the restaurant.

'I just hope they haven't got Ian there, too,' said Libby, drying her hands on a tea towel before throwing it into Hetty's washing basket.

But they hadn't. When they arrived, Harry, still in his chef's whites and checked trousers, was in his customary position on one sofa, with his legs on Peter's lap, while James and his girlfriend, who, they learned, was unaccountably called Portia, occupied the other. Libby sank into her favourite saggy chintzy armchair and Ben went to fetch drinks from the kitchen.

'I am *erzhausted*, dear heart,' said Harry, waving a languid hand. 'Fetch me more wine.'

Ben topped up his glass. 'Why particularly today?'

'You would not believe the number of people who came to poke their blasted noses into our poor boys' deaths.' Harry shook his head. 'People in general can be ghastly.'

'It's the witchcraft angle,' said Portia, in her surprisingly cut-glass accent. They all stared, and she

168

went pink. 'The ballet last year. We did a research project on seventeenth-century witchcraft at the university and came to see it as part of our research. There's a lot of interest. Rather prurient, I'm afraid.'

'Oh, you're at the university?' said Libby.

Portia smiled. 'Not Kent and Canterbury,' she said. 'I'm a lecturer in History.'

'Oh.' Ben, Peter and Harry all looked rather cowed by this information and James laughed.

'For goodness' sake! You've met history lecturers – professors, even – before! Andrew Wylie, and that Edward person you met over the Civil Wars.'

'You know Andrew Wylie?' said Portia eagerly. 'He's one of my heroes.'

'Really?' said Libby. 'He'd be delighted to hear that. We'll have to introduce you.'

'So did you touch on any modern witchcraft practices in your research?' asked Ben, bringing them back to the subject of the murders.

'A little, but it didn't really impact on our subject,' said Portia. 'I could look up my notes and see if there's anything relevant there.'

'The problem, if I remember rightly,' said Libby, 'is that the real modern witches have a very rigid organisation and history and one of their tenets, I think, is Perfect Love. And not in the – um – naughty sense. So they get very teed off with the people who use it for a cover for said naughtiness. Or worse.'

'I think I remember that,' said Portia, frowning slightly. 'And although they hold Aleister Crowley in some esteem, I don't think they go along with everything – do they, Libby?'

'I'm not terribly sure of the details, which isn't surprising, as the whole movement is somewhat mysterious. But I reckon that whatever was going on back in the days when Clive and Danny were at school, it wasn't real witchcraft. They get a really bad press, mostly.'

'I don't know why you don't know more about it, you old trout,' said Peter. 'The amount of times the whole subject's cropped up in your jollies.'

Portia was now looking shocked. Peter patted her hand. 'I did explain about my family, didn't I? Libby really doesn't mind being called an old trout.'

'Wouldn't make any difference if I did,' said Libby with a sigh. 'Anyway, Portia, if you do come across anything, I'd be very glad to hear it. And as I said, we'll have to introduce you to Andrew.'

'And Edward,' said Harry. 'He's got his – what did he call it? Tenant?'

'Tenure,' said Libby. 'Yes he has. Medway, isn't it? He and Andrew are still in touch, I think.'

'Who's Edward?' asked Portia.

'Dr Edward Hall. He's a historian too.'

'Oh. A bit above my pay grade,' said Portia. 'I'm just cannon fodder.'

'Really?' James looked at her, surprised. 'But you lecture.'

'But we aren't all senior lecturers,' said Portia.

'Anyway,' said Libby, 'it looks as if we're right out of the equation now.'

'Is that likely to stop you?' said Harry.

'I can still look into the historical aspect, can't I?' said Libby.

170

'Historical?' repeated Harry.

'She means when the boys were at school,' said Ben. 'I suppose you can, if there's anything to find out.'

'Only in the public domain, though,' said Peter.

'Hmm,' said Libby, eyeing Portia speculatively.

'No!' said the four men together.

It was Monday morning before Libby called Fran to update her on Sunday's events.

'What do you want to do, then?' asked Fran. 'There isn't much point in us looking into anything, is there? The police are on top of it all, and while Clive's identity is protected we'd never get very far.'

'I know, but I can't help wondering if there's some connection locally.'

'Well, of course there is, if Clive is Wayne. He went to school the other side of Canterbury.'

'But something that got him killed.'

Fran made an exasperated sound. 'Well, yes!'

'I mean rather than something else in his life, like music – or a woman, perhaps.'

'Look, Libby, that's exactly what Ian and his team are looking into. They'll be taking apart every aspect of his life in Manchester and London, and trying to find out if there's any sort of carry-over from his previous life – once they've established that he is Wayne Fulmore. There is absolutely nothing we can usefully do.'

'Hmm.' Libby scowled at the floor. 'It feels like giving up.'

'Well, go and do some research on real witches, then, just for information's sake. We found quite a lot out before, didn't we?'

'Yes, but as I said to Portia yesterday, real witches don't do such horrendous stuff. And the other lot don't advertise.'

'There's the Dark Web, or whatever it's called.'

'But we can't get into that, and I'm not sure I want to.' Libby sighed. 'I'd quite like to know what exactly this bunch of so-called witches were up to back then, though. How could we do that?'

'Internet, of course, and probably newspaper archives.'

'Jane?' suggested Libby hopefully.

'I don't know about that,' said Fran, 'but I don't suppose it would hurt to ask.'

After a little desultory tidying-up, Libby, wary of calling Jane at work in her capacity as editor of the *Nethergate Mercury*, sent her a text message, and followed it up with a private message on Facebook. Jane could then choose to answer, or not.

With nothing to do except finish the current painting on the easel in the conservatory, Libby decided to go and buy something for this evening's dinner before getting down to work.

The village was quiet. The weekenders had gone back to London, the locals had gone to work, and visitors, at the beginning of autumn, were thin on the ground. Libby bought some home-made sausages from Bob the butcher and crossed the high street to buy potatoes from Nella's farm shop. Just as she was crossing back towards the Pink Geranium, she was hailed by a shout.

'Libby! Hi!'

She turned to see Dick Fowler waving from the doorway of his shop.

172

'Morning, Dick.' She changed direction and went back towards him.

'Sorry to bother you, but I thought you might like to see something I found.' Dick was looking excited. 'It was something your DCI Connell said the other day.'

'Oh? What was that?'

'Papers. He was interested. I found some papers. In the flat over the shop.'

'Oh?' Libby vaguely remembered something about that.

'Yes! Newspapers – from about fifteen years ago. All local ones. And there's a great big piece about witchcraft!'

Chapter Twenty

Libby felt her mouth drop open.

'W-w-witchcraft?'

'He found that symbol or whatever it was, didn't he?' Dick was sounding a little testy now.

Libby's mind was racing. How much did Dick know?

'Oh, yes...'

'Well, I thought you'd be interested. Connell thought you would, too.'

'He did? You told him?'

'I phoned the incident room. I don't think the officer who answered the call thought it was anything interesting, but when he mentioned my name to the boss, Connell came on the line.' Dick looked smug and pleased with himself.

'Oh.' Libby tried to look bright and interested. Not avid.

'Do you want to see, then?'

'I'd love to.' Libby looked down at her basket. 'But I ought to get this into the fridge. Can I come back?'

'Oh – yes. Or you could pop it in my fridge – there's a little one in the kitchen there.'

'Good idea!' said Libby, wondering if it was. 'Lead on, MacDuff!'

Looking as though he wanted to ask who MacDuff was, Dick ushered her inside the shop and through to the back, where a narrow staircase led up to the first floor and a small, light, empty room, painted a nostalgic cream and pale green.

'Here,' he said, dragging a wooden chest into the middle of the room. 'I decided to check it out before getting rid of it all. I thought it was just rubbish that had been left behind.'

Libby bent down and carefully dislodged the top newspaper, yellowed at the edges and distinctly fragile.

'Actually, of course, it is rubbish,' Dick went on, 'but your DCI Connell thought it might be useful.' He cocked an anxious eye at Libby. 'What do you think?'

'Can I put my sausages away first?' asked Libby. 'Then I'll have a look and tell you.'

The little kitchen, like the other room, was very light and bright, containing only a stainless steel sink unit, a small fridge and an electric hob. The window looked out, as did the other, over an untidy patch of garden and the back fences of Lendle Lane. Dick plugged in the fridge and switched it on. 'I hope it doesn't take too long to – er – what's the opposite of warm up?'

Libby sighed. 'Never mind. It'll be better than nothing. I'll just have a quick look through these and then – I don't know – perhaps I could take away any I thought might be useful?'

Dick nodded doubtfully. 'If you know what they are. Did you want to phone DCI Connell and ask...?'

'No, I won't disturb him.' Libby returned to the other room and squatted down by the chest. 'What else was in here?'

Dick shrugged. 'Just a few leaflets – advertising, that sort of thing.'

'OK. I'll have a quick look. Thanks, Dick.'

Libby saw immediately what had captured his attention. Across the front page of the top paper was splashed a 72-point headline: *Witchcraft!*

She sat down to read the piece, but discovered it was simply a taster referring to a longer editorial inside. She turned to the next paper.

After twenty minutes she had discovered several pieces relating to what was obviously a thriving cult. She realised that a cursory glance through them all wasn't going to suffice if she wanted to make sense of them.

'Dick!' she called down the stairs. 'Can I take these home? They're really interesting, and I think Ian will find some of them useful.'

Dick's head appeared halfway up the stairs.

'Are they about the murdered boy?'

'Not as far as I can see, but possibly a link to the witchcraft lead,' said Libby, crossing her fingers.

'Well, OK, then. I haven't got time to look through them myself.' He came up and helped her take the papers out of the chest. 'I'll put them in a black sack, shall I? Easier to carry than this chest.'

'OK, thanks,' said Libby. 'Oh, look! What's this?'

A dog-eared flyer lay on the bottom of the chest.

'Oh, good Lord!' she almost shouted. 'Look!'

'What?' A bemused Dick leant over, frowning.

'It's our production of *Nicholas Nickleby*!' Libby

turned to him, excited. 'My old company. We did one week of the first part, and the second week of the second part. It was fabulous.'

'Oh?' Dick was looking mystified.

'That dates it, you see! Most of these papers seem to be around the same dates, which is very strange. You'd normally expect them to be over a period of a few months, or even years, but these all seem to be around the same time. Months, I suppose, but no longer.'

'Ah.' Dick tried to look as though he understood, but obviously didn't.

'I wonder why they were kept?' Libby stared down at the pile of papers. 'Seems odd, doesn't it?'

'Er – yes.' Dick frowned. 'Well, I suppose I'd better fetch that sack...'

Ten minutes later, Libby left the shop, a black plastic sack full of newspapers slung over her shoulder.

'Good job I haven't got to go far,' she said to Dick with a grin, and went to cross the high street.

'Hi, Lib!' A shout made her turn in the middle of the road and risk imminent peril from an ageing tractor.

'Sorry!' she mimed, and struggled to the other side. 'What did you do that for?' she grumbled at a grinning Harry.

'I'd have rescued you,' he said, relieving her of the sack. 'What the...?'

'Papers.' Libby flexed her arm. 'They're heavier than they look.'

'Newspapers?'

'Yes, old ones. From about the time Clive – or Wayne – murdered his brother. Very odd.'

'You had better come and tell me all about it,' said Harry, leading the way back towards the Pink Geranium. 'I need to know.'

Settled at the large round table in the right-hand window, Libby opted for coffee rather than wine.

'Are you getting sensible in your old age?' asked Harry, placing the cafetière in front of her.

'No. I just need a clear head.' Libby pushed down the plunger.

'What for?' Harry sat down opposite her. 'To read newspapers?'

'Well, yes. I want to know if there's anything to be learnt about this odd witchcraft craze. What it's got to do with Wayne Fulmore.'

Harry picked one of the papers out of the sack. 'Are they all from the same time?'

'Yes. That's what's so odd. And this was all that was left in the flat, as far as I can make out.'

'Did Dick actually say that? Did you ask?'

'Er – no.' Libby was startled. 'No, I assumed. He said he'd phoned the incident room about them and Ian suggested he showed them to me.'

'That sounds like Ian passing the buck, if you ask me,' said Harry, leaning back in his chair.

'What, not really interested, you mean? Throwing both Dick and me a bone, sort of?'

'Well, doesn't it?'

Libby nodded reluctantly. 'I suppose so. But it still doesn't explain why all these papers were there. I mean – why just these?'

'Who had the flat before Dick?' Harry was leafing

through one of the papers.

'No idea. You'd have more idea than I would.'

'No, I wouldn't. What was it?' He checked the date. 'I wasn't here, then. Neither was Pete, come to that. Nor Ben. We've all arrived since then. Hetty might know, or Flo. Flo more likely.'

'True,' said Libby. 'I'll ask her. But Dick would know, wouldn't he? If he bought the shop and the flat?'

'Unless it was done through a third party – executor's sales sometimes are, aren't they?'

'Oh, heavens, I don't know.' Libby heaved a sigh and finished her coffee. 'I'd better go home and start sorting through these. I expect I ought to get them back to Dick ASAP.'

'Why? He can't want them.'

'I don't know.' Libby shrugged. 'I just thought I ought to. And I've got dinner to sort out, too.'

'That's the trouble with going out for Sunday lunch,' said Harry. 'No leftovers.'

Once back at home and with dinner in the slow cooker, Libby sat down and began to go through the papers. After about half an hour she was feeling puzzled, and by the time she'd read all the articles concerning witchcraft, she was definitely mystified. She called Fran.

'And there is not one mention of Wayne Fulmore or his twin,' she concluded. 'Not one.'

'What are they all about then?' asked Fran.

'About this group of people who said they were witches and warlocks and so on, who had nasty little parties – like those up at the Tyne Chapel – and who in

179

their real lives did favours for each other – you know, secretly. Brown envelope jobs, and giving contracts to each other, and selling a pub to a developer under a parent's nose.'

'Eh?'

'Oh, there was this pub apparently, and the daughter didn't want to run it, so she sold it to a property developer under her dad's nose. Village was up in arms, it says.'

'How could she do that? If it was her dad's pub? A Free House, I assume?'

'I don't know. I just know that was one of the cases cited in the papers. There were others. And a certain amount of prostitution.'

'Goodness! And were they all indictable offences?'

'I think so. It appears that they were caught out in a Black Mass, or something, and they were defiling church property, as the church or chapel, or whatever it was, hadn't been de-consecrated. And then all these other things came to light.'

'And nothing about the Fulmore twins?'

'Nothing. So either we've been barking up the wrong tree – which doesn't seem likely – or this particular witchcraft strand is nothing to do with the murder.'

'Which murder? The twins' murder?'

'Well, yes. It would hardly have anything to do with the present-day ones, would it?'

'I suppose not.' Fran was quiet for a moment. 'And it was Dick who drew your attention to it?'

'Well, he drew Ian's attention to it.'

'And he didn't know anything about the witchcraft thing?'

'He didn't seem to. He'd just put two and two together, I suppose.'

'You could ask him. When you take the papers back.'

'I could. I might have a flick through them all again first, though. To look at other stories.'

'Right. I'll call you if I think of anything else. And how about dinner at Harry's again on Wednesday with Patti and Anne?'

'Good idea,' said Libby. 'I'll tell Ben.'

'Or ask him, perhaps.'

'Hmph,' said Libby.

Later in the afternoon, when she was sure Harry would have finished serving lunches, Libby called to make the reservation for Wednesday.

'It's all right – Fran's already done it,' he said. 'How are the papers coming on?'

Libby told him. 'And I've been going through them to look at other stories, but there's nothing relevant.'

'Hmm,' said Harry. 'What actual dates are these? If there's nothing relevant, and no mention anywhere of the Fulmore twins, then perhaps it hadn't happened yet.'

'The murder? Do you think so?'

'If there's a fuss in the local press about witchcraft and the Fulmore murder was connected to witchcraft, you can bet they'd have been linked in the minds of the press, even if they weren't,' said Harry.

'That's true. I wonder why we can't find a date for

181

the Fulmore murder.'

'Have you tried? You were going to go online to search, weren't you?'

'Oh, yes! And I got distracted by the papers. I'll try that next.'

She ended the call and pulled the computer towards her.

And the telephone rang.

Chapter Twenty-one

'Is that Libby?' asked a soft voice.

'Yes?'

'I hope you don't mind me calling. This is Jenny Dean.
I met you last week with Belinda.'

'Jenny! No, of course not.'

'Bel thought I ought to tell you something.'

'Oh?' Libby frowned. 'Not the police?'

'Er – no.'

'Have they spoken to you?'

'Yes.' The voice was so quiet now Libby could barely
hear it.

'Did they call you? Did Bel ask you if she could pass
on the number?'

'Yes.'

Like drawing teeth, thought Libby.

'What do you want to tell me?'

'Well...' Long pause. 'It's about Clive.'

Well, duh, thought Libby.

'Yes?'

'You see, I wasn't quite truthful.'

What a surprise, thought Libby.

'Go on.'

'He – um – he was actually – er – sort of a bit...
well, into witchcraft.'

Libby felt her mouth fall open in surprise. 'Was he now?' she managed eventually.

'Only not like the band.'

'Not ... ? I'm not sure I know what you mean.'

'No.' Jenny gave a soft sigh. 'It's very difficult to explain, actually.'

Libby pulled herself together. 'You mean the band said they were Satanists and Clive said he was into proper witchcraft?'

'Yes.' Relief sounded in Jenny's voice.

'And did he tell you anything about it?'

'He tried to get me to join.'

'Join? What, a coven?'

'That was it.'

'And did you?'

'No. And then he left.'

'Do you think the rest of the band threatened him? You said they threatened you.'

'I don't know.' Jenny took a very deep, audible breath. 'But he went very suddenly.'

'You really should have told the police this, you know,' said Libby.

'I know.'

'And what about down here? In London?'

'I think ...' Jenny stopped. 'I'm not sure I should say any more.'

'Why?'

'I don't know...'

'Don't know why you shouldn't say any more?'

'I don't know anything ... not definitely.'

Libby was beginning to get annoyed.

184

'Look, Jenny, if you have anything that might help the police find out who killed Clive, you really must tell them. That's why Belinda told you to tell me, isn't it? So that I would relay it to the police?'

'Yes.'

'Well, I have to tell you that the police won't accept what I say. They will have to hear it from you. And they will need something a little more concrete than what you've told me.'

'Oh.'

'Look, I'll pass it on to the incident room here, and after that it will be up to them. Thank you for ringing me, and thank Bel for me, will you.'

'Yes, I will. And thank you, Mrs – I mean Libby.'

Libby ended the call feeling frustrated. Was Jenny telling the truth? Was Clive really into witchcraft? After his childhood experiences – if he was Wayne Fulmore. It all sounded a bit made up. She made an exasperated sound and found the number of the incident room.

She repeated what Jenny had told her to a dubious-sounding officer who said, unconvincingly, that he would pass it on, then went back to her aborted search for the online mentions of the Fulmore Twins Murder.

There was less than she'd expected. And it was several months after the flurry of witchcraft activity. The articles she did read, although not very detailed, made no mention of a link to the high-profile recent trials, and there was obviously a news blackout on the actual trial of Wayne Fulmore, as Fran had already found out.

She sat back in her chair and stared thoughtfully at the screen. It looked as though her researches had come to the end of the line.

'Why don't we go for a drink after dinner?' suggested Ben later. 'You could ask Tim if he knows anything about that pub that was being sold.'

'Why would he know anything about that?'

'Didn't he come from over that way? He took over a failing pub, didn't he? I thought he might know.'

'I suppose it's possible,' said Libby grudgingly, 'but I don't see how that would help.'

'It might tell you something about the witches' conspiracy, which might help.'

'It doesn't look as though it's got anything to do with the Fulmore twins after all, though.' Libby sighed. 'Still, we might as well.'

Ben sent her an ironic grimace.

'Don't do me any favours,' he said.

As it was Monday and the Pink Geranium was closed, Harry and Peter elected to join them.

'You'd think we'd want to stay in for a quiet night in front of the TV, wouldn't you?' said Peter, with a sigh, as they settled round their favourite table. 'But he can't stay bloody still.'

'Well, I've got news for the old trout, haven't I?' Harry sent Libby a wink.

'What news?'

'I think it's news, anyway, although with your contacts in the police, it probably isn't.'

'Well, what then?'

'They're packing up the incident room.'

'What?' Libby sat up straight, her mouth open in surprise. 'But we only saw Ian yesterday, and he didn't say a word.'

'Well, that's what it looked like,' said Harry. 'This afternoon I was putting away an order and doing some of the paperwork –' he made a face, 'when I saw them. Don't forget, I'm right opposite Maltby Close.'

Libby looked at Ben. 'I wonder why.'

'Well, for one thing, Danny Coleman wasn't found here, and we don't know what the investigation into Clive Eddington's murder has thrown up – discounting his possible old identity – and there's probably nothing else to link him to the village.' Peter looked round at them all. 'Don't you think?'

Ben sighed. 'You're probably right. It won't stop madam here ferreting about, as Ian says. Which reminds me – we were going to ask Tim a question about his former pub.'

'You were?' said Harry. 'Why?'

'If we can get him over here, you can hear what I ask him,' said Libby, waving at Tim, who was behind the bar talking to one of the regulars. When he'd seated himself at the table, she continued. 'Your old pub, Tim. You turned it round, didn't you?'

'Yes?' said Tim, looking puzzled.

'Why was that? I mean, why was it failing?'

'It was – hang on, why do you want to know?'

Peter, Harry and Ben all turned to look at Libby.

'It's a bit difficult.' She looked a trifle sheepish. 'Anyway, it was Ben's idea.'

'Oh?' Tim looked Ben with raised eyebrows.

Ben sighed. 'OK – it was like this.' He explained his idea and the reasons behind it. 'So, you see, I thought you might know something about it.'

'My pub, or this other one?' asked Tim.

'The other one.'

Tim laughed. 'Well, I just might! I have to say, if I'd thought it was anything to do with our little local murder I'd have told your Ian straight away. Meanwhile, I might as well tell you.'

'Before you start – does anyone want another drink?' asked Peter.

Tim stood up. 'I'll get them.'

'No you won't,' said all three men, which made Libby laugh.

When they had come back with new glasses, Tim leant forward, elbows on the table, and grinned round at the four friends.

'You know Betty and I were managers for a big chain in London?'

They all nodded.

'And we bought a Free House which was run down and turned it round?'

'Yes.'

'Do you know where it was?'

'I think we thought Sussex,' said Libby.

'The first one was, yes.'

'The first one?' said Harry.

'There was more than one?' said Peter.

'Oh, yes,' said Tim, taking a sip of his drink. 'The first one was over on the border.'

'Romney Marsh?' said Ben.

Tim nodded. 'It was supposed to have been a smuggler's pub – actually called The Owler, although I don't suppose it was called that back then – but they hadn't exploited that. Anyway, we managed to start making it pay, and then one day this couple came in for lunch. They'd been years before, it seems, and so they asked what had happened to the old place. Couple of the regulars told them, and they said they could do with us over their way.'

He stopped for a drink. Libby fidgeted.

'So,' he continued, 'they told us all about their village pub, The Dolphin.'

'Was it by the sea?' asked Peter.

'No.' Tim shook his head. 'It was in Dungate.'

'Dungate!' exclaimed Libby. 'But that's –'

'The other side of Canterbury,' Ben finished for her. 'Yes. Go on, Tim.'

'Well, it seems there'd been some sort of dispute over ownership – we heard all sorts of rumours, but we couldn't be certain of the facts. Anyway, we went to have a look. It was still just about open, being run by an old boy who'd been there forever. It's a pretty pub, in a tiny village, but we could see it had potential, and the upshot was, we put The Owler on the market and bought The Dolphin.'

'And that's the story of your pub,' said Ben. 'And what about the other one?'

Tim laughed again. 'Not got it yet? Blimey, you're slow! There isn't another one! It's the same one.'

The men laughed with him and Libby scowled.

'Now what's the matter with the old trout?' asked Harry.

'Wrong-footed,' said Ben, patting his beloved's hand.

189

'Tell us more, Tim. You said you only heard rumours. But you must have known more about it when you bought it – who did you buy it from?'

'Solicitors who were – what d'you call 'em? Not trustees.'

'Executors?' said Peter.

'No. Sounds American.'

'Oh – power of attorney?' suggested Libby.

'That's the one.'

'What was the story, then?' asked Harry.

'Well, this old boy had run the pub for years and it was a really popular traditional village boozer, y'know? But he was getting on and his daughter wanted to turn it into – oh, I dunno, a gastropub sort of thing. The regulars didn't want that, and neither did the old boy. Anyway, somehow or other the daughter gets some crooked solicitor to work out a way for her to take over. And she was getting all these quotes from builders and what-have-you, closed the pub and tried to get the old boy out – he lived up top, see?'

'Goodness!' said Libby, eyes wide. 'And then what?'

'According to the regulars there was some big witchcraft scandal locally, and the crooked solicitor and the daughter were caught up in it. They were both put away – although I reckon they'd be out by now. The old barman opened up until they knew what was going to happen, but the old boy – the owner – he'd lost heart and put it up for sale. They was all sorry – they'd loved their pub.'

'And then you came along,' said Harry.

'Yeah.' Tim smiled modestly. 'And we got it going

again. We did start doing food, but nothing like a gastropub. Home-cooked, see, like we do here.'

'Why did you leave?' asked Libby. 'Not that we're not glad you did.'

'The old boy – the owner – was still living upstairs and we didn't want to turn him out, so we were renting round the corner. And it was a tiny village, with only a small regular clientele, as they say, although we did very well at weekends. And once again, it was word of mouth. Somebody came in the pub from over this way and said this was on the market, so we came and had a look. And here we are.'

The four friends broke into spontaneous applause and Tim went pink.

'Why didn't you think to mention it when Ian first told us about the sigil?' asked Libby.

'Sigil?' repeated Tim.

'I don't think Tim knows anything about that,' said Ben. 'But you did know there was supposed to be a connection to witchcraft in the first murder, didn't you?'

'Only vaguely,' said Tim. 'There was a bit of a mention of it in the paper, but that's all.'

'That's the trouble,' said Peter, sitting back in his chair. 'Because we – or you, Lib – have been so tied up with the witchcraft thing, we forget that not everybody knows about it.'

'So tell us about it, then,' said Tim. 'See – there was this whole scandal about it over Dungate way. I told you. Reckon it was all linked up?'

Chapter Twenty-Two

'We – and the police – think there's a possibility that Clive Eddington was in the UKPPS – ' began Libby.

'Hang on – what's that?' asked Tim.

'The modern name for the Witness Protection Scheme,' said Ben.

'Right. Carry on. Why?'

'For murdering his twin, with witchcraft overtones,' said Libby bluntly.

Tim looked shocked. 'Bloody hell!'

'Yes. You never heard anything about that? When you were in Dungate?'

'No. When did it happen?'

'As far as we can tell, well over ten years ago.'

'Might have been when we were still in London,' said Tim. 'We moved to the Owler about fourteen years ago, then to Dungate about seven years ago. As far as we could tell, the scandal had been some time before.'

Libby fished one of the local papers out of her bag. 'About this time?'

Tim looked at the headlines and the date. 'That'd be it.' He read on. 'Look – it mentions The Dolphin!'

'Not by name,' said Libby, 'but that's what made Ben think of asking you.'

'You've got very strange brains, you lot,' said Tim.

'What else have you linked up?'

'Only that if Clive is this other boy, he was at school with Danny Coleman, the other victim,' said Ben.

'But the police aren't telling us anything, although they must have found out quite a lot by now.' Libby took a mournful sip of her drink. 'And the incident room's gone.'

'Didn't your Ian tell you that, even?'

'No, he didn't. And we don't even know if he's found out if Clive is the other boy. Apparently they keep everything very close to their chests, these protection people.'

'Who is this other boy?' asked Tim.

'Wayne Fulmore.'

'Nope.' Tim shook his head. 'Never heard the name. He lived over our way, did he?'

'Yes – he and Danny went to Eastfields Primary School together.'

'Oh, I know Eastfields. Most of the kids in Dungate went there. The local school had been closed down years before.'

'Like so many village schools,' said Peter. 'Scandalous.'

'So you didn't know much about this witchcraft scandal then?' said Libby. 'Only that this woman who tried to sell your pub was connected with it.'

'That's it. It used to get mentioned in passing, you know, the way things do in pub conversations, but that's about it. Sorry I can't help more.'

'What about the old boy, Tim?' said Harry. 'Is he still around?'

193

'As far as I know,' said Tim, 'although he doesn't have anything to do with the pub these days – except living there, of course.'

'How did you manage to sell it with a sitting tenant?' asked Libby.

'We were dead lucky. We sold it to the owners of another big pub a few miles away, so they continue to live there. They hire local staff for The Dolphin and it benefits from discounts that a small pub wouldn't normally come in for.'

'But still a Free House?' said Peter.

'Oh, yes.'

Libby sat back. 'Well, that's about it, then. We know as much as we're likely to know.'

'Can I get anyone another drink?' asked Tim. 'You don't look very cheerful.'

Glasses were hastily drained, and Peter went with Tim to the bar.

'Cheer up, petal,' said Harry, reaching across to pat Libby's hand. 'You can't always be in the thick of the action.'

Libby sighed. 'I know, I know. It's just this feels personal.'

'Because it all seems to start from where you used to live?' asked Ben.

'Partly, and because the first murder was here, in our own back yard.'

Peter and Tim came back with fresh drinks.

'Pete and I have just been talking,' said Tim, as he sat down, 'and we thought perhaps Libby would like to go over to The Dolphin and meet old Paddy.'

194

Libby sat up straight. 'Really?'

'Well, wouldn't you?' said Peter. 'That might satisfy the nosy itch for a day or so.'

'They're very rude to you, aren't they?' said Tim, looking amused. 'Anyway, would you? Betty won't mind looking after things for a couple of hours. We could go tomorrow lunchtime, if you're free.'

'You'd take me?' said Libby, eyes wide. 'Yes, I'd love to.'

'Good, that's settled, then. The old regulars come in weekday lunchtimes, not so many DFLs.'

'DFLs?' Harry looked puzzled.

'Down From Londoners,' explained Libby. 'You get them all over the place, but mostly seasides where they buy up houses for holidays and weekends. Nethergate's got them, too, but Whitstable over on the other coast is a hot spot, although a lot of them have been absorbed now.'

'There's a mixed reaction these days,' said Ben. 'Some people say they've kept the towns alive with increased trade, but others say they've changed the character of the towns.'

'Anyway,' said Tim, 'they're good for the out of town pub trade at the weekends, but they leave us alone during the week. So tomorrow lunchtime would be a good time to go. Half past eleven suit you?'

Tuesday was another bright early autumn day. The trees were just beginning to turn, and very occasionally, Libby caught a whiff of woodsmoke on the air when she let her window down.

'Second time I've been this way this week,' she said, as they breasted a hill and looked across to the sea.

'Oh, when you went to see Old and Filthy, you mean?' said Tim.

'Old and Filthy?'

'That's what we used to call it in the trade. Very good stuff. I hope Ben manages to get his going.'

'I thought they were only growers? The owner said he had an arrangement with a craft brewer.'

'That's right – but it's a very close relationship. That's what you need. Unless Ben fancies setting up the brewery himself.'

'Eh?' Libby turned to look at Tim. 'You're joking!'

'Very keen, is Ben.' Tim smiled straight ahead at the unfolding countryside and Libby scowled.

Eventually, they turned off into a network of narrow roads and lanes which led them to what was no more than a collection of houses and cottages, with a rambling, low, red brick pub opposite a T-junction.

'Centre of the village,' said Tim, with a grin, and swung into a miniscule car park.

Inside, The Dolphin was a typical country pub. A lot of polished wood, old village photographs on the wall, and mismatched old tables and chairs. Behind the bar was a comfortably plump and well-preserved blonde barmaid, who greeted Tim with a beaming smile.

'Tim! How lovely to see you! Hey, Dodger, look who's here.'

At the end of the bar, nursing a pint of what certainly looked like Old and Filthy, an elderly man in a well-worn donkey jacket and a flat cap looked up.

'Well, well. Young Tim. What brings you over here?'

'Libby, meet Daphne, who's been here since before my time, and Dodger, who's been here even longer.'

Libby shook hands with Daphne and Dodger, and accepted the bar stool Dodger pulled forward.

'I'll have a tonic with ice, Daph, and Libby – what will you have?'

Libby chose a half of lager and waited while the transaction was made.

'So come on then,' said Dodger. 'What brings you here? Showing your friend the sights?'

'I used to live near here,' said Libby, 'although I don't ever remember coming out here.'

'Lives over in Steeple Martin now,' said Tim. 'Regular in the new pub.'

Tim then fielded questions about his 'new pub', and unsurprisingly, comments on the murder at the Beer Festival.

'Well, that's what we came over for,' he said confidingly, hitching himself closer to the bar. 'We wanted to talk to old Paddy.'

Daphne and Dodger shook their heads sadly.

'Too late, mate,' said Dodger. 'Gone this last coupla months.'

'Gone?' Tim looked shocked. 'He died?'

'No, Tim – in a home,' said Daphne. 'Couldn't manage no more. Old Doc Hargreaves tried to put together what he called a "care package", but it weren't no good. Weren't good fer business, neither, if truth be told.'

'Oh, that's a shame. I ought to go and see him. Where is he, do you know?'

'That won't do you no good neither,' said Dodger, shaking his head. 'Wouldn't know you.'

'Oh, bloody hell. Poor old Paddy.' Tim stared mournfully into his tonic water.

'What d'you want to see him for?' asked Daphne.

Libby looked anxiously at Tim. This didn't seem the right moment to be talking about what could only be sad memories.

''Bout that Maureen, I'll be bound,' said Dodger suddenly.

Tim, Libby and Daphne all looked sharply at the old man, who took a long, comfortable swig of his pint.

'What makes you say that?' asked Tim cautiously.

'You got a murder. Two murders, with the Coleman boy.'

'Ye-es,' said Tim slowly.

Dodger shrugged. 'Nasty business. And all of a sudden you comes over to talk to Paddy. Wouldn't be fer Paddy, now would it? But Maureen – she was mixed up in nasty business, wasn't she?'

'But not murder!' said Daphne.

'Don't know that, do we? All that shenanigans with lawyers and such, and them so-called witches. No more'n a bunch o' crooks.'

'Well, yes,' said Libby. 'We just wondered... There was that horrible business of the boy who murdered his twin.'

'That was nothing to do with Maureen!' said Daphne, shocked.

'To do with witches, though.' Dodger nodded thoughtfully. 'Not the same boy, though, was it?'

'The boy who got murdered at the festival was Clive Eddington from Manchester,' said Libby, neatly avoiding the question.

'Ah,' said Dodger, and wiped froth from his mouth.

Tim indicated that Dodger's glass should be refilled. As she did so, Daphne asked 'So what did you want to talk to Paddy about Maureen for?'

'Just to see if he remembered anything, really,' said Libby, rather shamefaced. 'We shouldn't have thought of it, you know, Tim. It would have been unkind.'

'Ah.' Dodger lifted his fresh pint to his lips. 'Wouldn'a minded. Liked to talk about the old days, right, Tim?'

'That's right, Dodge. That's why I thought we'd come.'

'Course, that business with that twin.' Dodger's eyes became fixed in the past. 'Said it was summat to do with witches.'

'Were the parents part of the –er – witches thing?' asked Libby.

Dodger shrugged again. 'Didn't know 'em. Moved away, I heard.'

'I suppose they would,' said Libby.

'So what about Maureen?' asked Tim. 'She must be out now. She not come to look after her dad?'

Daphne and Dodger made rude noises.

'After what she did? He wouldn't have had her anywhere near,' said Daphne. 'Not that she'd have wanted to. Gawd knows where she went.'

'So everyone who was around then has gone, then?' said Libby.

'More or less.' Dodger nodded wisely. 'Anyone anything to do with that lot, anyway. Plenty here who've been here since Adam was a lad, though.'

'In Dungate?' Libby asked.

Dodger nodded. 'Only fly-be-nights like this one who comes and goes.' He jerked a thumb at Tim, who buried his face in his glass.

'Hasn't worked out bad, though, Dodge,' said Daphne comfortably. 'New lot kep' us just as we liked, didn't they?' She moved down the bar to serve some newcomers.

'Is it all right, though, Dodge?' asked Tim. 'No complaints?'

'Better if we had a proper landlord,' grumbled Dodger, 'but not too bad. Paddy couldn'a carried on. Not up with the times.'

Libby hid a smile.

'Well, that wasn't much help, was it?' said Tim, as they emerged into the sunshine half an hour later. 'Sorry to drag you all the way over here.'

'I enjoyed it,' said Libby. 'And –'

'You was askin' about them Fulmore boys, wasn't you?' said a voice behind them. 'It was all 'er, it was. Put away, she was.'

Chapter Twenty -three

Libby and Tim swung round to see a wizened gnome in a wheelchair piloting himself out of the pub.

'Bernard! I didn't see you!' said Tim.

The gnome's deep-set eyes twinkled up at them. 'Nobody does. Useful.'

'How are you?' Tim held out his hand. 'This is my friend Libby.'

'Ah. Betty know about 'er?'

Tim laughed. 'Course she does. Libby's a regular in our new pub.'

'Ah. I 'eard. You wanted to know about the Fulmore boys.'

'Well –'

''Twas the mother. In with them witches. Got them twins involved. The one boy thought 'e'd be better off without the other, see.'

'How do you know this?' asked Tim.

'Remember, don't I? I bin in this blasted chair so long, I don't 'ave much else to do. Even remember 'er name, I do. And 'is.'

'The mother?' Libby gasped.

'And the father. Evelyn and Raymond, they was.'

'Well, thank you – er – Bernard,' said Libby.

'Pleasure.' The eyes twinkled up at them again. 'Do me good to go rememberin'.'

Tim laughed. 'You old rogue. Go on, then, go back and tell Daph I'll stand you a pint.'

'Do you think he's right?' asked Libby, as they made their way back to the car.

'Oh, he'll be right,' said Tim. 'What was it they used to call him? The Memory Man. Always asked him to put 'em right on dates and things. Wouldn't let him join the quiz team because they said it wasn't a fair advantage.'

'Well, I'm blowed.' Libby climbed into the car. 'Why didn't you think of him straight away?'

'Because I was thinking about Paddy. Anyway, it means you've got something else to look at, you and Fran.'

'Certainly does.' Libby turned and beamed at him. 'Thanks, Tim.'

Fran was in the shop relieving Guy at lunchtime when Libby rang.

'Hey – slow down!' she said, as Libby poured out a torrent of news.

'Sorry!' Libby took a deep breath. 'But I can't remember where you're up to. So much has happened.'

'I thought you said nothing had happened?'

'Well – both,' said Libby. 'Look, can I come and talk to you? Are you busy this afternoon?'

'Once I've finished here, no. Not officially.'

'What do you mean "not officially"?'

'Nothing. No, I'm not busy.'

'Hmm,' said Libby suspiciously. 'Well, can I come?'

'Yes. Have you had lunch?'

'No – only a half of lager. I've got some soup in the

fridge. I'll have that before I come. See you about half past two.'

Harbour Street was far emptier now than it had been a couple of weeks ago. Only a few people walked the beach, and a solitary black labrador waddled happily along the surf line.

Coastguard Cottage gleamed white in the early autumn sun. Guy had found someone to paint the outside during the summer, and now, with fresh blue window frames and door, it looked the very epitome of the idyllic seaside cottage.

'Are you ready for tea, yet?' asked Fran, as Libby made straight for the window seat.

'Not yet – the soup's only just gone down,' said Libby, holding her hand out to black and white Balzac, who joined her, purring loudly.

'All right then – tell me what's been going on.' Fran sat down in the rocking chair and waited.

'Well, you know I took all those old papers from Dick Fowler.'

'Yes. And you told me about the so-called witches who seemed to be more an underhand Rotary Club than anything else. About the pub?'

'Right,' said Libby. 'So we went for a drink last night, and guess what!'

Fran sighed. 'What?'

'It was Tim's old pub!'

'Good Lord. I thought that was in Sussex?'

'That was the first one, apparently.' Libby told the tale of Tim and his two pubs. 'And then Tim suggested taking me over to The Dolphin to meet the old owner.'

'Is he still alive?'

'Well yes, but it turns out he's in a home, so we couldn't talk to him, but amazingly we met two of the old regulars, one who actually remembered the name of Wayne Fulmore's parents! *And* the fact that the mother was part of the witchcraft business.'

'So if Clive Eddington really was Fulmore, Ian will be able to speak to the parents.'

'I don't know. The mother was put away, as Bernard the gnome said. And I expect the father – what was his name? Raymond, that's it – moved away.'

'Ian would still be able to trace them and speak to them,' said Fran. 'That is, if the protection services have allowed him to know the truth.'

'And we're not being kept in the loop, now,' said Libby gloomily. 'I can't believe he just closed down the incident room without telling us.'

'And moved out of the Manor?'

'Oh, I didn't think of that. I suppose so.'

'Well, I suppose we can always do a search on the names, if you think it's really important.'

'Don't you?'

'As I said, Ian will be on it, I'm sure.'

'And what about what Jenny told me?'

'You left a message at the incident room, didn't you?'

'But now I know they were in the middle of moving out, I wonder if it got passed on.'

'It will have been logged, won't it? Don't worry about it.'

'Hmm.' Libby turned to look out at the sea. 'But Jenny might not talk to Ian. Or whoever talks to her.'

'Look,' said Fran, beginning to sound exasperated, 'Ian's on the case, with, as we know, far more resources than we have, so I think we ought to leave it to him.'

They were quiet for a moment. Then Libby said, 'But do you think we ought to have another word with Edna? She might know more about the whole witchcraft Rotary thing than she let on.'

'And where will that get us? Nowhere.'

'Oh.' Now it was Libby's turn to be exasperated. 'It's all so frustrating.'

'Just think how much more exasperating it is for the police,' said Fran. 'And they've got two murders to solve, not just one.'

'Oh, yes, poor Danny Coleman. I'd almost forgotten him.'

Fran stood up. 'Come on, let's have that cup of tea. Shall we go down to Mavis's instead of here?'

Libby brightened. 'Good idea. Let's.'

Mavis's café, The Blue Anchor, stood next to the Sloop at the end of Harbour Street, on the small jetty. When they arrived, neither of the two captains of the pleasure boats were at their usual table outside, although both boats were tied up, rocking gently in the slight breeze. Mavis herself came out to take their order.

'Really is the end of the season now,' said Libby, 'if Mavis hasn't got any help.'

'She'll be closing up soon for winter,' said Fran. 'Half term, probably.'

'So, Danny Coleman,' said Libby, when their tea had arrived. 'Where does he fit in?'

Fran sighed. 'Not going to give up, are you? I expect he saw something on Saturday night and threatened whoever it was.'

'With blackmail?'

'Well, yes. "I saw you and I'll tell if you don't -" I don't know, "give me a thousand pounds." Or something.'

'A thousand isn't much.'

'Just an example. That's the most likely, isn't it?'

'He couldn't have recognised Clive?'

'We said, if you remember, then it would be more likely that Clive would have killed *him*.'

'But he *was* killed.'

'But not by Clive!' Fran put down her cup with a bang. 'Look, Lib, we just don't have enough to go "ferreting about", as Ian puts it. And it's not our business, it isn't anyone we're connected to and no one's asked to look into it. Give it up.'

'Oh, all right.' Libby frowned at the sea and shifted in her seat. 'Right then. So what were you doing that wasn't "official" this afternoon?'

'Eh?'

'You said, on the phone. "Not officially", you said.'

Fran sighed. 'If you must know, I've been trying to start a novel.'

'A novel?'

'Yes. I told you I might have another go at writing, didn't I?'

'Yes, you did, but I suppose I didn't take you seriously.'

Fran looked slightly embarrassed. 'Well, it's only an attempt. A sort of tentative beginning.'

'What's it about?' asked Libby, starting to get interested.

'Oh, nothing much. I don't really want to talk about it,' said Fran, fixing her gaze on the horizon.

'Why not? I'd like to read it.'

'Oh, no,' said Fran firmly. 'No one gets to see it until – and if – I finish it. And maybe not even then.'

'What's the point, then?' said Libby reasonably. 'Why write it if no one can read it?'

'Because it might not be good enough. Probably won't.'

Libby shook her head. 'Well, why don't you write something shorter first? A short story, perhaps?'

'I'll see.' Fran picked up her cup. 'More tea?'

Libby held out her cup. 'One more, then I'll have to get back.'

Fran's eyebrows rose. 'Why? What for?'

'Dinner.' Libby cleared her throat. 'I haven't bought it yet.'

'Ah,' said Fran, with a knowing smile.

Dissatisfied, Libby returned home, and, after a quick trip to Bob the butcher, began an internet search on the names Evelyn and Raymond Fulmore.

Raymond produced very few references, but Evelyn was more productive. However, there were few links to her son Wayne, although he was mentioned in a couple of press reports.

'Very much kept under wraps,' Libby said to herself.

'It's really quite odd,' she said to Ben when he came in half an hour later. 'There are quite a few links to her arrest and trial, and mentions of this group of – I don't know –

witches? Except that they weren't. They were all secretly getting together to do nasty stuff and doing each other favours in order to keep each other quiet. And the only mentions of her son – or sons – are as a sort of sidelight.'

'Don't worry about it,' said Ben. 'I expect Ian's got to the bottom of it by now. I doubt if he'd have pulled out of the incident room if he hadn't.'

'Do you think he'll turn up tomorrow?'

'After dinner? No idea. He doesn't always.'

'He's left the Manor, I suppose?'

'Of course. No point in staying there now. Did you find anything about the father?'

Libby shook her head. 'No. He seems to have disappeared from the face of the earth. Hardly gets a mention anywhere. I can't even find a mention of what he did for a living. I mean, it usually says "Joe Bloggs, forty-eight, a fisherman", doesn't it? I always object to the insistence on providing an age.'

'Because it's misleading?'

'Well, yes. The same as if it says "Maisie Bloggs, grandmother". The image conjured up is entirely wrong. I mean – you wouldn't say "Fran Wolfe, grandmother", would you? It gives entirely the wrong impression.'

'All right, it does. So there's not a whisper about whatsisname Fulmore. Not in the reports about the twins either?'

'There's hardly anything about them anyway,' said Libby. 'Ready for tea?'

The landline rang half way through the ten o'clock news.

'I got your message, Libby. Thanks for letting me know.'

208

'Oh. Well, I didn't know if you would want to know or what. You could have already spoken to her for all I knew.'

'When did she call you?'

Libby frowned. Ian sounded perfectly relaxed, and she could hear the faint sounds of a Satie *Gnossienne* in the background. 'Are you at home?'

'Yes, Libby.' Ian sounded amused. 'Now, when did Jenny Dean call you?'

'Yesterday afternoon. After I'd got the papers.'

'Papers? What papers?'

'Apparently you said he should show them to me.'

Ian hissed. At least that was what it sounded like. 'Libby – start at the beginning.'

Libby did. For once, Ian listened in silence.

'And what have you found out since?' he asked when she finally came to a stop.

'When Tim took me over to Dungate, you mean?'

'Oh, he did, did he?' Well, yes. But that can wait for a moment. I meant about Jenny Dean.'

'That? Oh, nothing. It was the other stuff –'

'Forget that for now, Lib. You see, Jenny Dean has disappeared.'

Chapter Twenty -four

'Eh?'

'I'm afraid so. You see, further to your information – for which thank you very much, even though I did get it rather late –'

'Well, I didn't know you were dismantling the incident room, did I?' said Libby, in an injured tone.

'So I called. And there was no reply. So I'm afraid I called Belinda. She was the only person I could think of with a link to Jenny. She said she had no idea where Jenny was, and wasn't particularly close to her in any case. But she suggested –'

'Don't tell me – Terry,' said Libby.

'Yes.' Ian didn't sound surprised. 'But he didn't know. In fact, he went round to her flat – well, her aunt's flat, actually – and her aunt didn't know either.'

'There's a cousin...' said Libby. 'Jenny told us.'

'Has no idea,' said Ian. 'So today we've been looking for Jenny Dean. I had hoped you might have dug up something.'

Libby swallowed the words "Oh, useful now, am I?" and simply said 'No.'

Ian sighed. 'It may be nothing, but connected to at least one murder, we have to take it seriously.'

'Her disappearance, or what she said?'

'Both, of course. Because it would be stupid to think the two weren't linked.'

'So do I take it from this you've had it confirmed that Clive Eddington *was* Wayne Fulmore?'

'Yes, Libby. As if you doubted it.'

'All right. Well, can I tell you what we found out at Dungate?'

'Something to do with what you found in the newspapers?'

'Well, yes, actually.' And Libby told Ian everything she'd found out from Tim, Dodger and Bernard at The Dolphin. And the little that appeared online.

'Right,' he said, when she'd finished. 'If you hear anything else, let me know.'

'Hoy!' she said. 'Aren't you going to tell me why you pulled out? What's been going on?'

'If you mean the incident room, there was no further reason for it to be here. We learned as much as we could about Eddington/Fulmore's murder from here, and Coleman was found in Canterbury.'

'And what about him? Do you know any more?'

'Libby. You know I can't tell you anything else. You've got a lot more out of me than I should have told you anyway. And I'll see you tomorrow.'

'Oh. OK.' Libby was mollified. 'If I have anything to tell you, which number shall I ring?'

'All of them, as usual,' said Ian.

Libby reported the conversation to Ben and contemplated ringing Fran to tell her.

'No, Libby. I've missed half the news as it is. Come and sit down, it'll keep until tomorrow.' Ben handed her a glass. 'Here – nightcap.'

But it wasn't destined to be. The phone rang again at a quarter to midnight.

'Mum,' gasped Bel. 'Jenny's here. She was kidnapped!'

Libby struggled upright in bed. 'Wha -?'

'I think it was those two girls.'

Libby swung her legs out of bed. 'Start at the beginning,' she said groggily.

'Oh, God, I woke you up,' said Bel. 'I'm sorry.'

'Doesn't matter,' said Libby. 'Come on, tell me.'

'Did you know Ian had been looking for Jenny?'

'Yes, and he called you and Terry.'

'Oh, right. Well, after Jenny had phoned you the other day she got a bit worried. She'd seen some people who were – oh, I don't know – connected in some way to Clive, and she thought she'd better go and see them.'

'She'd seen them? Where?'

'At a gig with Terry. They've got quite close, you see.'

'I gathered that. So what happened?'

'They spoke to her at this gig and one of them gave her a phone number.'

'So she phoned that after she spoke to me?'

'Yes. And they said come over.'

'Silly girl,' said Libby.

'Yes, well. Anyway, off she went to this place in West Ken, and as far as I can make out they wouldn't let her out.'

'Why?'

'Oh – some nonsense about Clive and what they did together. She says they weren't happy and didn't seem to

212

know what to do.'

'How very strange.' Libby frowned as Ben came round the bed with a look of enquiry. 'What happened after that?'

'She had a fight with one of them, but they locked her in a room. She managed to get out by wanting the loo, and ran for it. Look, Ma, I'll have to get back to her. She's with Terry and George, but she's in a state.'

'What do you want me to do then?'

'Tell Ian? He'll have to know.'

'Oh, joy,' said Libby. 'All right.'

She explained to Ben on her way downstairs to find all Ian's numbers in her mobile.

'As long as they don't want me to go up there,' she finished and keyed in Ian's home number. He answered quickly and briskly.

'Do we assume she means the two girls we spoke to?' Ian asked.

'Bel thinks so.'

'Is she sure Jenny's telling the truth?'

'Heavens, I don't know! I don't suppose she does either. What shall I do?'

'Ring Bel back and tell her someone will be with her shortly. Where's her flat?'

Libby gave him the address, rang off and rang Bel's number.

'He's sending someone round,' she said. 'And he asked if you thought she was telling the truth.'

'God, Mum, I don't know! I just assumed she was – she's in such a state.'

'All right. Sorry you got mixed up in this, darling.'

'Not your fault. It was Dom and me getting you to

book Ellis, wasn't it?' Bel sighed. 'If only we'd known.'

'The world is paved with "if onlys",' said Libby sententiously.

Bel giggled. 'That's a mumism.'

'OK, mock if you like. I'll ring you in the morning – or you ring me, if you like.'

Libby explained the bits Ben hadn't deduced as they made their way back to bed.

'So goodness alone knows what this is all about – and where it leaves Ian's investigation. I shall never go to sleep now.'

But she did.

Belinda was on the phone bright and early next morning while Libby was drinking her first cup of tea.

'Couple of plain clothes coppers from the local station came round, and after we'd all been questioned, suggested she go with them until Ian could tell them what to do with her, but Terry vetoed that, and said she'd be quite safe in his flat. So one of them phoned Ian, who must have said that was OK, and off they all went. That's all I know so far. And I'm knackered.'

'Sorry, darling. Are you at work?'

'Yes, I am, and propping my eyelids open with matchsticks. Let me know when you hear anything.'

'I will,' said Libby.

'What do you think?' she said to Ben.

'I've no idea. What do we know about the two girls?'

'Not much. I can't even remember their names. Fiona, was it?'

'Were they sisters? They looked alike.'

214

'No, they had different surnames. But it looks as though they were involved with Clive, doesn't it?'

'It also looks as though he hadn't shed his old ways with his old name,' said Ben.

'I thought that.' Libby reached for the teapot. 'I suppose we can't ask until tonight.'

'And he might not tell us then. Patti and Anne will be there.'

'He doesn't usually mind them. I think he relies on Patti's essential goodness.'

When Ben had departed for the estate office to start investigating the purchase of hops and machinery, Libby rang Fran.

'I thought they might be a couple,' said Fran.

'The girls?' Libby was startled. 'But they were groupies.'

'Were they?'

'Well, they said they'd been fans of George and Kyle before Terry and Clive came on the scene, didn't they?'

'They might have been. But Clive might have inveigled them into something different. Just because they liked a band doesn't mean to say they weren't gay.'

'But −' began Libby, and stopped.

'Ian will tell us tonight,' said Fran. 'Don't be impatient. Go and do something else.'

Libby virtuously decided to do some necessary housework, then stared at the current painting on the easel in the conservatory for a while, before deciding it was finished and could therefore be taken down to Guy in Nethergate.

As she drove down the hill towards the town, she hesitated. Perhaps it would be a good idea to pop in and

215

see Edna while she was here? Before she went on to see Guy and Fran? And before she knew it, she was parked in the car park on the cliffs at the end of Victoria Place.

When she reached Cliff Terrace, she paused. Should she tell Fran what she was doing? She turned and leant on the railings overlooking the town and The Alexandria. Actually, what was she doing?

'Libby? Did you want me?'

Jane Baker appeared by her side.

'Jane! No, I was...' Libby stopped and let her eyes slide back to the sea.

'Going to see Edna?' suggested Jane.

'Eh?' Libby was startled.

'I'm a newshound, Lib!' said Jane with a grin. 'A rather mild-mannered one, admittedly, but I saw you the other day when you and Fran went to see her. What do you want this time?'

'I wondered if her connection to the motorbike witches gave her any idea about the ones who were operating a few years ago. Who someone described as an evil Rotary Club.'

Jane cocked an eyebrow. 'She might – but so do I.'

'You do?' Libby's own eyebrows shot up.

'Why surprised? Told you – I'm a newshound. Actually I'm very surprised you don't know yourself. Most of it was concentrated over the other side of Canterbury, where you used to live.'

'Well, I do know about The Dolphin at Dungate,' said Libby, omitting the fact that she only learnt about it yesterday.

'It was in all the local papers,' said Jane.

216

'Yes, I've seen quite a few of them, but there wasn't much about the witchcraft aspect.'

'Strangely, a lot of that was kept out of the media.' Jane made a face. 'The owner of the Kent Telegraph Group was one of them.'

'Oh, I see. So it was fairly widespread?'

'Oh, yes. Do you want to come in for a minute? Or do you have an appointment with Edna?'

'No – she doesn't know I'm here. I was supposed to be delivering a painting to Guy, but he doesn't know, either. I'll come in.'

Settled in the big window overlooking the bay with a coffee percolator between them, Jane began her story.

'I was working for the other paper then.'

'Oh, yes – I saw them. Mostly them, actually. The *Telegraph* wasn't very well represented.'

'Where was this?'

Libby told her about the papers found in Dick Fowler's flat.

'So someone had collected them all. For a reason, do you think?'

'It looked like it.'

'I guess it was someone with a reason to want to know about it all,' said Jane. 'It was such a scandal that it mostly got buried. I started digging off my own bat and worked a lot of it out, but when my editor got to know what I was doing, even I, a lowly junior reporter, was pulled off it.'

'So it's bigger than I thought?'

Jane nodded. 'You know about The Dolphin and the solicitor who was involved in that?'

217

'Yes – although I know more about the woman he was helping. Maureen something.'

'She was a minor case, although she was put away. The solicitor was heavily involved.'

'But in what way? I don't really understand it.'

Jane poured coffee. 'You've been involved with the Hellfire Club in the past, haven't you?'

'Not involved, exactly,' said Libby. 'But come across it, yes. The Notbourne Court business, for example. You know all about that.'

'And the dancers,' said Jane.

'It wasn't exactly the dancers,' said Libby.

'No, but there was a connection in the background. Well, this was more or less the same. A modern Hellfire Club.'

'Another one? Blimey. How many are there, do you suppose?'

'A lot, I suspect. Anyway, this was the usual thing – a group of people getting together for rather unpleasant goings on, usually sex. And keeping quiet about each other for obvious reasons.'

'So what else did you find out?'

'The worse thing was after the whole thing was out in the open. One of the women implicated, although she wasn't that high-profile, had been particularly involved in the grubby little rituals. And when she was prosecuted, it happened.'

'What did?'

'One of her twins killed the other.'

Chapter Twenty-five

Libby almost choked.

'What's up?' Jane looked concerned.

Libby shook her head, belatedly realising that the news that Clive Eddington was really Wayne Fulmore was not common knowledge.

'I know it's shocking, but that's what happened. Apparently, the boy had been watching and even probably participating in some of the rituals, or whatever they were, and it was thought that he killed the other boy to get more power. Or something.'

'After his mother was sent to prison?'

'Must have been.'

'There was nothing about that in any of the papers I saw.'

'It was after the scandal broke – but even that was kept fairly quiet. Although I think that was more because the children were young.'

'Did you cover it?'

Jane shook her head. 'No. The editor himself did. Oh – and Samantha Potter.'

'I remember her. She used to cover our shows at the theatre.'

'What – at the Oast?'

'No, when I used to live over there. But I suppose that

would have been before all this happened.'

'I wasn't with the paper then.' Jane sat back and sighed. 'It was all horrible. And it all just disappeared.'

'Did it? What about the twins' father? If his wife went to prison – and I suppose his son did too?'

'I've no idea. I went back to London.'

'Oh – oh, of course.' Libby sat and thought. 'Have the police been on to you?'

'Of course they have. That's how I knew about the witchcraft connection. Not that I believe in it any more than you do. As we both know, it's simply a cover for bad behaviour.'

'That's putting it mildly,' said Libby. 'So would Samantha Potter know any more about all this than you?'

'She might, but I doubt it. I even managed to find out names!' Jane grinned wickedly. 'I've got enough blackmail material in my little black book to last a lifetime.'

'But about the twins?'

'She might.' Jane frowned. 'There's something behind this isn't there?'

'Well, yes. Two murders.' Libby buried her face in her coffee mug.

'Libby.'

Libby looked up cautiously.

'What's going on?'

'I can't tell you,' said Libby, faced screwed up in anguish. 'Ask Ian.'

'Oh – and he's likely to tell me, isn't he?'

'He might. You never know.'

220

'Come off it, Libby! You know perfectly well he won't.'

'What did the police ask when they got in touch with you – or with the *Mercury*?'

'What we'd heard about the murder at the beer festival. That was all. We told them. The other murder wasn't on our patch. They're connected then, are they?'

'I've no idea,' said Libby. 'It just seems a coincidence.'

Jane looked at her through narrowed eyes. 'I don't believe you.'

'Oh, look, Jane. I only know what I know because it all happened at our beer festival and Ian was involved. Otherwise, we've been kept right out of it.'

'That'll be the day,' said Jane. 'Oh, all right, I know you can't tell me, but you will when you can, won't you?'

'Of course. Otherwise I wouldn't be able to ask you to look things up for me, would I?'

'No, you certainly wouldn't!'

Libby laughed and stood up. 'Well, I'd better go and deliver this painting to Guy. My pin money depends on it.'

'Give Samantha a ring,' said Jane, as she saw Libby off on the doorstep. 'She might know something. I think she still lives in Canterbury.'

'I will, if I can find her number.' Libby leant forward and gave Jane a kiss on the cheek. 'Love to Terry and The Kid.'

Guy took delivery of the painting and told her Fran was at home.

'Writing furiously, as far as I know,' he said with a

grin. 'And she won't show me.'

'No, she won't show me, either.' Libby shouldered her bag and left for Coastguard Cottage.

Fran was surprised to see her.

'I've just seen Jane,' Libby told her. 'I thought I'd report. But actually I was here to give Guy a painting.'

Fran looked suspicious. 'You could have given him that this evening.'

'I know. But I needed something to do. I thought I might talk to Edna again.'

'Edna? Why? You said you'd seen Jane.'

'Jane saw me just before I knocked on Edna's door and invited me in for coffee.'

'Well,' said Fran, leading the way through to the yard at the back of the cottage, 'you won't want any more, will you?'

'No. Do you want to know what she said?'

Fran sat down and closed her laptop which sat on the table under the umbrella. 'Go on, then.'

Libby told her everything Jane had said, including her suggestion to ring Samantha Potter.

'So you'll do that when you get home?'

'I thought so. She might know something. I don't know how I missed it all, but I suppose I was far more taken up with the theatre over there – and the kids, of course.'

'What will you ask her?'

'What she knows, of course. And if she knows if this coven, or whatever it called itself, really was into witchcraft.'

'What? But witchcraft's been on the cards all the way through!'

'Just because of the sigil,' said Libby. 'I've got the feeling that it was probably the media which brought it into the equation in the first place.'

'How do you mean?'

'The first prosecutions of that little group. Jane mentioned the Hellfire Club – well, that wouldn't resonate with the general public like witchcraft would, so they probably did what the media usually do – made it up.'

'Did Jane say that?'

'No, and I didn't suggest it. And let's face it, we've had quite a bit to do with fake witches over the years. It's easy for us to jump to conclusions.'

'But the police have, too.'

'I'm not sure,' said Libby.

'So is that what you'll ask Samantha?'

'Among other things.'

'And where will it get you?'

'I don't know. I just want to *know*.'

'You always do.'

'So do you, usually.'

Fran smiled. 'But not as much as you. And it doesn't affect me as much as it does you. Now, is there anything else? Because I'm rather busy, and you will see me this evening.'

'OK.' Libby sighed and stood up. 'Perhaps I'll speak to Samantha before tonight.'

'Don't pester the poor woman. She might not remember you.'

That was true, Libby reflected as she drove home. And was Fran right? Was it all rather pointless? After all, the police were still investigating, and if they didn't seem to

223

be getting anywhere on the surface, it was pretty certain that an awful lot had been going on *under* the surface.

When she got in, she unearthed her old address book, barely used these days, and found a landline for Samantha Potter. Then she looked her up online.

Among several links given, she found one which actually listed articles by Samantha Potter in the last twelve months, the most recent being nearly a year ago, and published in the online version of the group she had worked for when Libby knew her. So it looked as if she'd retired. There were also social media links for her, assuming it was the right woman, but Libby decided to try the phone first. A rather surprised voice answered.

'Hello, er – is that Samantha Potter?'

'Yes – who's this?'

'It's Libby Sarjeant. I don't know if you remember me'

'Libby Sarjeant? Bloody hell! Remember you? How could I forget? Well, well, well. To what do I owe the honour?'

Libby laughed nervously. 'Well, it's a bit difficult, actually...'

Now Samantha laughed, a deep throaty laugh, reminding Libby that in her smoking days she and Sam had frequently been the two who sneaked outside for a quiet fag.

'What do you want, Libby? Something to do with your new career?'

'My -?'

'Your sleuthing. Or your lovely new theatre.'

'Oh.'

'Oh, yes. I've followed your exploits. Well, not followed, exactly, but had them thrust down my throat. You've featured quite heavily in the local media over the last few years.'

This wasn't going to be as easy as Libby had hoped.

'I'm sorry,' she began.

'What for? Go on, ask away. I can always get a freelance piece out of you in payment.'

Libby cleared her throat. 'Well, it's like this. We ran this beer festival, you see...'

'Oh, yes. The Steeple Martin Roll Out The Barrel Festival. And – surprise, surprise – you had a murder. You sure you don't do them all yourself?'

Libby tried to laugh.

'Oh, go on, sorry. Don't mind me. So you had that murder. And then there was the other one. Don't know if that's connected, but the vic was also a muso, wasn't he? From Fat Dragon?'

'I don't know much either, but it seems possible – and this isn't for publication, freelance or otherwise – that there's a connection to witchcraft, and we – I mean I – wondered if you remembered anything about that witchcraft scandal that involved some bigwigs in the Canterbury area some years back.'

'Oh, God, that! Well, I can put you right straight away – it was no more witchcraft than the Boys Brigade.'

'Ah!' said Libby.

'You sound as if you knew?'

'I sort of guessed. I wondered if it was a label the media attached to make it more interesting. Sorry if that offends.'

'You're right, as it happens – but it wasn't me. It was our brothers and sisters in the national press. I can't for the life of me remember who started it, but it caught on. Not that I knew much about it.'

'So there were no scary rituals or Black Masses?'

'Not as such. They seemed to have taken their cue from a group of high-flyers in the sixties who used to meet for, shall we say, recreational purposes. And they all knew so much about each other they did each other all sorts of favours.'

'Sort of modern Hellfire Club?'

'Oh, you have been doing your homework! So tell me, what has that to do with your little local murder?'

Now Libby was in a cleft stick. Her original purpose, to ask Samantha about Wayne Fulmore, looked a little risky now. Could she afford to give any more information away?

'Someone mentioned a witchcraft connection,' she said hesitantly, 'and – well, you might know we've had a couple of fake witch stories over our way in the last couple of years.'

'Yes, I did know. I covered most of them. Just because you're now on the other side of Canterbury doesn't mean you don't get Potter the Piranha on your trail.'

Libby's heart sank.

'Let's see,' Samantha carried on, 'the boy who was killed was part of a London band, wasn't he? And came from Manchester? Hmm. But the boy who was with Fat Dragon – now, they're a local band – he came from round our way, didn't he? All those years ago? He would have been a kid. Let's think... oh – got it.'

226

'Have you?' quavered Libby.

'Didn't take much working out. He was Wayne Fulmore, wasn't he?'

Chapter Twenty-six

Libby stuck her tongue out at the phone.

'Not as far as I know,' she said, as nonchalantly as she could. 'But I'm not in the confidence of the police.'

'Oh, no? That's why you're asking me then? You think he is?'

Libby swore silently.

'I just wondered, that's all. And I thought you might know,' she lied.

'I can take an educated guess from what you've said. But I don't understand how you made that leap.'

'Oh – it was the mention of witchcraft,' said Libby vaguely. 'And I wondered why I hadn't heard of any scandals when I was still living over the other side.'

'You were too busy being head honcho at your little theatre. I've been to your new one, by the way. Very nice.'

'Have you?'

'Oh yes. Seen a couple of pantos – well, I had to, didn't I? – and that ballet. That was about witches, wasn't it? And I came over for your first one – the one which had the murder connected to it.'

'Not unusual,' said Libby morosely. 'So did the ballet.'

'So what you're actually doing is trying to work up

another case for yourself and that psychic woman you go about with these days.'

'You seem to know a lot about me,' said Libby.'

'I keep my ear to the ground. And I still do reviews. I did one of that play you did in the old monastery.'

'Oh.' Libby just stopped herself asking if it was a good one.

'Anyway, Libby, good to hear from you. Let me know if there's anything I can use, won't you? I still have my contacts.'

Well, that went well, thought Libby after ending the call. Samantha knew no more than she'd been able to find out herself. But, she wondered, as she went into the kitchen to make herself yet another cup of tea, who was the group of people in the sixties who were a sort of Hellfire Club Samantha had referred to? How could she find out about them? Were they the same as the group they had come across during the infamous ballet murder? She sighed, and took her mug into the conservatory to ponder.

Later, at the Pink Geranium, she and Ben joined Fran, Guy, Patti and Anne at the big round table in the window.

'Any news?' asked Anne eagerly, almost before they were seated.

'She's been very good,' said Fran, amused. 'She hasn't asked me a thing.'

Anne blushed.

'It's the only excitement she gets,' said Patti, giving her friend a poke in the ribs.

'Don't mock the afflicted,' said Anne. 'You know you're just as interested.'

Before they could update her, there was food and wine to order. Adam wasn't working tonight, and to Libby's surprise, Harry's old right-hand woman, Donna, appeared to serve them. She was greeted rapturously.

'Well, I never actually left,' she said. 'Libby suggested Harry keep me on to do the books at home, which is what I've been doing. And some ordering and stuff. And I said I'd come and help out if I could get a sitter. It's not fair to go out when the old man has a night off – they're so rare.'

Donna's husband was a registrar at the hospital.

'So,' said Anne, when the orders had been taken. 'What's been happening?'

Between them, they told Patti and Anne what had happened over the last week, without revealing that Clive Eddington was Wayne Fulmore.

'So there's no more evidence of witchcraft?' said Patti.

'Well, there is and there isn't,' said Libby.

'What's this connection with the scandals of ten years ago, or whenever it was?' asked Anne.

'That was in the papers I found in Dick Fowler's flat,' said Libby.

'There's quite a lot you aren't saying,' said Patti shrewdly. 'But I expect Ian's told you to keep quiet.'

Libby sighed. 'He has. He's also not told us very much, especially since he moved the incident room away.'

'What about the other boy?' asked Anne. 'Last time we saw you he wasn't dead.'

'No. That's a bit of a puzzle,' said Fran. 'And we have no idea if it's connected to the first death or not.'

'But you think it is,' said Patti, laying her cutlery neatly side by side on her plate.

The two men looked at each other and shrugged.

'Are you going to go on dissecting the murder all evening?' asked Guy.

'Sorry.' Patti smiled at him. 'I expect you came out to get away from it.'

'If I wanted to get away from it I'd go a long way away from Steeple Martin,' said Guy.

'Like Africa,' said Ben.

Luckily, Donna arrived to collect plates and ask if anyone wanted dessert. The lift in tension was, however, transitory, as a few minutes later Ian Connell opened the door.

'Oh, you're all still here,' he said.

Libby couldn't help giggling, and Anne snorted loudly from behind her napkin.

'What?' said Ian.

'Oh, come and sit down, Ian,' said Ben, pulling out the empty chair next to him. Harry appeared from the kitchen and asked if Ian wanted anything to eat, or simply coffee.

'Just coffee, Harry, thank you. Not joining us?'

'Later in the pub, if that's where you're going,' said Harry. 'Pete'll be back by then.'

'I take it you've told Patti and Anne everything that you've found out this week?' said Ian, when Harry had gone.

'Not everything,' said Libby. 'We didn't think you wanted us to.'

Ian nodded approval. 'As it happens, I may well tell them the rest. You'll see why when I tell them.'

Everyone looked at him in astonishment. Libby recovered first. 'What's happened?'

231

'I'll tell you when we get to the pub,' said Ian, accepting his coffee from Donna with a maddeningly smug smile.

'If you've gone and solved this without telling us –' began Libby with an awful glower.

'No, I haven't, but there are a few things you don't know.' He turned to Ben. 'How's the research going?'

'Research?' whispered Anne to Libby.

'Hops,' said Libby. 'He's going to re-open the hop garden.'

'You mean the one where...'

'Where his mum and dad met, yes,' said Libby.

Patti looked uncomfortable. 'And that play...'

Libby sighed. 'Yes. We can never get away from that.'

'Well, it was the opening production at the theatre,' said Fran. 'Bound to be remembered.'

'Yes. Even Samantha –' she stopped.

'Samantha?' prompted Anne.

'Potter.' said Fran. 'Well, of course she would. She reviewed it.'

Libby looked surprised. 'You knew that?'

'Oh, yes,' said Fran airily and Libby didn't believe a word.

'Deflection technique,' she said to Libby as they left the restaurant half an hour later. 'That would have given the game away.'

'I know – I realised that,' said Libby. 'Speaking before engaging brain again.'

Safely ensconced in the old lounge bar, which was, as usual, empty except for themselves, Ian sat back in his chair and fixed Patti with a thoughtful gaze. She looked

232

nervously round at the others.

'Before I start, I want to know something, Patti. All of this is both confidential and highly sensitive, so if you're not happy with that, tell me.'

Patti frowned. 'I don't know until you tell me what it is, do I?'

Ian smiled. 'True. So what have Libby and Fran told you so far?'

Anne recounted the little they had been told.

'In that case you've all got some catching up to do.' He looked round the table. 'As you know, I shouldn't be talking about this, but there are a couple of things you're already involved in.' He turned to Patti and Anne. 'Did they tell you about Jenny Dean and the two girls?'

Both women shook their heads, wide-eyed.

'Jenny confessed to Libby that while she was in Manchester Clive Eddington had been involved in some kind of witchcraft, or occultism and had tried to get her interested. When she came south after he did, it was a coincidence that they met again. And then later, at another gig, she met the two girls we questioned here.'

There were a couple of gasps.

'They gave her a phone number, seemed friendly and told her to ring any time. After Jenny had talked to Libby, she called the number, and they told her to come round.'

'Where was this?' asked Patti.

'West Kensington. And when she got there, they locked her in.'

'When did you hear about this?' Patti looked at Libby.

'Last night. I had to phone Ian at midnight – or somewhere around there.'

233

'So what's happened now?' Patti was looking serious.

'The two women have been questioned under caution, but haven't said anything of great importance yet. They are, by the way, in a civil partnership.'

Fran nodded. 'Thought so.'

'To go back to last week, you remember we were speculating about Clive Eddington having been in the UKPPS?'

'Well, we were, to be fair,' said Anne.

'He was. Now this is definitely top secret at the moment, but necessary for what I want to ask you. As an expert witness.' He gave Patti a crooked smile.

'Oh, Lord,' said Patti.

'Clive Eddington was originally Wayne Fulmore. When he was eleven, he killed his twin brother, Stephen.'

Patti reached out and gripped Anne's hand.

'Very little got into the media, and the trial was held almost completely *in camera*. As it turned out, the event followed in the wake of a scandal that had broken out locally which concerned, according to the press, the practising of witchcraft. Has Libby told you about finding out about a publican who was almost turned out of his own pub by his daughter?'

'I glossed over it a bit,' said Libby.

'A few high-profile, supposedly law-abiding, local figures had got involved with something, and were doing one another favours to keep each other out of the law's grasp.'

'By something,' said Patti, frowning, 'you mean illegal?'

'Remember we heard about the Hellfire Club?' said

Libby. 'All that nastiness?'

Patti and Anne nodded.

'That sort of thing.'

'It also transpired, thanks to Libby and Ben researching hop gardens, that young Danny Coleman had gone to school with Wayne Fulmore.'

More gasps.

'So it's all coming together?' murmured Anne.

'Let's say there are links,' said Ian.

'Can we know what happened to Wayne Fulmore after the trial?' asked Fran.

'He was sent to a secure unit and eventually released, on license with his new identity, into the Manchester area. While inside, he'd taught himself to play guitar and drums, and began gigging around the pubs, playing with anyone who asked him, eventually joining Lucifer's Maiden.'

'Was he –' began Libby, but Ian held up a hand.

'They were a flamboyant band with a rather spurious interest in the occult. They scared Jenny Dean, their singer, who is rather quiet and shy. Odd for a singer.'

'Not really,' said Libby. 'Lots of performers are shy underneath. I am myself.'

A howl of derision rose round the table and broke the tension.

'As far as we have learnt from the officers sent to interview members of Lucifer's Maiden, Eddington was contemptuous of their so-called Satanism, and kept himself to himself.'

'But –' Libby began again.

'All right, Libby. I'll –'

'Why did he kill his brother?' Patti broke in sharply.

'Ah.' Ian gave her a rueful smile. 'You've pre-empted me.'

'His parents were part of this Hellfire Club, weren't they?'

'His mother was, yes.'

'And he was following her instructions?'

'Not exactly.'

'But that's what gave him the idea?'

'Yes.'

'Was that released to the press?' asked Libby.

'No. There was speculation, but everything was brushed under the carpet fairly quickly. Fulmore's mother had been convicted of fraud and various other charges, and the father stayed practically out of sight.'

Everyone was quiet for a moment. Libby finished her drink.

'So what did you want to ask me?' said Patti eventually.

'Have you personally, or the Church, ever heard of chaos magic?'

Chapter Twenty-seven

Patti looked surprised.

'Yes,' she said.

'And could you explain what it is?' asked Ian.

'Not really. Everyone associated with it seems to have their own ideas.'

'I've heard of it,' said Fran thoughtfully. 'Isn't it some sort of cult where all the rules are turned upside-down? And where people are supposed to believe in one thing and the next minute believe in the exact opposite?'

'Put simplistically, that's about it, although as with all these things, there are impenetrable stages of immersion, if you know what I mean. Gnostic states come into it very heavily, I believe.' Ian sighed. 'Basically translated, adherents are told they can do what they bloody like.'

'Are you telling us that this was the cult that sparked the scandals when Wayne Fulmore was a boy?' asked Ben.

'Exactly.'

'How did you find out? Was it in the old files?' asked Guy.

'It was mentioned, although glossed over, rather. It was when I started looking into sigils that I stumbled across it. There is actually something called sigil magic, the basis of which is where the words of a statement of intent are reduced into an abstract design or sigil – heaven knows how – which is then charged with the will of the creator. That technique, known as sigilisation, has become a core element of chaos magic. And don't ask me to explain any further, because I haven't got a clue.'

'Glorified mumbo-jumbo?' suggested Libby.

'Dangerous stuff,' said Patti. 'It did come into my theology degree as an also-ran sort of thing, but was considered less of a threat than Satanism. Nobody seemed to understand it.'

'So it gives *carte blanche* to people to do exactly as they like,' said Anne. 'Bloody hell.'

'What's a gnostic state?' asked Guy suddenly.

'Deep meditation, or trance,' said Ian. 'There's one form which relies on – forgive me, Patti – intense arousal.'

'Ooh, I bet they love that,' said Libby.

'And then there's the Multiplicity of Self.'

There was a sudden silence round the table.

'Is that schizophrenia?' asked Anne hesitantly.

'It can be, but in this context, it seems to be literally what it says, creating as many personas as you want to fit different situations.'

'And killing them off?' Libby suggested softly.

This time there was a longer silence.

'Killing a twin,' said Patti eventually.

'I've absolutely no evidence for that, but reading the old files, and the psych reports on Wayne, both before and after he was sent away, it seems possible.'

'Golly,' said Libby.

After another short silence, Guy stood up. 'Another drink, anyone?'

Ben went with him to the bar and Libby turned to Ian.

'It's all very well, but all this seems to point to Wayne – or Clive – as a murderer, and he wasn't. He was the victim.'

'Could it be,' said Patti slowly, 'that it was someone who was upset about what he did as a child? His mother perhaps?'

'His *mother*?' said Libby and Anne together.

'Isn't it possible, though?' said Fran. 'After all, she'd be out of prison now, wouldn't she? And eaten up with resentment, I would think.'

'But Wayne didn't put her in prison,' said Ian. 'She did that herself.'

'Where is she now, do you know?' asked Anne.

'I haven't been told, but I could find out, now I've been given the go ahead on the investigation.'

'What do you mean?' said Libby. 'You've been investigating it for a week or more!'

'As Clive Eddington. Remember I couldn't do anything about Wayne Fulmore until I'd gone through all the UKPPS hoops.'

'I know this sounds daft,' said Anne, 'but I suppose it is the real Clive-stroke-Wayne? Not someone pretending?'

'Fingerprint and DNA evidence confirm it,' said Ian, 'even if I shouldn't be telling you.'

'So where does the chaos magic theory get you?' asked Libby, being careful not to say "us".

'A motive for what he did as a child, and a possible

239

reason for his attitude to Lucifer's Maiden.'

Guy and Ben arrived back with drinks just as Peter and Harry came through the door.

'I must be mad,' said Ian with a sigh, as he embarked on his second explanation of the night.

'The idea, then,' said Harry, when he'd finished, 'is that he thought Lucifer's Maiden were a bit – well – silly?'

'Infantile?' put in Fran.

'Yes. And his form of magic was the real thing. Would he still have been convinced of that all these years after? And after treatment?'

'That's the theory we're working on at the moment,' said Ian. 'I really just wanted to ask Patti if she knew anything about it – and she does. So I can take it seriously.'

'Can I ask another question?' said Peter. 'There was something about a kidnap and those two girls from the festival. May we know what that was all about?'

Ian sighed again. 'Well, Libby's entitled to know, and she'd tell you anyway, so you might as well know.'

'Would you rather we found out by ourselves?' asked Fran, earning her a sharp look from Ian.

'Difficult, I'd have thought,' said Libby. 'I reckon they'll still be in custody for false imprisonment.'

Ian laughed. 'You'd be right, they would. And I'll tell you what London have found out for us so far.'

'You aren't doing it yourself?' said Patti, surprised.

'My job, believe it or not, is to direct operations from behind a desk,' said Ian. 'I could get out and about more as a DI, and even more as a DS, but as a DCI it's difficult.

240

And the two girls are in London, where the victim lives and where the crime was carried out.'

'Oh, I see.' Patti looked chastened.

'Don't worry,' said Libby. 'None of us really knows what goes on behind police closed doors, and if we did, I think we'd find it very boring. Ian just tells us the good bits. When he can.'

'And so far that's all I can tell you.' Ian took a sip of his cooling coffee. 'As Jenny Dean told you on the phone Libby, Clive, as he still was, was into a very particular form of magic which he did not want to share with a lot of men.'

'But he did with women,' suggested Fran.

'Indeed. Usually on a one-to-one basis. This is what sounds like chaos magic to me. As far as we can tell, the two women, Fiona Dawson and Tracey Field, were fans of Ellis before Eddington was recruited, and at some point he tried recruiting them. He didn't manage it, and they admitted they thought it was weird, but decided to ignore it. They *did* give Jenny Dean their number, but simply because she seemed a bit lost and lonely. Which is why they invited her round last night. Their story is that she began to get as weird as Clive – Wayne – had been, and then ran out of the flat.'

'Curiouser and curiouser,' said Patti. 'And, as I said, dangerous.'

'So you've got very little from the two girls?' said Fran.

'As I said – so far. We have hopes.'

'Well, I'm sorry I can't help you any more,' said Patti. 'Can't you find a sort of high priest of chaos magic or something? They might help.'

'We're trying,' said Ian. 'It isn't easy, believe me. I think they would be more willing to talk to the media than the police.'

'Surely you could get a contact from the media to do it, then?' said Libby. 'Only not Samantha Potter.'

'Why not?' asked Ian. 'What have you been up to?'

Fran told him.

'I've not had much to do with her,' said Ian, 'but I remember being told she was one of the worst locally. Any stick to beat the police – or the politicians, come to that – with. So don't talk to her anymore, Lib.'

'What about Jane Baker then?'

'I wouldn't imagine high priests of any kind would bother with a small regional, Lib,' said Ben.

'Don't worry, we'll get there,' said Ian.

'Well, that didn't get us any further,' Libby said to Ben as they walked home a little later.

'You know about chaos magic now,' said Ben. 'And Ian and his team are still working hard on the case.'

'But what about Danny Coleman? He keeps getting ignored.'

'I don't suppose he's getting ignored by the police. They probably know an awful lot more about it than we do. Or should I say – than *you* do.'

'I expect they do,' said Libby with a sigh. 'We don't even know if the two deaths were linked.'

'I thought you'd established that they were?' said Ben. 'They went to the same school.'

'And presumably were at that school when Wayne...' Libby broke off. 'I don't even like saying it.'

'I know.' Ben put his arm round her shoulders. 'Let's go in, have a nightcap and forget about it.'

But Libby couldn't.

The next morning she called Jane Baker.

'Have you got any more on the murder of Danny Coleman?'

'*You* asking *me*?' said Jane. 'Goodness me – has the Libby and Fran rumour mill let you down at last?'

'We just feel we've got a sort of vested interest, but the police won't tell us anything.'

'Why a vested interest? He wasn't killed at the festival, was he? I thought he was found in the boot of his own car in Canterbury.'

'That's all I know,' said Libby. 'But the other victim came down with the band my kids recommended, and we think he knew Danny Coleman. So it could be...'

'I see. Tenuous, but I see. How did you find out they were at school together? I thought Eddington came from Manchester?'

Too late, Libby realised that the news about Eddington's real identity hadn't been released to the press.

'Police again,' she said vaguely. 'We're completely in the dark about both investigations, but Ian lets the odd bit slip.'

'Nothing I could use, I suppose?'

'No,' said Libby regretfully. 'Although I did suggest he spoke to you about something yesterday.'

'Oh? What?'

'I can't tell you if he hasn't been in touch. I think it was a bit sensitive.'

'Now you've got me really intrigued,' said Jane. 'You shouldn't have told me!'

'No, I know. My big mouth. I'm sorry.'

'Oh well, no doubt someone will tell me eventually.'

'I expect so. But listen – I spoke to Samantha Potter yesterday. She's much more – I don't know – abrasive than I remember.'

'And retired,' said Jane.

'I gather she doesn't take that seriously,' said Libby. 'Anyway, you don't know anything else about Danny Coleman.'

'No. I know that his car was parked near one of those nightclubs in Canterbury. I must say, I thought they'd all closed down. We never hear about them these days.'

'I don't think I knew that. Who found him?'

'No idea. I expect it's in the report, but I'd have to look it up.'

'OK.' Libby chewed her lip. 'Well, if you do hear anything, will you give me a ring?'

'I doubt I'll hear anything before you do, but yes, I will.'

Libby ended the call and sat down at the table in the window with the laptop. The online version of the *Nethergate Mercury* seemed her best bet. Sure enough, within seconds, she had the relevant report up on screen. But, as was frequently the case, the report was a truncated version of the one which appeared in print, and had no information other than that which Jane had told her. There was a photograph of the car however. She stared at it, then called Fran.

'The car they found Danny Coleman in,' she began.

'I've seen it before.'

'How do you know? You don't go round taking number plates, do you?'

'No – but it was an old Volvo estate. Remember those cars they called "the brick"? Well, it nearly ran me down in the high street.'

Chapter Twenty-eight

'How do you know it was the same one?' asked Fran, sounding dubious. 'And when you say ran you down, do you mean like they do on television – you know, attempted murder?'

'Well, all right, I suppose it could have been a different car, but how many do you see these days? The one in the village was yellow, but the photograph is black and white, so I can't tell. And it came up behind me really fast. I jumped out of the way and it just carried on.'

'Hmm,' said Fran. 'Coincidence, probably.'

'And don't forget I'd just seen Danny and told him Ian wanted to speak to him.'

'So he was running away? You know, everything seems to point to Clive – Wayne – being the murderer instead of the victim, doesn't it?'

'It would make much more sense if it was,' said Libby. 'All very puzzling.'

'What did you make of the chaos magic theory?'

'Makes sense, doesn't it? Can't quite say the same for Jenny Dean. I hope young Terry isn't too smitten with her.'

'Now, don't start getting all protective about them. They aren't your children. I expect he's got a very nice mother of his own.'

'Don't laugh at me,' said Libby. 'She just looks and sounds like trouble to me, and I sort of feel responsible for those poor boys in the band. After all, it was our festival, and my kids who persuaded them to come down.'

'Look, Libby – you've nothing to do with this. Jenny met Clive when he was in Manchester and Terry and the rest of the band in London. Nothing to do with the festival or you.'

'All right.' Libby heaved a sigh. 'What shall I do, then?'

'I don't know. Paint a picture? Start work on the pantomime? Turn out the spare room?'

'Gee, thanks. You don't think I ought to tell Ian about the Volvo, then?'

Fran sighed. 'If you must. But I'd send him a text, if I were you. Then he can ignore it if he wants to.'

After ending the call, Libby laboriously sent a text to both Ian's numbers, personal and work. Then it was time for lunch.

The day was warm enough for her to take her ham sandwich outside to eat under the cherry tree with a book and the portable radio for company. Sidney joined her and stretched out at her feet.

'No wonder you couldn't hear me,' said a voice, and she looked up to see Ian peering over the back fence at her.

'Did you knock?' she asked as she opened the gate for him.

'Yes, loudly. Sorry, have I disturbed your lunch?'

'I've finished,' said Libby. 'Would you like tea?'

'No, I won't thank you. This is only a flying visit. I got your text.'

'Oh. Fran said to do that so you could ignore it if you wanted to.'

'Very sensible.' Ian pulled out the other garden chair and sat down. 'Now tell me exactly what you meant.'

Libby told him.

'But Fran said it could be a coincidence, and I couldn't tell what colour Danny's car was from the photograph because it was in black and white.'

'It was yellow.' Ian was frowning. 'I hate to say it, but I think you were right.'

'That it was Danny's car? Or that it was trying to run me down?'

'Both. Oh, I don't say he set out with that intention, but he'd just spoken to you and you said I wanted to see him, so he picks up his car from wherever he left it and there you are in the high street.. I did actually speak to him, though. I told you at the time. It was probably a sudden impulse, and I doubt he meant to kill you, just to frighten you perhaps'

'Oddly, it didn't, at the time. I just hopped out of the way and thought what an idiot the driver was.'

'I'll get someone to ask around in the village to see where the car was spotted. It wasn't at the Manor or anywhere near our incident room. And, by the way, Hetty said he didn't go back to pick anything up. Oh – which direction was it going? Towards Canterbury?'

'Yes. I wonder where he'd parked it, then? Not in Maltby Close or the Manor Drive. Up the lane towards Steeple Farm? Or the Nethergate Road? It would be hard to miss.'

'You'd be surprised at what people miss.' Ian stood up. 'If we could find out what he was doing here, we'd be a lot closer to Wayne's killer. And his own.'

Libby got up to see him out. 'So do we – er, you – think Danny saw who killed Wayne and threatened to blackmail them? So they killed him, too?'

'It seems like the most likely scenario,' said Ian, following her into the house. 'But don't spread it around.'

'So that's nothing to do with chaos magic, if that's what it is?'

'I don't think so.'

'Are you going to ask Jane?'

'I might. You haven't told her anything, have you?'

'No. I actually rang her to ask if she'd heard anything, but she hadn't. She only knew what had been in the papers.'

'Well, don't. And remember, no speaking to the Potter woman, either.'

'All right, all right.' Libby opened the front door. 'Sorry if I'm interfering.'

Ian swiftly bent to kiss her cheek. 'You're not. Don't worry.'

Libby watched open-mouthed as he strode back to his big, black, anonymous saloon, and wondered afresh why Fran had turned him down all those years ago.

'And I don't suppose we'll hear any more about it until next week,' she finished up after telling Ben all about it when he came home.

'Why didn't you tell me about that?' He was scowling at her.

'I forgot all about it. Sorry.'

'Honestly, Libby, you'll be the death of me. Or yourself.'

Libby was surprised. 'But that wasn't my fault! Nothing to do with me.'

'That time, maybe not, but think of all the other times. On that boat, for instance, or in that shed...'

'Yes, yes, all right.' Libby gave him a hug. 'I'm sorry I'm a nuisance. Even though Ian told me today I wasn't.'

'Did he? That was big of him. You watch it with these dark-browed, smooth-talking Scotsmen.'

Libby grinned. 'Oh, yes. He's bound to go for a stunted, frizzy-haired blob like me.'

'He's very fond of you,' said Ben. 'And so am I.'

The following day, Friday, Libby and Peter had called a preliminary meeting of the Oast Theatre committee, such as it was. Although the theatre was owned by Ben's family, having been converted by him from the redundant Oast House, a few regular members of the acting and backstage company had places on an ad hoc committee - mainly, as Ben and Peter said, to temper some of the most outrageous schemes Libby put forward. This meeting was to discuss the forthcoming pantomime, a popular pro-am production which funded the theatre for the following year, along with the hirings.

They met in the foyer of the theatre, Peter opened the bar and the first ten minutes, inevitably, were spent talking about the recent murders.

'I didn't realise that boy discovered in the car was connected,' said Dr Nigel Peasegood. 'I saw him a few

250

days after the festival.'

All eyes turned on him.

'Go on, then, Nigel – where?' Libby urged.

Nigel frowned. 'Lendle Lane, actually. He was getting into that huge car – that's how I recognised him in the paper. Well, not him, the car.'

'Would that be just after you spoke to him, Lib?' asked Peter. 'Which way did he go?'

'Well, I thought he set off for the Manor – that's where he said he was going.'

'And you didn't see him cross back?' said Ben.

'Obviously not. I'd have said.'

'He'd have to, to get to Lendle Lane,' said Bob the butcher, half of the perennial double act and occasional Dame.

'Why park there, though?' asked his partner, Baz the undertaker. 'Perhaps he'd already been to the Manor?'

'No.' Libby shook her head. 'Hetty said he hadn't been there at all. Remember the police were still in the village then.'

'Wonder why they didn't see him then?' said Tom, former Dame now returned to the village.

'No idea,' said Libby, 'but I shall tell Ian if you don't mind, Nigel. He really wants to know why Danny Coleman was here.'

'Coleman?' Tom frowned. 'Danny Coleman? I used to know a Coleman family, and they had a son called Danny.'

'Was that when we were with the other company, Tom?' Libby was on the alert.

'It was. Poor little sod went to school with that kid

251

who killed his twin.'

There were gasps throughout the foyer.

'I remember that,' muttered a few voices.

'Witchcraft or summat, weren't it?' said someone.

'Some stupid sect or something, I heard,' said Tom. 'Don't you remember, Lib?'

'Yes, vaguely,' said Libby, feeling uncomfortable. She looked to Ben and Peter for rescue.

Peter rapped on his glass. 'OK, let's leave a very unpleasant subject and turn to another one.'

This raised a laugh and broke the mood.

'*Jack and the Beanstalk*,' said Tom.

'No – *Puss-in-Boots*,' said Libby. 'We've lost a fair few of our old regulars, one way and another, and most pros I could call on are already doing something for the season.'

'Besides, ours is only a two-week run, and doesn't pay a lot,' said Ben. 'So we've got some heavy recruiting to do.'

'Libby's got to be the Fairy Queen,' said Baz.

'Not again,' said Libby.

'Or the Queen,' said Tom.

'Or just the director, perhaps?' said Libby.

Nigel, a fairly new member of the company, looked from one to another. 'Do I have to audition?'

'We'll see,' said Libby. 'We'll put out a notice for all interested parties. Now, lighting and sound.'

The meeting turned technical.

'Should I ask Nigel to call Ian with that information?' Libby asked Ben, as they helped Peter close up the bar later.

'I should. It will be better coming from our respected doctor.'

252

'Nigel!' called Libby. The doctor, who had been stacking chairs, came over.

'Would you let DCI Connell know about seeing Coleman, please?'

'Oh ... I thought you would?' Nigel's eyebrows rose in surprise.

'It would be better coming from you,' said Libby. 'Ben says it will lend an air of respectability.'

Nigel grinned. 'I can feel myself becoming less and less respectable the longer I'm in this village. What's the number? And do I do it now? It's rather late.'

'Send a text,' said Ben. 'Then he can answer it or not, depending how important he thinks it is.'

Nigel keyed the number into his phone and wandered off, composing a text.

'How easy it is these days,' said Libby with a sigh, as she watched him.

'Communication? Certainly is,' said Ben. 'But we're still doing glasses the old-fashioned way. Come on.'

As they approached the pub, Nigel appeared from his surgery and home on the corner of Maltby Close.

'Your mate's just phoned me back,' he said, jogging across the road. 'He's on his way home, apparently, and said if I was still up he'd like talk to me.'

Libby grinned. 'In the pub?'

'Well, yes. I said you'd told me to call him.'

'Suggested,' said Libby. 'Nobody does what I *tell* them.'

'But where's he on his way home *to*?' Libby whispered to Ben as they entered the pub. 'That's what I want to know.'

253

Ian joined them less than ten minutes later, and with Tim's permission, took Nigel into the office.

'So what's the doc done?' called a voice from the public bar, followed by a surge of raucous laughter.

Tim quietened them good-humouredly, and turned to the rest of the theatre crowd. 'To do with our murders, is it?'

'Expect so,' said Peter.

Tim cocked his head. ' Like that, is it?'

Ben grinned at him. 'It is.'

Libby had an idea. She went up to the bar and peered over Tim's shoulder. 'Is Dick in?'

'Dick Fowler? Yes – shall I call him over?'

'Please. Don't make it too obvious though.'

Tim turned and made a gesture with his head. Seconds later, Dick was pushing through the crowd to get to the bar.

'Hello, Libby.' He looked from her to Tim. 'Did you want me?'

'Just a long shot, really,' said Libby, 'but a couple of days after the – er – murder, did you see a big old Volvo estate parked in Lendle Lane? That's where you live, isn't it?'

Dick looked startled. 'I don't know about the date, but around that time, yes. I saw it from the flat over the shop.'

Chapter Twenty-nine

'I only noticed it because it's so unusual to see them today,' Dick went on.

'What time was it, do you remember?' asked Libby, almost hopping about from excitement.

Dick frowned. 'I don't rightly know. Morning, sometime? I can't even remember why I was up there...It wasn't the day I showed you those papers, was it?'

'No – but they were fascinating, Dick. Must find out who used to have the shop. So it was morning, definitely?'

'I think so.' Dick looked anxious. 'Is it important?'

'It might be.' Libby gave him a friendly grin. 'Hang on a minute.'

She darted out of the bar and knocked on the office door. Ian's face appeared frowning.

'Sorry,' she said, 'but I've just heard. Dick Fowler saw it, too.'

Ian sighed. 'So now it's all round the village?'

'No, just Dick.'

'Ask him to come in, then.'

Libby went back to the bar and mouthed "Office" across to Dick. Tim grinned and lifted the hatch to allow him through.

'So what was that all about?' asked Ben.

'Another witness,' said Libby. Bob, Baz and Tom looked interested.

'He saw the Volvo too,' said Libby, 'but don't you dare say anything to anybody round the village.'

'Don't you think, though,' said Baz, 'that it would be a good idea to ask a bit more around the village?'

'I thought the police had done that when they were here last week,' said Ben.

'Baz is right,' said Peter. 'They only asked the people they knew had been at the festival. And that wasn't all that many.'

'They asked the motorbike people, didn't they? Edna's lot?'

'We don't actually know who they asked,' said Libby. 'They do an awful lot we don't know about.'

'Why don't you ask, then?' said Tom. 'You're no stranger to asking questions about murders.'

'Poking her nose in, you mean,' said Peter.

'Only you could get away with that,' said Bob. 'But yes – don't you think that's a good idea?'

'I suppose it might be,' said Libby. 'But not now – not with Ian here.'

'Why not?' asked Ben. 'I can't think it could be called interfering. He's already questioning Nigel and Dick.'

'Somebody else can do it then,' said Libby.

'Go on, Baz,' said Peter, 'it was your idea.'

Baz got up, went to the bar and called Tim. Libby saw him nod, glance over at her, then ring the bell. A surprised hush fell over the crowd in the public bar.

Baz cleared his throat. 'Er – hi, everybody. Um – can I

ask if any of you were at the beer festival the other weekend?'

There was a chorus of 'Yeses' and a few 'Nos'.

'Were any of you on the field when they finished on the Saturday night?'

'When that guy was killed?' said someone.

'A lot of us were,' said someone else. 'We helped clear up. Where's Libby?'

Libby stood up and waved across the bar. 'I'm here.'

'Lot of us clearing up, weren't there, Libby?'

'Yes, but I don't know everybody.'

Various people identified themselves.

'And Dick was there,' said somebody. 'Where is he? He was here.'

'Talking to DCI Connell,' said Libby and suddenly another silence fell.

'You didn't tell us that,' someone said accusingly to Baz.

'It's all right,' said Libby hastily. 'This isn't official. We just wondered if the police had asked everybody.'

'There were a few lying about pissed,' said someone. 'Did they ask them?'

'Who were they?' asked Tim. 'I saw a few, but I assumed they'd been moved on.'

'Several of them were,' said Libby.

'But a lot of the Regionals were there. I bet they didn't get moved on,' said someone else.

'The police talked to them,' said Libby.

'Not all of them, I bet,' grumbled a voice from the snug.

Everyone tried to see into the snug, which sat behind

257

the saloon bar and only shared a tiny corner of the bar counter.

'Now, Giles,' said Tim, 'you don't know that.'

'I know I had 'em in my field when they was turned off the field here.'

'Giles Turner,' whispered Ben. 'The original Farmer Giles.'

'But you've had the Regionals on your field before, haven't you?' called Libby.

The door to the snug opened and Giles stood there, check shirt, corduroy trousers and unbuttoned tweed waistcoat making him look as if he'd just stepped out of the wardrobe department of a television drama.

'I have,' he said, glowering at Libby. 'But only on sufferance. They were a bliddy nuisance, truth be told.'

'Oh.' Libby subsided back into her chair. Bob and Tom went and joined Baz at the bar, and joined the conversation between the saloon and the public. As they did so, the door from the reception area opened and Nigel and Dick came in, followed by Ian.

'Thank you, both,' said Ian formally, and shook hands. 'And thank you, Libby. I'll be in touch.'

Libby opened her mouth to speak, but was forestalled by Ian frowning over at the bar.

'What's happening there?'

'They're chatting,' said Ben. 'That's what people do in pubs.'

That earned him a scathing look. 'They're talking about the murder of Clive Eddington.'

'For goodness' sake – why shouldn't they?' asked Peter. 'It happened here – among them. Of course

258

they'll talk about it.'

'What have you been doing, Libby?'

Libby went pink despite the fact that she hadn't, for once, done a thing. 'Nothing to do with me. They're villagers. I'm still not quite a villager.'

Dick grinned. 'I know what you mean. Neither am I.'

'They say it takes at least fifty years,' said Nigel, with an answering grin.

Ian gave them all a disgusted look and left.

'There,' said Ben. 'Now we've upset the constabulary. Anyone for another drink?'

'What are they talking about?' asked Dick. 'I've got a drink waiting in there, but I don't want to barge in.'

'Oh, Baz wanted to know if the police had talked to everyone who was left behind on the field when the victim was murdered,' said Peter. 'We know you were there, helping Fran and Libby.'

Dick nodded. 'There were several of us. But I've been through all this with the police.'

'What about people who were left sleeping it off on the field?' asked Libby.

'I thought we got rid of them?'

'I thought we did, too, but Baz said he thought there were some left. And Giles Turner said the Regionals were a nuisance – although they weren't in his field that night.'

'Hang on,' said Dick. 'Now I'm lost. Regionals? I thought we talked about them the first time DCI Connell spoke to me. In here.'

'We did. It sounds as though we might have missed a couple, although I didn't see anyone when we came in the next day,' said Ben. 'And Giles is the farmer -'

259

'I know who Giles is,' said Dick. 'I don't see what he's got to do with anything.'

'No, neither do I,' said Peter.

Dick went back to the public bar, where, by the sound of his welcome he was roundly teased about his interview with the police. Baz, Tom and Bob came back to the table and sat down.

'Interesting,' said Baz. 'A lot of them weren't spoken to by the police at all.'

'Really? Do you mean the people who were at the festival, or the people helping clear up.'

'Mainly the people helping clear up.'

'No one seems to have noticed anyone in particular hanging about when they all left,' said Tom. 'But there seems to be divided opinion about the Regionals.'

'Isn't that normal for bikers?' said Libby. 'Some people hate them on principle.'

'True,' said Tom.

'Well, I think I shall go and see Edna again,' said Libby. 'See if she can shed any light.'

'She couldn't last time,' said Ben.

'Different question,' said Libby, lifting her glass.

The following morning Libby phoned Fran.

'It's Saturday,' said Fran. 'I'm helping in the shop.'

'But I thought things had quietened down now?'

'It's still the busiest day, in season or out of it. And since the internet business has taken off there's always packing to do.'

Libby, who was rather vague as to the exact nature of internet business and hadn't even caught up with supermarket deliveries, despite living in a rural community, made an indeterminate but disappointed sound.

'Anyway, what did you want?'

'I'm going to see Edna again.'

'What for?'

Libby explained about the impromptu session in the pub.

'I don't think you ought to bother her again,' said Fran. 'She couldn't tell us anything last time, really, could she?'

'This is different.'

'She's not likely to say anything that could place any of her friends in a difficult situation, is she? And she said she couldn't see anything from her tent.'

'She said she saw Clive – Wayne – talking to someone, didn't she?'

'She couldn't identify them, though.'

'No... Do you think I could phone her?'

'I think she might resent it.'

'Oh.'

'Look Lib, Ian is obviously still working on both cases, and I think all you're likely to do is put people's backs up.'

'OK.' Libby sighed. 'I'll try and concentrate on something else, then.'

'Your trouble is you don't have a job,' said Fran. 'It's not as if you're retirement age yet.'

'I do my paintings!' said Libby indignantly.

'One every now and then,' said Fran. 'How much do they actually earn?'

'Not very much,' admitted Libby.

'And you're no longer a working actor.'

'I do a lot of work for the theatre,' said Libby.

'Now and then,' said Fran.

'All right, all right.' Libby sighed again. 'What do I do? Get a job?'

'Difficult in this day and age, especially at our age.

'I'm not that old!'

'No, but it's difficult everywhere these days.'

'So what do I do then? Unless we start a proper private investigation company, like I suggested before?'

'I doubt if we'd ever get a licence, and it would be a lot more hard work than what we do now. No, I think you should volunteer somewhere.'

'What, you mean a charity shop or something?'

'Something like that. Why don't you ask Bethany if she can think of anything? Perhaps you could do something for the residents of Maltby Close.'

Libby's heart sank as she contemplated this gloomy prospect. 'I'll think about it,' she said.

Saturday morning. Ben was out on what was left of the hop garden of the Manor estate with his estate manager and a visiting agronomist and hop producer. Libby sighed again, collected her old basket and decided to see if Beth was available.

No one was in at the vicarage on the corner of Allhallow's Lane, so she walked across to Maltby Close, past the church and up to the village hall, until so recently the venue for the police incident room. The door was locked, so Libby turned and began her walk back, when Bethany Cole appeared from the back of the church.

'Hello!' she called. 'What can I do for you?'

Libby brightened.

'I don't know, really. It was an idea of Fran's.'

Beth cocked her head on one side. 'A murder idea?'

'No. A keep-Libby-out-of-trouble idea.'

Beth laughed. 'Come and tell me all about it,' she said. 'We're serving teas in the narthex. Just the place for ideas.'

Chapter Thirty

Libby accepted a cup of tea and a slice of Victoria sponge, waved at Flo Carpenter who was presiding over a tea urn, and sat down at a table in the corner opposite Beth and a bookcase full of hymn books.

'What trouble are you in this time?' asked Beth.

'Oh, I'm not, not really, but this murder – well, both murders really – I can't find out anything about it, and it's bugging me. And Fran says as I haven't got a job, I should start volunteering.'

Beth frowned. 'You do quite a lot of that already, don't you? None of your work for the theatre is paid, is it?'

'No, but I suppose it's a bit hit and miss.'

'And you still paint – commercially.'

'Not that much,' admitted Libby.

'And Fran thinks if you had a job of some sort you wouldn't want to get involved in these murder cases?'

'That's the top and bottom of it.'

'I see her point, but isn't it a bit pot and kettle?'

'She's got a job. She helps Guy with the shop, and she's often in charge if he's painting or away on buying trips or at exhibitions. And she's trying to write again.'

'Again?'

'Oh, you didn't know us when she was taking creative

264

writing classes with Amanda George, did you? Our friend Rosie?'

'Now I'm confused,' said Beth. 'Rosie took classes? I've heard of Amanda George.'

'Rosie *is* Amanda George. She taught a term of creative writing classes which Fran attended. Then we did her a favour and she became a friend – and a bit of a liability. Anyway, Fran decided she'd have another go at writing and she's trying her hand at a novel. She won't let me see it though.'

'I should think not!' Bethany said. 'You wouldn't be objective.'

'I would!' Libby was indignant.

'No, you wouldn't. You'd pick huge great holes in it. Anyway, good for Fran. So part of the reason for suggesting you do voluntary work is to keep you out of her hair?'

'I suppose so.' Libby made a face. 'I expect I am a bit irritating.'

Bethany patted her hand. 'Only in the services of justice. Why did Fran suggest you came to me?'

'I suppose because you oversee a lot of voluntary services.'

'But they're all church-based, and you're not a churchgoer.'

'Do you have to be? What about the food banks? Don't they need people?'

'Libby, do you honestly see yourself working in a food bank sorting food donations? It would drive you bonkers, as well as upsetting you. Which is why I wouldn't suggest you go and work in an animal sanctuary either.'

'Ooh, no, I couldn't do that.' Libby shuddered. 'Pretty useless then, am I?'

'No, of course not. I would have said that the work you do with the theatre is as valuable as anything else – and you raise money for charity. Also – think of the crimes you've helped solve. That's work, too, isn't it?'

'No, it's interfering.' Despite herself, Libby laughed. 'But I can't seem to help it.'

'Where have the police got so far?' asked Bethany. 'I quite liked having them here.'

'I'm not absolutely sure,' said Libby, 'but they have placed the second victim here a couple of days after the first. I saw him, and his car was parked in Lendle Lane. Two people saw that – Dr Peasegood and Dick Fowler from the photography shop.'

'What sort of car was it – and is it important?'

'Well, yes. He was found in the boot of it a day later.'

Bethany made a face. 'What was it?'

'A yellow Volvo estate.'

'Yellow?' Beth looked surprised. 'A big squared-off sort of thing?'

'That's it. Why, did you see it?'

'Yes, I did – and I'm surprised the police didn't. It drove round the back of here.'

'Round the *back*? How?'

'Although Lendle Lane looks like a dead end, it leads onto a track which skirts the wood and comes out behind the village hall, across a field and joins up with the Nethergate Road, although I can't imagine anyone wanting to do it. All right for a four-by-four, but no good for an ordinary car. Anyway, I saw it. I'm 'surprised the police didn't.'

'That explains why I saw it coming from that direction in the high street,' said Libby. 'I'll tell Ian, but I don't suppose it helps. Oh,' she paused as another thought struck her. 'Ian was asking Patti if she'd ever heard of something called chaos magic. Have you?'

Bethany's face changed.

'Yes. Don't touch it.'

Startled, Libby drew back. 'I wasn't going to! Why?'

'What do you know about it?'

Libby explained what they had found out so far without mentioning the Clive Eddington/Wayne Fulmore connection.

'Right.' Beth looked down at her feet. 'Look, I don't feel comfortable talking about it in here. Come outside.'

Libby followed Beth outside into the graveyard and on into Maltby Close. The vicar paced slowly, head bent, hands clasped behind her back.

'Before I came here I did an interregnum at a church the other side of Canterbury. It was before this post came up and just after I'd finished my curacy.'

Suddenly, Libby knew what was coming.

'The reason I was sent there was because the former parish priest was in jail.'

Libby let out a long breath. 'Don't tell me – he'd been part of this strange brotherhood, or whatever it was.'

Beth looked sideways at her. 'Yes. What else do you know?'

Libby told her about the strange case of The Dolphin in Dungate.

'I remember that. I was taken there not long after I

arrived by some parishioners who were only too keen to show me all the places that had figured in the case. Their case.' She looked up. 'There were others all over the country of course, but I somehow guessed this would be what you were talking about. I did a lot of reading up about it afterwards – and very unpleasant it was too. Pseudo-religious, part Satanism, part witchcraft, taking the worst and most depraved elements from everything, including their own imaginative touches.'

'So I gathered,' murmured Libby.

'Of course, it was all over when I went there, although some of the trials were still going on. But a lot of it was kept under wraps, especially a particularly nasty one about child murder.' She looked quickly at Libby. 'And that's what you're concerned with, isn't it?'

Put on the spot, Libby could only nod.

Beth sighed. 'I don't suppose you can tell me anything else, so I won't ask, but if you or your Ian want to ask *me* anything, I'll do my best. I'm sure the diocese would want to keep it as far under wraps as possible, but I'm afraid you can't, with this sort of thing.'

'Would you rather tell me or Ian?'

'Both of you together rather than have to go through it more than once,' said Beth with a small smile. 'Let me know if and when.'

Impulsively, Libby leant forward and kissed her on the cheek. 'Thank you, Beth. I'll call you, shall I?'

Bethany nodded, and Libby watched as she turned and walked slowly back to the church, cassock swinging around her feet.

Libby sent Ian yet another text - *Bethany has*

something to tell us re murder. Both of us. - then set off to the Pink Geranium to treat herself to lunch.

Peter was on the sofa in the left-hand window, newspapers spread over the coffee table in front of him.

'Ah – it's the old trout.' He moved some of the papers aside and brandished a cafetière. 'Join me?'

Libby sat in the armchair. 'Go on, then. I actually came in for lunch. Well, soup and a roll.'

'Ben off gallivanting?'

'Researching this hop garden idea of his.'

Harry appeared with a mug. 'Have you come in for a reason, petal? Not that you need one, but you've usually got one.'

'No, I just fancied lunch.'

'When you've finished the coffee you can both be guinea pigs for the new soup, then.' Harry gave a theatrical wink and sauntered off to the kitchen.

'No reason?' Peter sent her a quizzical look.

Libby sighed. 'Not really. Fran told me I need a job, so I ought to start volunteering. I went to see Bethany.'

'That's an odd thing for Fran to say.'

'Well, she's got her own life now, hasn't she? I think I'm a bit of a thorn in her side.'

Peter looked shocked. 'You can't say that! Why, you two have been like salt and pepper for years.'

'More like chalk and cheese these days,' said Libby. 'She's always been calmer and less impulsive than me, and what with the shop and Guy, and now her writing...'

'Writing?'

'She's gone back to it. Remember she took classes with Rosie years ago?' Peter nodded. 'She's started again.'

269

'Not classes with Rosie, I hope?'

'No, writing a novel. So I'm a bit in the way.'

Peter looked thoughtful. 'She hasn't had any of her "moments" recently, has she?'

'No, she hasn't. Well, not to my knowledge, anyway. I quite miss them.'

'And they were often what gave the police the final solution, weren't they?'

'Yes. What are you getting at?'

'Do you think she feels she's nothing to add these days, so she'd rather stay out of things?'

'Maybe.' Libby looked doubtful. 'But she's always been a much more logical thinker than I am.'

'Look, my darling.' Peter leant forward and took her hands. 'You have to bear in mind that this hobby of chase the murderer is just that. You aren't a detective, private or otherwise, and neither is Fran. Perhaps she's just realised it's time to hang up the handcuffs.'

'I know.' Libby shifted uncomfortably. 'Anyway, I don't really think I'm the volunteering type.'

'What you do at the theatre is voluntary, isn't it?'

'That's what Beth said.'

'You told Beth, then?'

'Yes. She said she wouldn't recommend me to work in a food bank.'

Peter threw back his head and roared.

'It's not that funny!' said Libby, rather hurt.

'Oh, it is! Was she scared you'd eat all the donations?'

Libby giggled in spite of herself. 'No – she said I was too soft-hearted.'

Harry's lunchtime waiting help arrived with two

270

large mugs on a tray.

'He said it was easier to have mugs while you were sitting here,' said the boy. 'Is that all right?'

'Fine,' said Libby, taking a mug and sniffing at it. 'Do you know what it is?'

The boy shook his head. 'No. An experiment, he said.'

'Could be anything,' said Peter. 'I think I'll let it cool down first.'

Libby put her mug down on the coffee table. 'So you think I should just give up on this murder, do you?'

'Ian will tell you anything you're allowed to know. He'll probably do his usual Poirot-like gathering at the end of the case anyway. I think it helps him unwind.'

'But suppose I find out something that could be important?'

'Why? Are you still poking around?'

'N-no, not exactly.' Libby picked up the soup mug and blew on it. 'But people tell me things.'

'Who's told you something now?' Peter squinted suspiciously at her over the top of his own mug.

'Beth.'

'Beth?' Peter's eyebrows shot up. 'What on earth could she have to tell you?'

'She saw the Volvo estate.' Libby wasn't quite ready to share Beth's other information.

'Where? In the village?'

Libby told Peter about the track from the bottom of Lendle Lane.

'Yes, I knew about that, but I thought it had fallen in disuse years ago. How do you get across the field to the Nethergate Road?'

'I don't know – is there a track there too?'

'Alongside the hedge, yes, there used to be. Sounds as though he didn't want to be seen, doesn't it?'

'There, you see – you're interested too!' said Libby in triumph, 'and we didn't go looking for it.'

Peter grinned reluctantly. 'I'll give you that.'

At that moment, Libby's phone rang.

Chapter Thirty-one

'So what's the Reverend Bethany got to tell us?' said Ian curtly.

'Something about chaos magic and Wayne Fulmore, I think.'

Ian sighed. 'Can I send someone else?'

'She wants to tell us both together. She doesn't want to go through it twice.'

'Really?' Ian's tone has sharpened. 'Any ideas?'

'I don't want to talk about it over the phone,' said Libby with dignity, and Peter pulled a face at her.

'When can we speak to her?'

'I'll call and ask her. Weekends are her busy time. She might have a wedding today, and she'll be dashing off somewhere first thing tomorrow for early service – Steeple Mount, I think.'

'So we have to wait until Monday?' Ian made an exasperated sound.

'She's volunteering the information,' said Libby. 'Don't knock it.'

'I wasn't!' Ian sounded surprised. 'I'll ring her then, shall I? And let you know?'

'Thank you, yes. Have you got her number?'

'Libby, I'm a policeman,' said Ian, and rang off.

'That went well,' said Peter.

Libby shrugged. 'I'm not getting involved.'

'Oh, yes, I remember. You're going to go a-volunteering.'

'Look, I can't help it. I didn't ask for the information Bethany just gave me, but I had to pass it on to Ian.'

'But you didn't tell him about the Volvo,' said Peter.

'Oh, no.' Libby felt herself going pink.

'The other information's more important, isn't it?'

'Well, yes.' Libby picked up her soup mug again. 'This soup's nice.'

Peter smirked and didn't answer.

Libby was on her way home when Ian rang for the second time.

'Are you free this afternoon? Bethany hasn't got a wedding today, although she's got one tomorrow, she tells me.'

'Yes, I'm free. What time and where?'

'The vicarage at three?'

'Fine. I'll be there.' Libby switched off her phone.

When she got home, she called Ben's mobile from the landline.

'So I won't be home until fourish, I should think,' she concluded. 'I didn't know exactly where you were.'

'Standing outside the hoppers' huts,' said Ben. 'You know we've never pushed these hard enough, have we?'

'Well, no.' The hoppers' huts and the family-owned Steeple Farm were all designated holiday lets, although nothing very much had been done with them, and Steeple Farm tended to be a temporary refuge for anyone needing a bolthole.

'We could do more with them. And if we get the hop garden up and running it would be great to have

274

accommodation on the site.'

'What – for workers?'

'No! For tourists.'

'Oh,' said Libby.

'You don't sound very enthusiastic.'

'I'm thinking about what Bethany's going to tell us.'

'Oh, I'm sorry. Is this new information?'

'I think so. I would rather she just told Ian, frankly, but she said she wanted to tell us both together.'

'You'd only have pestered him to know what it was.'

'Yes...' Libby frowned at Sidney who had approached looking hopeful.

'OK – well, you can tell me all about it when you get in. I'll see you then.'

Libby switched off the phone and scowled again at Sidney. 'It is not time for food and you've already got some anyway.'

She wandered out into the conservatory and stared at the empty easel. Should she try and up her output of Interesting Views of Nethergate? Was it worth it? She was aware that she was very lucky to sell any work at all, and certainly, without Guy's gallery-shop, she wouldn't be able to. He had some of the paintings reproduced as postcards, which didn't sell terribly well these days, as few people sent them, and had been contemplating producing a calendar, but she couldn't see that as a significant income. Although it wasn't an income she was thinking about, was it? It was occupation. She had been able to invest a considerable portion of the money she received from the old marital home, and this provided a satisfactory income, provided she wasn't extravagant.

Ben, of course, now contributed to household expenses, but, as she frequently said, she had no intention of becoming a kept woman. Hard, in Ben's opinion, if you were the owner of the home.

Just before three o'clock, she left number seventeen to walk the hundred yards or so to the corner of Allhallow's Lane and the vicarage. Ian's car, she noticed, was already parked outside.

Bethany showed her into the kitchen at the back of the house, where Ian was sitting at the large table wearing his best forbidding expression. Libby looked at Beth and made a face.

'Tea, Libby?' asked Beth. 'I've made a pot, especially in your honour.'

'In that case it would be churlish to refuse,' said Libby with a grin, hoping to diffuse the situation. Ian's expression didn't relax.

When they were settled, Beth and Libby with cups of tea and Ian with nothing, he began.

'I gather that you have told Libby you know something of the case we are investigating.' He fixed Beth with a baleful eye. 'I must warn you not to discuss this with anyone outside this room when we've finished.'

'But inside it I can discuss what I like?' said Beth calmly.

Ian looked furious for a moment, then his natural good humour reasserted itself and he gave a reluctant grin. 'Very well, Vicar. Carry on.'

'It's either Bethany or Beth,' said Beth. 'On no account call me Reverend.' She leant forward and put her elbows on the table. 'First of all, I told Libby I had seen

276

the yellow Volvo you've been investigating leaving Lendle Lane and going round the back of the churchyard into the Nethergate Road.'

Ian had to have the topography explained to him. 'That's why I saw him coming from that direction,' said Libby. I couldn't work out why, if he'd been in Lendle Lane – normally, he would have turned round and gone straight into the Canterbury Road and not come through the village.'

Ian nodded. 'And then what, Bethany?'

'I don't know how much Libby's told you, but before I came here, I did a interregnum at a parish the other side of Canterbury. The reason for this was the vicar –'

'Thomas Elliot,' broke in Ian, 'was on trial for offences committed while a member of a so-called chaos magic group.'

'You knew!' Bethany's eyes widened.

'Not that you were there,' said Ian. 'We're only just finding our way into all the offences committed under their aegis. Is there anything you can tell us?'

'Only a little. I was taken to The Dolphin at Dungate by some of the parishioners, and I had various people pointed out as having figured in the scandal. One was a woman called Evelyn Fulmore.'

'She was put on trial, wasn't she?' asked Ian.

'Yes – although I wasn't entirely sure of all the details. You've got to remember it all happened before I got there, and I expect you could find all this out for yourself.'

'If we knew what we were looking for,' said Ian, with one of his nicest smiles, and Libby breathed a sigh of relief.

'All I knew was that in the parish's eyes, the worst of her crimes was "corrupting a minor".'

'Ah!' Ian breathed out the word with satisfaction. 'And this was to do with her son?'

'With her sons, yes.' Beth looked down. 'You see, one twin had killed the other.'

'Yes. Wayne killed his brother Stephen.'

'You did know.' Beth looked up accusingly.

'We knew that – it's a matter of public record – but little more. Why he did it, for a start, although there's much speculation.'

'Apparently – and this is only gossip from the parish – his mother encouraged it as part of the ritual part of this chaos magic. Which, incidentally,' Beth drew herself upright in her chair, 'has been completely debunked by the Church.'

'I'm not surprised,' said Ian. 'Go on.'

'Well, there isn't much more. Evelyn Fulmore never came back to the town after she was released from prison. She didn't serve a long term, and I only heard vaguely that she was out. I believe she changed her name.'

'As did Wayne, although his was changed for him,' said Ian.

Bethany went pale. 'Was that the boy in the Volvo?'

'No, the boy who was killed at the festival,' said Libby gently.

'Oh, how awful!' Beth's hands flew to her face.

'What happened to the father?' asked Ian.

Beth looked surprised. 'Do you know, I've no idea! I assume there was one, but I never heard of him.'

'His name was Raymond,' said Ian. 'So he wasn't

278

implicated in any of the – what shall I call them? - witch trials.'

'Not that I heard.'

'So he disappeared, too,' said Libby.

'Wouldn't you?' said Ian. 'Well, thank you, Beth. That was very interesting.'

'But not as revelatory as you'd hoped,' said Beth. 'You knew most of it.'

'But not all of it, and you've connected some dots for us. By the way, you don't remember what either of the Fulmore parents did for a living, do you? It might help to track them down.'

Bethany shook her head. 'No idea. But I am in touch with the current priest over there. I could ask him – privately, of course. He might be able to find out.'

'We might take you up on that,' said Ian, with another smile. 'Meanwhile, I'll try and find out myself.' He stood up. 'Thank you again for the information – I'll see myself out.'

He left them sitting at the table, and they heard the front door close behind him.

'Why was he so cross at the beginning?' asked Beth.

'He doesn't like me interfering, and he thought that's what I'd been doing.'

'But you've helped in the past, haven't you? You and Fran?'

'The police don't approve of members of the public trying to solve their crimes for them.'

'Hmm.' Beth sat back in her chair and gazed reflectively at the table. 'So what's to prevent me asking the priest I'm in touch with just for interest's sake?'

'Nothing.' Libby looked up, surprised.

Beth grinned. 'Let's do it, then.'

'I thought you were uncomfortable with the situation?'

'With the appalling crimes, yes. But I want murder to be punished as much as you do.' She leant forward. 'Do you think that's what this murder was, then? Punishment?'

Libby frowned. 'The first one? It could be, I suppose. We were puzzled about it because if it had been that he was recognised as Wayne Fulmore he would have been more likely to kill than be killed.'

'And what about the second one? The poor boy in the yellow Volvo? Could he have been a witness? Seen something suspicious?'

'Yes ... and threatening to tell. So he had to be shut up.'

'Well, I suppose your Ian's team will have thought of that. They'll be trying to find out who saw the car, and when, won't they?'

'But it was in Canterbury. Not quite such a limited field as Steeple Martin.'

'No,' said Bethany. 'Well, shall I call my friend?'

'Who? Oh, the priest. Why not. Are you going to do it now?'

'I thought so.' Bethany stood up and retrieved her phone from the dresser. 'I hope I've still got the number.'

Libby tried not to listen as Beth exchanged greetings with the priest, whom she hadn't seen for some time, it transpired. Then:

'Yes, that's right, it was. Actually, Matthew, that was one of the reasons I was ringing. Yes – no, nothing to do with that! No, but you remember the scandal that was actually the reason both you and I were shipped in? Well, I don't suppose you've heard any follow-up?'

Matthew obviously spoke for some time. Beth made several expressive faces at Libby.

'Where?' she said eventually. 'Really? So close? I wonder she didn't go further away? And the father?'

A few minutes later she ended the call.

'Well!' she said coming back to the table. 'That was interesting.'

'What was?'

'Evelyn Fulmore is still in the area.'

Chapter Thirty-two

'What?'

'She's in Ashford – or on the outskirts. And she's still Evelyn Fulmore, believe it or not.'

'Bloody hell!' said Libby. 'Sorry, Beth. And you asked about the father?'

'I did, but apparently he moved away and nothing's been heard of him since. But whatever possessed the mother to come back to the area?'

'Perhaps she didn't want to move right away from the area because all her family were here?'

'But after what she did would her family acknowledge her?'

'I don't know. So what do we do now?'

'I don't know. What would you and Fran do?'

'Look her up, I suppose.' She stopped and thought for a moment. 'Do you think Ian already knew this?'

'I would have thought he must have done,' said Beth. 'If he'd got the information that the boy was really Wayne Fulmore, he would have got all the relevant information, wouldn't he?'

'Thinking about it, that could be the reason he was cross,' said Libby. 'Us coming up with something he already knew. But how could we have known?'

'He doesn't know the parent's jobs, though, does he?

He asked me about that. I forgot to ask Matthew.'

'I'll go home and have another look on the internet for Evelyn Fulmore,' said Libby. 'I wonder why she didn't change her name? You thought she had, didn't you?'

'I'd heard that she had. Can't remember where, though.'

'Well, I bet the police know everything we've – or you've – told them today.'

'Except that I saw the yellow Volvo.'

Libby sighed. 'But I don't suppose that actually helped. They already knew he was here, and both I and Dick Fowler saw it, too.'

She stood up. 'Well, thank you, Beth. At least I've got something to look into, even if Ian knew it all already. That's the trouble with the police. They don't tell you anything.'

Libby wandered back up Allhallow's Lane thinking hard. Although interesting, Bethany's information hadn't helped towards finding out who murdered either Clive Eddington or Danny Coleman.

To her surprise, Ian appeared on the doorstep of number seventeen half an hour later.

'Hello?' she said, standing aside to let him in.

'How much have you told Bethany about the police investigation?' He remained on the doorstep.

'Almost nothing.'

'Then why did she volunteer this information?'

Libby sighed. 'Look, come in and sit down. I do not want to stand here having an argument.'

Reluctantly, Ian stepped inside and Libby closed the door.

'Now,' she said. 'Beth found me wandering about near the church this morning.'

'Why? What were you doing there?'

Libby fixed him with a baleful eye. 'None of your business.'

'Yes, it is.'

'All right – I was on my way to see Beth about volunteering, if you must know.' Libby lifted her chin and Ian began to laugh. 'Yes, I know, laughable. But Fran – of all people – thought it might keep me out of trouble.'

'All right, go on.' Ian looked more relaxed now. 'Then what?'

'Beth took me into the narthex for a cup of tea and we talked about it. Then she asked whether I'd heard anything about the investigation, and said she'd quite liked having you here. So I said I hadn't, except that we'd seen the yellow Volvo. I thought she would have heard about that, but she hadn't, and then she told me about seeing it drive round the back of the hall and the churchyard. Then I simply asked her if she knew anything about chaos magic, and she went all serious and told me what had happened in her old parish. So I told you. And that,' she finished, glaring at him, 'is all.'

Ian sighed. 'Thank you, Libby. You can't blame me for wondering, can you?'

'Maybe,' said Libby, unwilling to concede anything. 'Anyway, you knew about everything Beth told you already, didn't you?'

'Most of it. Once we had permission to look into Wayne Fulmore's life it all came to light. His mother was convicted of various offences, but by the time she came to

284

trial, Stephen had already been murdered and there was a certain amount of sympathy for her. Consequently, she received a lighter sentence than she might otherwise have done. She is, incidentally, not living far away.'

'I know,' said Libby morosely. 'Ashford.'

'How do you know?' Ian narrowed his eyes at her.

'The priest who took over from Beth at that church told her.'

'And did he tell her that she's still living under her own name?'

'Evelyn Fulmore – yes.'

'Actually that isn't quite right. She's reverted to her maiden name.'

'What's that?' asked Libby.

'Why do you want to know?'

'Just wondered.'

'You might be surprised.'

'Why?' Now it was Libby's turn to be suspicious.

Ian leant back in his chair, crossed his legs and steepled his fingers. 'Coleman,' he said.

Libby almost leapt to her feet. '*Coleman*?'

'Danny's aunt on his father's side.'

Libby opened and shut her mouth a couple of times and Ian laughed again.

'You see, we do get there without you sometimes, Lib.'

'Oh, I know, you always do. So now you know who the murderer is as well, I suppose?'

'Not quite. As I said earlier, I could bear to know what both Fulmores did for a living. I do know what Evelyn did – and what she does now. But I have no idea about Raymond.'

285

'So what does Evelyn do?'

'She's a hairdresser and beautician. She works from home and goes to clients' houses. The local force keep an eye on her.'

'Tell me more about the Coleman connection.'

'Nothing much to tell. And aren't you going to offer me tea?'

Libby stood up. 'Didn't you have enough at Beth's?'

'I can always drink more.' He grinned at Libby.

When Libby returned from the kitchen with two mugs, Ian was scrolling through his smartphone.

'No further news,' he said. 'I checked for you.'

Libby handed him a mug.

'I knew Danny and Wayne were friends at primary school. The owner of the hop garden we went to visit told us, but there was obviously a family connection too.'

Ian nodded. 'And it makes me wonder why Danny didn't say anything when we questioned him. He must have recognised Wayne.'

'Perhaps he didn't. After all, he was – what, when he last saw him? Eleven? People change a lot. Or if he did, perhaps he didn't want to say as it would have looked suspicious.'

'Perhaps.'

'But they were cousins...' Libby shook her head. 'Did you find out any more about the whole chaos magic thing? And Stephen's murder?'

'As far as we can find out, as usual, the whole chaos magic cult is a convenient blanket to throw over a lot of reprehensible behaviour. "Do what you will" appears to be their motto. This particular crowd wore hooded robes and indulged in ceremonies around a fire – all very familiar. They derived their practices from various different sources – there are mentions of Astaroth, Hecate, Ba'al and Belial, and even Druid worship.'

'They seem rather confused,' commented Libby.

'Oh, they were, very. But young Wayne used to spy on them, and eventually his mother confided in him to a degree. According to transcripts of some of the interviews, he was convinced that if he killed his brother he would become cleverer, stronger and able to protect his mother.'

'From what?'

'She apparently told him he had to keep it a secret because people were out to harm her. Which was true, in a way.'

'I expect,' Libby mused, 'it got worse when Stephen passed the Kent Test and Wayne didn't.'

'Ah! Now that I didn't know. Did you get that from the hop grower, too?'

'No, Fran found it on the internet. There wasn't much information there, though. I suppose that was because of the UKPPS?'

'And because he was a minor.'

'So we know quite a lot about the background now,' said Libby, 'but nothing that would lead us to the murderer.'

'Yes, "we" do, don't we?' said Ian, amused.

'What about Fiona and Tracey? And Jenny?'

'I can't say they were very clear, any of them, as far as I can tell. I didn't see any of them. But it would appear that Jenny was far closer than she told you originally to

287

Clive, as she knew him. He recruited her into what he hoped would be a recreation of his mother's cult. How his mental state wasn't picked up before his release I have no idea.'

'I wonder how Terry's coping with her? Perhaps I'd better ring and find out.'

'Don't start questioning the poor girl. Leave her to us.'

'It wasn't really very serious, though, was it?' Libby frowned at him. 'She was playing at it.'

'She certainly wasn't terribly upset about his death,' said Ian.

'You don't think she had anything to do with it?' Libby was shocked.

'She wasn't there, Libby.'

'But...' Libby stopped. 'She wasn't here when Danny was killed, either. And how would she have known about him, anyway? She's a fantasist, isn't she? Kidnapped, my eye!' She thought for a moment. 'So do you think the murderer was the same person? And was it someone who knew both Wayne and Danny as children? I suppose there must be a lot of them; after all, they lived in the same area – the same town? – went to the same school, Eastfields Primary, and they were cousins.'

Ian sat forward and put his mug down. 'Have you still got those papers you got from Dick Fowler's flat?'

'Yes. I don't think he wants them back.' Libby stood up and went to root around on the shelves by the fireplace. 'Here. They're all around the time of Wayne's trial. There isn't that much information in them, either.'

Ian had a cursory look through the top few of the pile. 'I wish I knew why these were there. Why these were

288

kept. Who lived there before Dick Fowler?'

'I asked Harry and Pete, and they weren't living here then. Neither was Ben. I haven't asked Flo or Hetty.'

'I could go to the Land Registry, I suppose.'

'He did say it was a photographic shop before he had it, didn't he? He found old negatives and slides there. I didn't see any of those upstairs.'

'I'm surprised you haven't googled it,' said Ian. 'Easy parameters, I'd have thought. "Photographic shop or studio Steeple Martin".'

'Shall we do it now?' asked Libby.

'No, I've no doubt you'll have great fun doing it after I've left.' Ian drained his mug. 'I am now going home, hopefully to have at least one day off this weekend.'

'You can always come to Hetty's for lunch tomorrow,' said Libby hopefully.

'Much as I love Hetty's roasts, I think I'd like to have a day clear of Steeple Martin.' He bent to kiss Libby's cheek. 'And next time you stumble over a murder, do it somewhere else.'

Libby took the mugs into the kitchen and put them in the dishwasher. So now she had more leads to follow, which was gratifying until she realised that it was only for her own amusement. The police had found out everything she had, and in fact made her feel a bit of a fool.

She went to the table in the sitting room window and pulled the laptop towards her. These days, she knew most people would be on their smartphones looking things up as they even thought of it, but so far, she hadn't caught up. Tablets she was familiar with, but smartphones, no. 'I haven't got the thumbs for it,' she told her children.

She typed the words Ian had suggested. "Photographic shop or studio Steeple Martin".

The first link, predictably was for Fowler's Photography.

The second was for the Steeple Martin Studio, est. 1911.

Proprietor: Edward Fulmore.

Chapter Thirty-three

'Look, Libby, I know it's a terrific coincidence, but that was back in 1911,' said Fran. Libby had been practically gibbering when she called her. 'It could have changed hands many times before the Fulmore scandal.'

'I know – but –'

'If you're worried, tell Ian. Although I expect he knows.'

'No, he doesn't, I'm sure. He's only just left.'

'Has he?' Fran's voice sharpened. 'Why was he there?'

Libby sighed. 'A few things have happened since I spoke to you this morning. Do you want to know about them or not?'

'Why wouldn't I?'

'I got the impression you'd had enough of going adventuring with me. Or, more precisely, you'd had enough of me.'

There was a silence at the other end of the phone. Libby waited as long as she could, and just as she took a deep breath, Fran spoke.

'I'm sorry it came across like that. Honestly, Lib, I'd be really upset to lose your friendship. Apart from Guy, you're the closest friend I've ever had.'

Embarrassed, Libby muttered an incoherent response.

Fran retrieved the situation.

'So what happened after we spoke, then?'

'Well, I went to see Beth, as you suggested.' Libby went on to tell Fran all about Beth's revelations, then about Ian's visits.

'Oh, and I saw Pete and Harry, too. I had guinea pig soup.'

'You had *what*?'

'It's what I call it. When Hal's testing a new recipe. He often tries it out on me.'

'Oh. And what did they have to say?'

'Hal didn't say a lot, he was busy in the kitchen. But Pete and Beth both said I did enough voluntary work without trying to do more.'

Fran sighed. 'That rankles – I'm sorry. Anyway, why did you decide to look up Dick's shop?'

'Ian wondered why I hadn't already done it. He was interested in why all those old papers had been kept. He even suggested the search parameters.'

'Why didn't you do it while he was there?'

'He said I could have fun doing it after he'd gone.'

'And you did.' Fran paused. 'So now you tell him what you found. You don't think you should ask Dick about it first?'

'I could, I suppose. Ask him who he bought the shop from.'

'He might nor even own it,' said Fran. 'He might be renting. He's got a house in Lendle Lane, hasn't he?'

'Yes. I thought that was rather convenient, because the back gardens join onto the backs of the high street buildings, including the shop. Dick says he can look straight into Lendle Lane from the windows of the flat. Well, I know you can, because I've been up there. And that's where he saw the Volvo from.'

Fran was silent for a moment. Then, she said, slowly, 'Just tell Ian what you've found. Send him a text if you think he might be driving.'

'He said he was going home,' said Libby. 'Do you think he'll want to be disturbed?'

'I think you should,' said Fran.

'What is it?' Libby was suddenly on high alert. 'Fran! What is it? What shall I do?'

'Just tell Ian,' said Fran. 'Ring me afterwards.'

'Not Dick? You don't want me to ask him after all?'

'No need,' said Fran. 'Go on, ring Ian *now*.' She ended the call.

Libby rang.

'Libby? What is it?' Libby could hear the surprise in Ian's voice. She could also hear Liszt in the background.

'Are you at home? I'm sorry,' she said. 'But Fran told me to ring you now.'

'Oh?' Ian's tone sharpened.

'She says I'm to tell you that Dick's shop was once called Steeple Martin Studios and it was owned by an Edward Fulmore.'

'*Fulmore?*'

'Yes. When I told her, she said it could have been bought and sold loads of times since 1911, but then she changed, and insisted I call you *now*.'

'She had one of her "moments",' said Ian.

'That's what it sounded like to me,' said Libby. 'She

hasn't had one for ages. What do you think it means?'

'I think,' said Ian, 'it means I'd better come back to Steeple Martin.' He sighed. 'I might just as well take up permanent residence with Hetty at the Manor.'

'Shall I do anything?' asked Libby.

'No. Just get on with whatever you were doing.'

And that's nothing, thought Libby, putting down her phone. As she did, the landline rang.

'Is that Libby Sarjeant?' asked a female voice.

'Yes. Who's this?'

'My name's Evelyn Coleman. I believe you found my son.'

It took several seconds for this to register. Then Libby was conscious of her heart picking up speed and her mouth going dry.

'Er –' was all she managed.

'Wayne Fulmore. I'm sure you know his real name by now.'

'Yes.' Libby's mind was searching frantically for reasons for this call and coming up with none.

'And you know about me. The police do, at any rate.'

'Yes.'

'And what about my – *husband*. Have you found him yet?' The voice was harsh and rasping.

'Er – no.' Libby swallowed. 'I don't know if the police have.'

'Oh, come on. I know all about you. I know all about your snooping at The Dolphin.'

'Do you?' Now Libby was at a complete loss.

'And I know you're hand-in-glove with the police. You and that friend of yours. If you know where my husband is you'd better tell me.'

'But I don't! And how did you find me?'

'You're in the phone book. You should go ex-directory, you know, if you don't want people you've annoyed coming after you.'

Stiffening what backbone she had left, Libby said: 'Why have I annoyed you?'

'Because you snoop. You pry. You're a nosy bitch.'

'Ms Coleman,' said Libby, adopting her best director's voice, 'I am very sorry about your son, and your nephew. All I have done is assist the police in their enquiries, which are ongoing in their search for the killer of Wayne and Danny.' She was quite proud of this speech.

'Then carry on assisting and find my fucking *husband*' roared Evelyn Coleman, and ended the call.

Libby immediately dialled 1471, which of course told her the number was withheld. Just as she was picking up the mobile phone to text Ian again, Ben came in through the back door.

'What's going on?'

'Eh?' said Libby. 'What do you mean?'

'I've just had Ian on the phone telling me to get back here. What have you done now?'

'I haven't done anything,' said Libby, bewildered. 'It's all been happening to me, I didn't do any of it.'

Ben now looked thoroughly confused. 'Why did Ian...'

'I don't know. Look, I've got to text him again. Something very strange just happened.'

Ben handed over his phone. 'Call him on that. He's expecting my call.'

'Libby!' Ian's voice sounded relieved.

295

'Yes. Now, why did you tell Ben to get back here? No, save that. I've got something else to tell you. I've just had a call from Evelyn Coleman.'

'You *what*?'

'You heard. Accusing me of snooping and asking where her husband was. What's going on?'

'Ah,' said Ian. 'That makes sense.'

'It does? Well, it doesn't to me.'

'I'll explain when I get to you. Just – be careful.' He rang off.

Libby turned to Ben. 'Why have I got to be careful?'

Ben opened his mouth just as there was a bang on the front door. Libby turned to open it, but Ben pushed past her. Dick Fowler stood on the step.

'Oh, hello, Ben,' he said. 'Is Libby in?' He peered past Ben and saw Libby standing open-mouthed behind him. 'Oh, yes. Libby, do you think I could have those newspapers back, please?'

And suddenly everything fell into place.

Chapter Thirty-four

'Newspapers?' said Libby. She cleared her throat. 'Oh, yes. I've got them right here.' She turned to pick them up from where Ian had left them.

'I thought you were up at the estate, Ben.' Dick had somehow got into the sitting room behind Libby.

'I was.'

'Thinking of turning it back into a hop garden, I'm told.'

Ben frowned. 'How –'

'Oh, I think Tim at the pub mentioned something,' said Dick vaguely. 'Thanks, Libby.' He smiled at them both and made for the door. 'It's been nice knowing you both.'

'What do you mean?' Ben was suddenly aggressive and blocked his way. 'Where are you going?'

'I have no idea at the moment,' said Dick calmly. 'But don't bother looking for me. And I wouldn't mention that you've seen me this afternoon, either, if you know what's good for you.' He turned to Ben, whose face had lost most of its colour. 'And try and keep that nosy bitch of yours under control. She'll cause serious trouble one of these days.'

The door flew open and Ian, at his most satanic, stood there with a uniformed officer behind him.

'Luckily for you, Fulmore,' he said, 'it's *your* serious trouble.'

'Fulmore?' gasped Ben.

Libby nodded wearily. 'I tumbled to it just now. This is Wayne's father, Raymond Fulmore.'

The newspapers had dropped to the floor, and Dick - Raymond - looked more like a rather weak village photographer than a deranged killer. Ian handed him over to the officer, and for the first time, Libby noticed the back up team of armed police.

'Goodness!' she said.

Ian grinned back. 'I'll have to take statements from you both, but that can wait. I'll get through this as soon as I possibly can, and unless you're doing anything special tonight, I'll join you later and explain.'

'Were we?' Ben asked Libby, who shook her head. 'In that case, we'll eat in the pub, and you can join us there.'

'I shall,' said Ian. 'Oh – and try not to talk about this until after I've arrived.'

'You mean don't tell anyone?' said Libby regretfully.

Ian looked stern. 'No, Libby.' He relented. 'Except Fran, of course.'

'And I don't suppose I should tell Evelyn Coleman I've found her husband, either?' she said mischievously.

Ben provided a large whisky 'for the shock', he said and Libby called Fran, who when informed of the revelations of the last hour announced her intention of joining them at the pub later.

'And you should ask Bethany, too,' she said. 'She'll be bursting with curiosity.'

And so it was that when Ian finally arrived just before ten o'clock, he found not only Libby and Ben, but Fran, Guy, Bethany and her husband, John, gathered round a table in the Lounge Bar. The Public and the Snug were packed with regulars, but somehow, Tim had managed to keep the lounge free.

'I hope you don't mind us being here,' said Bethany, as Ben and Guy arrived with a tray of drinks. 'Libby said it would be all right.'

Ian smiled at her. 'You gave us a lot of help,' he said.

'Most of which you already knew,' said Beth.

'Well, come on,' said Ben. 'Some of us don't.'

'First of all, Dick Fowler was, as you now know, Wayne Fulmore's father, Raymond. And putting it simply, when he came to the festival and saw Clive Eddington, he recognised him. He hadn't seen him since the murder of his twin, Stephen.' He looked across at John Cole. 'Are you following this, Mr Cole?'

'John, please.' He smiled. 'Yes, Beth told me all about it, after Libby explained it to her.'

'New recruits, Libby?' murmured Ian. 'Fine. So after the evening finished, Fowler hung around, hoping to find an opportunity to speak to his son.'

'But Ellis had packed up by then, they played the day before,' said Fran.

'They had, but Fowler assumed, rightly, that they would be staying at the site. As it happened Clive played right into his hands by coming back to the stage. We don't know why, but you remember Edna saw him go up and speak to someone? She thought they'd arranged to meet, but in fact, Fowler was poking around backstage to see if he could find anything that would tell him where Clive was.' He sighed. 'He's not saying much, but it appears he tried to ask the boy why he'd killed his brother and Clive laughed at him. And that was it. He broke down when he told us. It's clear that he was completely traumatized by the original events. And of course he blames his wife for all of it.'

'And Danny?' asked Fran.

'Danny recognised them both. He didn't know his uncle was living here –'

'His uncle?' chorused half the company.

'Oh, didn't Libby explain that? Yes, Clive's – or Wayne's – mother was Danny Coleman's father's sister – his aunt. She was sent down at the time of the original scandal, and is now living under her maiden name as a hairdresser in Ashford.'

'Blimey!' said Guy.

'Yes. So Danny, who had seen nothing except his uncle loitering around the festival field, decided there was more to that than met the eye. At least, that was what we assume. Fowler says he didn't see him, but Danny came round to his house on the Monday morning –'

'So that's where he saw him, not at the studio!' said Libby.

'Yes, and according to Fowler, "tried it on". Fowler, of course, denied it, but agreed to meet Danny in Canterbury.'

'That was stupid of Danny,' said Libby.

'I don't suppose he suspected Fowler of anything. He looks too mild to be a threat.'

'But he suspected him of killing Wayne.'

'Yes, but I expect he thought that was a crime of passion – which it was. Anyway, we'll never know.'

'So what about my phone call this afternoon from

300

Evelyn?' asked Libby. 'That made sense to you?'

'Somebody was stirring the pot,' said Ian. 'We suspect it was your friend Bernard from The Dolphin.'

'The gnome in the wheelchair!' said Libby.

'He not only knew the names of the Fulmore parents, he knew where they both were, although he didn't tell you that. We know Evelyn received a call this afternoon on her mobile, and that after that she called you. I rather think that he called Fowler, too. We'll ask him.'

'I wonder if he'll tell you,' said Libby.

'So all the other things were red herrings?' said Ben. 'The fake stage suppliers and the witchcraft angle.'

'Completely,' said Ian. 'Although we have rounded up the fake stage suppliers. Fowler said he drew the sigil to make us think it was the old cult that had come out of hiding if we found out who Clive really was, not to lead us to the truth.'

'I bet that annoyed him,' said Libby. 'And he was so helpful, wasn't he? With all the pictures and everything.'

'Did you find out what he used to do as a living?' asked Beth.

'Yes.' Ian smiled round at them all. 'He worked in the editing suite of a film post-production company.'

'So practically in the same business as he ended up,' said Libby. 'And whose was the studio?'

'His. His grandmother had lived there in the flat above the shop even after it was closed, which it was, for years. If anyone had checked we'd have found out who he was sooner.'

'She must have kept the newspapers because it was her grandson's family that were involved.' Fran shook her head. 'How tragic.'

'It's a very tragic story,' said Ian.

'And it's the two victims who really come out of it worse, isn't it?' said Beth, her face grave. 'They were both evil.'

'Dick was just a grieving father, really,' agreed Fran.

'Evelyn doesn't come out of it too well, either,' said Libby. 'Can't understand why she didn't change her name.'

'Perhaps she didn't think anyone would connect Evelyn Coleman to Evelyn Fulmore,' said Ben.

'Well,' said Ian. 'That's the story, and here, I think come two more people who'll want to hear it. I leave it to you.'

'Fancy meeting you here,' said Harry, as he wafted up with Peter in his wake. ' I have a suspicion that we've walked in on a dénouement, dear heart.' He poked Libby's shoulder. 'And you're going to tell us all about it, aren't you?'

'Don't mind him,' said Libby with a sigh to Beth and John, who laughed.

'Ah!' Harry bestowed a sweet smile on them. 'And we've got two new members of Libby's Loonies, I see! Welcome to the madhouse.'

**Have a sneak preview of the next book in
the Libby Sarjeant Murder Mystery series**

Murder and the Glovemaker's Son

Lesley Cookman

Out 2019

Chapter One

'But,' asked Libby Sarjeant, 'is there any real proof that they came to Steeple Martin?'

The young man on the other side of the table almost bounced in his chair, and a lank lock of mousy hair fell forward over his eyes. He pushed it away impatiently.

'Yes, there is – I've actually seen it!' He looked at the other people seated round the pub table, his light blue eyes shining. Although that was probably incipient myopia, thought Libby.

Peter Parker, sitting next to Libby, his long legs stretched out before him and his own blonde hair more artistically draped across his brow, was frowning disbelievingly. 'And there are no other records anywhere? After all, the various tours were quite well recorded – Maidstone, Hythe, Fordwich, New Romney – but I don't recall any mention anywhere of Steeple Martin.'

His cousin Ben Wilde, Libby's significant other, leant his elbows on the table and bent an amused glance at the young man. 'And where, exactly, did you see this proof?'

A faint colour rose up onto the young man's pale cheeks. 'Well, I'm not actually allowed to say yet. You see, it's being investigated by people at the V&A –'

'Like Hamnet's Glove,' said Libby, apparently irrelevantly.

In the sudden silence, the three men turned to look at Libby.

'Well, that was investigated by experts at the V&A, too. Being a Shakespearian relic.'

Both Ben and the young man frowned.

'I've never heard of it,' said Ben.

'Then your education is sadly lacking,' said Peter with a laugh. 'Does Hamnet not ring a bell, Ben?'

'I know!' The young man's face lit up. 'Hamnet! He was Shakespeare's son who died when he was – what? – ten?'

'That's him,' said Peter.

'And you mean to say – ' the young man was now breathless ' – there's a *glove*? Where? How do I not know about it?'

Libby laughed. 'Don't get excited! Hamnet's real, but his glove isn't. It's part of a plot by Ngaio Marsh.'

'Who?' By now the young man was looking completely bewildered. Peter took pity on him and patted his hand.

'One of the longer lasting Golden Age detective writers. In fact that particular book was late sixties, wasn't it, Lib?'

She nodded. 'And one of my favourites. But I'm sorry, I interrupted.'

'That's all right.It's rather interesting, especially with our own mystery.' The young man swallowed the last of his coffee. 'Well – that's it, really. We would love to bring the tour here and include it in the publicity. After all, it's a National Shakespeare production, so very prestigious. And you never know, by the time it actually comes here we might be able to produce the actual documentary proof.'

'If the V&A lets it out of their sight,' said Libby.

'Did you know,' said Peter, after they had waved off their visitor and ordered more drinks from Tim the landlord, 'that there was actually some debate about whether there actually *was* a glove?'

'When?' Libby was incredulous. 'Don't be daft. I'd have known.'

'Why would you?' Ben put down glasses on the table.

'I just would,' said Libby. 'How do you know, Pete?'

'It was in my early days at Reuters. One of the stories I was sent off to research – but nothing came of it.'

Peter had worked for the international news agency for years, until he went freelance, a job which gave him the freedom to indulge his passion for theatre with Libby and Ben at their Oast Theatre, and to help when necessary at the little restaurant he owned with his partner Harry, the *chef patron*.

'Oh, that's a shame,' said Libby. 'Think what a scoop that would have been! Was Ngaio Marsh still alive then?'

'You should know,' said Ben. 'You're the fan.'

'Yes, she was, thinking about it. Early 80s she died, didn't she?'

'I don't know!' said Ben and Peter together.

'So what do we do about young Tristan's offer?' said Peter. 'Do we let them come?'

'I don't see how we can say no to National Shakespeare,' said Libby. 'And he might be right. They might be allowed to use the document, whatever it is, in the publicity – and think what a coup that would be!'

***

Steeple Martin, Nethergate and their denizens – an introduction

Steeple Martin is in Kent, although you won't find it on a map. It is somewhere to the south east of Canterbury, and Nethergate is a few miles further along on the coast. Set around these towns are villages – the other two Steeples, Steeple Mount and Steeple Cross, Heronsbourne, Cherry Ashton, Shott and Bishops Bottom among others. Along the coast northwards lies St Aldeberge, and in the other direction, on the edge of the marshes, sits Creekmarsh, the ancient house and gardens owned by television handyman Lewis Osbourne-Walker.

Libby Sarjeant and her siver tabby cat, Sidney, live in Steeple Martin, at number 17, Allhallow's Lane. Her partner, Ben Wide, lives with her, while his mother Hetty lives at the Wilde family home, The Manor. Next to the Manor stands the oast house which was once the heart of the Wilde family hop garden. Ben, an architect, drew up plans to convert it into a theatre, and Libby and Ben's cousin Peter Parker are directors of the management company.

Peter is a freelance journalist who lives with his partner, Harry Price, in a cottage on Steeple Martin High Street. They own The Pink Geranium restaurant also on the high street, of which Harry is chef patron, whose specialities include Chimichangas, Nachos Grande, Black Bean Tostadas, Heuevos Rancheros, Harry's Hot Pickled Vegetables and Smokey Stuffed Peppers. In the flat above the restaurant lives Adam, Libby's younger son, who works as an assistant landscape gardener and occasional waiter for Harry.

Opposite the restaurant on the other side of the high street is Maltby Close, which leads to the church. Maltby Close is the home of Flo Carpenter, who originally came to the village hop picking with Hetty Wilde. Hetty married Ben's father Greg, while Flo married the hop garden foreman, farmer Frank Carpenter. The Carpenters prospered, and the barn of their farm is now Carpenter's Hall on Maltby Close, while alongside it had been built a row of bungalows occupied by the over 65s of the village, including Flo, who now lives with her first love, Lenny, Hetty's brother. Flo is a fount of knowledge about Steeple Martin's past, and is at the centre of a group of elderly residents who all know where the bodies are buried.

Along the road at Nethergate lives Fran Wolfe with her husband Guy. Guy is an artist who runs a small gallery and shop on Harbour

Also in the Libby Sarjeant series

Street, where his daughter Sophie lives in the flat above the shop. He and Fran live in Coastguard Cottage further along Harbour Street, with Balzac the black and white cat. Further along still on the small jetty at the end, stand The Blue Anchor café and The Sloop Inn.

In Cliff Terrace at the other end of town live Jane Baker, deputy editor of the Nethergate Mercury, her husband Terry and their daughter Imogen. Jane's mother lives in the self contained garden flat in thir house. Below them, right on the litte promenade, stands The Alexandria, now restored to its former glory as an Edwardian Concert hall, and used by the Oast House company as a summer venue. Its Edwardian Concert Party, The Alexandrians, became quite famous in their day.

Nethergate itself centres around the little square at the bottom of the high street, where The Old Swan stands. It is an old fashioned seaside town, rather set in its ways, its two arms curving round a small bay, a little red and white striped lighthouse on the left hand arm, casting its beam across Dragon Island in the middle of the bay.

Of the villages that lie either side of the road leading between Steeple Martin and Nethergate, Steeple Mount is the biggest, with its prehistoric burial mound and monument, Grey Betty. St Aldeberg, named for its church and Saxon Princess, is home to vicar Patti Pearson, whose friend, Anne Douglas, lives in Steeple Martin.

Finally, living neither in Steeple Martin nor Nethergate, Chief Detective Inspector Ian Connell, an exiled Scot, has become a friend, nevertheless keeping his private life very much to himself. At one time, he was very interested in Fran, but she chose Guy, and since then, as far as Libby and Fran know, there has been no romantic nvolvement in his life. They don't even know where he lives, except that it must be somewhere in the area, but Libby will never give up trying to find out.

If you know the countryside of Kent south of the A28, that will give you some idea of the terrain. Surprisingly, for an area so close to London, there are some remarkably remote pockets, as Libby and Fran found out in Murder In The Dark. The whole area is rich in lawless history, from ancient invaders to more recent smugglers and even more recent people and drug traffickers. Also we have some pretty good national monuments, such as Canterbury Cathedral and the iconic White Cliffs of Dover. And of course, many individual food and drink producers, who, unlike the villages, you *can* find.